"I love you both," Rick said. And the breath stopped in my chest as he spoke. "I love Martine as my wife, you as my sister. That's how it's worked out, how it *should* have worked out, and I hope you won't take this the wrong way."

He'd said he loved me. That had never happened before, though once I'd desperately longed to hear it. The night stilled around us, and I couldn't speak past the lump in my throat.

"Trista?"

"Thanks for telling me that," I whispered. Then something twisted inside me, wrapped itself around my heart. I hugged my knees and willed the pain to go away.

Dear Reader,

Like you, I treasure my family photos. Because many of them were taken in South Carolina, where I lived when my children were young, they recall joyful memories of a state that was my home for a long time. So when I decided to write a novel in which photos document the development of a love relationship over the lifetimes of the two main characters, it seemed fitting to choose the hauntingly beautiful South Carolina Low Country as my setting.

If you haven't yet visited the Low Country, you are in for a treat. If you've already been there, perhaps you'll be glad to know that you're being welcomed back by two of my favorite people—Rick and Trista, who have a story to tell.

Though they became best friends when they were nine years old, they were too young and inexperienced to recognize the love they felt by the time they were teenagers. Later, Rick married Trista's twin sister, leading Trista to believe that he was lost to her forever. But sometimes life throws you a curve. And occasionally you get a second chance. Happily, so it was for Rick and Trista.

How they found their way back to each other is the story in *Snapshots,* and I hope it will touch your heart as it has mine.

Happy reading.

Pamela Browning

P.S. I love to hear from my readers! Please write to me through my Web site, www.pamelabrowning.com.

Snapshots

Pamela Browning

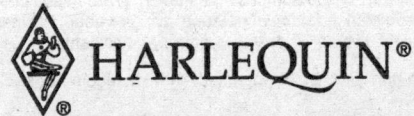

TORONTO • NEW YORK • LONDON
AMSTERDAM • PARIS • SYDNEY • HAMBURG
STOCKHOLM • ATHENS • TOKYO • MILAN • MADRID
PRAGUE • WARSAW • BUDAPEST • AUCKLAND

If you purchased this book without a cover you should be aware that this book is stolen property. It was reported as "unsold and destroyed" to the publisher, and neither the author nor the publisher has received any payment for this "stripped book."

ISBN-13: 978-0-373-65414-7
ISBN-10: 0-373-65414-6

SNAPSHOTS

Copyright © 2007 by Pamela Browning.

All rights reserved. Except for use in any review, the reproduction or utilization of this work in whole or in part in any form by any electronic, mechanical or other means, now known or hereafter invented, including xerography, photocopying and recording, or in any information storage or retrieval system, is forbidden without the written permission of the publisher, Harlequin Enterprises Limited, 225 Duncan Mill Road, Don Mills, Ontario, Canada M3B 3K9.

This is a work of fiction. Names, characters, places and incidents are either the product of the author's imagination or are used fictitiously, and any resemblance to actual persons, living or dead, business establishments, events or locales is entirely coincidental.

This edition published by arrangement with Harlequin Books S.A.

® and TM are trademarks of the publisher. Trademarks indicated with ® are registered in the United States Patent and Trademark Office, the Canadian Trade Marks Office and in other countries.

www.eHarlequin.com

Printed in U.S.A.

ABOUT THE AUTHOR

Pamela Browning lived in South Carolina for more than twenty-two years. She still cherishes fond memories of the Low Country and visits friends and relatives there as often as she can.

Thanks to Neill for "Joey" and the music, Melanie for Low Country lore and Bethany for chai tea latte and the prom (though like my heroine, she was never allowed to stay at the hotel all night, either). I love y'all!

This book is for Cameron, in happy anticipation of our snapshots together in the coming years.

Chapter 1: Rick

2004

To say that their marriage was in trouble was a classic understatement. Sure, he and Martine had their problems like any other couple. They'd managed, though. In the past they'd congratulated themselves on their strength under pressure, their determination to make the relationship work. But this time was different.

An unwelcome guest had hitched a ride earlier when he stopped to pick up Martine at work, and it began to whine in the vicinity of Rick's ear. He swatted at the mosquito, and the hum stopped, then resumed. He slapped at it again, harder this time, and the noise ceased.

Martine glanced out of the corner of her eye, still defiant but incredibly beautiful. "Bet you wish that was me," she said. "Bet you'd like to squash me flat."

"Stop it, Martine," he said, keeping his voice even.

She turned her head away, her pale hair glimmering in the headlights from oncoming cars. "*If* you insist on going to this stupid party for Shorty, I have to stop by the house to get a wrap," she said. The early-January breeze blew in on the promise of a cool night, more than welcome in Miami any time of year.

"Attendance is mandatory," Rick said. "All the guys are—"

She cut him off midsentence. "Just don't talk to me while we're there, okay?"

"Fine," he said curtly. It's not as though he really had anything to say to Martine, except *Why?*

"At least we're doing something together," Martine said. "For once you don't have to work late." She didn't even attempt to conceal her resentment.

Gunning the car's engine as he rounded the corner onto their peaceful palm-lined street, Rick spotted the white Impala immediately. It stood out in this manicured Kendall neighborhood; one rear window was broken out, and a spreading rust stain marred the trunk. At any other time, he might have paid more attention.

"I'll be right back," Martine said, reaching for the door handle.

"It's a surprise party," Rick reminded her. "We don't want to be late."

As she slammed the car door, Martine cast a scathing glance back over her shoulder. Under normal circumstances, Rick would have accompanied her, maybe changed out of his jacket, shirt and tie into more comfortable clothes, but he needed time to recoup. She disappeared into the house, a typical south Florida ranch with a red barrel-tile roof.

Rick drummed his fingers on the steering wheel. Ten years of marriage. Ten wasted years, and how long since he'd realized he'd made a terrible mistake? Seven years? Five? He'd wanted kids; Martine hadn't. His paralyzing discovery of those love notes in Martine's bottom dresser drawer, which he had opened innocently enough last night, had made so many things clear. All the nights she'd said she had to work late, the Saturday-afternoon shopping trips when she returned with no purchases, the cell-phone bills he never saw, not to mention the general air of secretiveness that he hadn't recognized for what it was. And all he'd had in mind when he opened that drawer was to check her bra size so he could buy her a sexy birthday present for the purpose of inspiring their almost nonexistent sex life.

He felt a sting on his left ear—that damn mosquito again. He opened the car window, figuring that maybe the insect would do them both a favor and escape into the night. While the window was down, he spared the derelict white car at the curb a cursory assessment. A car parked there was by no means unusual, since the teenage girl next door often entertained boyfriends who left their vehicles at the edge of Rick's property. Out of habit, Rick attempted to pick out the numbers on the license tag, but it was hidden in shadows from the surrounding shrubbery.

He punched the button to bring the window all the way up and massaged his eyelids for a long moment. It had been a quiet day in Homicide, affording him time to catch up on paperwork and mull over the situation with Martine. He'd never dreamed she was capable of betrayal. They'd been childhood friends, college buddies. Which proved that you really never knew another person, no matter how close the relationship.

Minutes ticked past, punctuated by the shrilling of crickets. What was taking Martine so long? Rick checked his watch. It had been half an hour since he'd picked her up at the law office where she worked, twenty hours since he'd read the incriminating letters. Last night she'd cried, he'd accused, she'd admitted everything. No, that wasn't quite true. Not everything—at least, according to a terrible suspicion that he'd never voiced and never would.

He sure as hell wouldn't be going to a party for his boss tonight if Shorty hadn't encouraged him and promised a promotion to chief detective before long. All Rick wanted, really, was to lick his wounds in private. To hunker down somewhere far from here and figure out whether he was capable of living without Martine. Or maybe he should be considering whether he could still live *with* her. Tappany Island, yeah, that was the place. Tomorrow he'd ask for a week off, depart on a road trip to South Carolina and just hang for a while.

The front door of their house swung open abruptly. Rick, expecting Martine to hurry out, waited impatiently for her to emerge into the yellow glare of the bug bulb in the porch light. Then, in the shadows inside the house, he saw the stocky dark-clad figure pressing a knife to Martine's throat, muscular arms gripping her in an awkward embrace. Instinctively, Rick reached for his weapon, a .38 semiautomatic tucked away in the shoulder holster under his jacket. He leaped from the car.

At this point, the action sped into fast-forward. Martine let out a small involuntary squeak at Rick's sudden movement. Lightning quick, the knife slit a shallow cut across the creamy skin at the base of her throat. Beads of blood appeared, dark red and out of place as they slid toward the scoop neckline of Martine's pale green dress.

"Stay away," warned her captor in an agitated voice, his accent guttural and Hispanic. "Unless you want your wife to become fish food at the bottom of a canal." The man seemed electric, wired, jittery, like an out-of-control marionette.

Rick recoiled, held himself back when all he wanted to do was to rush the man and blow his head off. Martine, who must have known his inclination, sent him a look of such dire pleading that it rocked him back on his heels.

All thought of their previous argument and of last night's discovery faded in the force of Rick's sudden, gut-wrenching comprehension. He recognized the man as Jorgé Padrón, an illegal immigrant who had been convicted on Rick's testimony some years ago. Padrón had created a fracas in the courtroom before they led him away, kicking over a chair and yelling in broken English that he'd get even with Rick McCulloch, no matter how long it took. Since Padrón was sentenced to ten years for armed robbery and aggravated assault, Rick had known he would eventually be back on the street, but he hadn't taken the threat seriously. The newly convicted often issued impassioned threats before being led away to serve their time.

"Drop your gun," Padrón commanded.

Rick hesitated, bile rising in his throat. It tasted metallic, coppery.

"Rick—" Martine gasped, her eyes begging him.

"Shut up," Padrón said, tightening his grip so that she winced. "Drop it," he said to Rick. "Unless you want me to add a few more red beads to this pretty necklace I gave your wife."

Bloodstains now covered the bodice of Martine's dress. Feeling a sense of futility, Rick dropped the .38. It landed with a thud on the grass.

"Hands up where I can see them."

Slowly, Rick raised his hands above his shoulders.

Padrón maneuvered Martine between him and Rick as he propelled her toward the white car at the curb. "No talk from you," he warned Rick. "I'll kill her without thinking twice."

"Take me, instead," Rick said urgently. "Let her go."

"You? You're no use to me. *Comprende?*"

Rick *comprend*ed, all right. The man was a convicted sex offender who had robbed a convenience store and raped the owner's wife. He'd carved the woman's face into ribbons for good measure.

"Open the door," Padrón ordered Martine as they approached the driver's side of the white car. *"Do it!"*

Martine's hand, the one with his wedding ring on the third finger, inched out. Rick watched, alert for any lapse on Padrón's part, any chance he might be able to jump the man before he reached the car. The steel skin of the .38 gleamed in the moonlight a few feet from his right foot.

"Hurry up!" Padrón said.

Martine pulled at the door; it opened. Padrón slid inside under the steering wheel and yanked Martine in after him.

"Padrón, let's talk about this," Rick said, refusing to panic. "We can solve your problems some other way. Let her go. Take me. I can help you."

"Like when you sent me off to Raiford Prison? Yeah, right." To Martine he said, "Turn the key. Start the car. You and me, we go for a ride." He tightened his choke hold around her neck.

Martine did as he said. The car's engine clunked to life, and a cloud of black exhaust spewed from the tailpipe. Rick hoped some of the neighbors would notice, but all the nearby houses were dark.

"Now put it in drive. No surprises, Mrs. McCulloch, and you will be okay."

Rage flickered up past the fear in Rick's throat, wrapped itself around his brain and squeezed. Martine...*Martine*. The white car began to roll slowly toward the intersection.

"Don't call police," was Padrón's parting command. "Anyone follows me, she dies."

This warning notwithstanding, Rick grabbed his gun and was behind the wheel of his Taurus sedan before the Impala rounded the corner. He grappled with his cell phone and managed to alert the police department, relieved to learn that his friend Wally was working the desk.

Rick did his best to explain, and Wally was no dummy. He knew who Padrón was. Wally had worked the case with Rick shortly after Rick had joined the force.

"Don't worry, Rick," Wally said, but by that time Rick was straining to keep track of the Impala, which was darting in and out of cars ahead. He almost lost it in the traffic on busy Kendall Boulevard.

Rick sped through traffic lights and ignored stop signs as the Impala bobbed and weaved, nearly running up on the sidewalk at one point, speeding up the ramp to the Palmetto Expressway. From what he could tell about the car's occupants, Padrón stayed pressed close to Martine, and he could only imagine her state of mind at present. His wife wasn't the most stable of women even in the best of times; in the past few months she'd been seeing a counselor for depression. *Hang in there, Martine,* he muttered. Despite their difficulties, she would expect him to do everything in his power to save her. Rick wouldn't disappoint her—the consequences were unthinkable.

The expressway was its usual tangle of passenger cars and

semis, with macho guys jockeying for every inch as they dodged from lane to lane, women laughing into cell phones pressed to their ears. Packs of commuters were scurrying home to outlying subdivisions. Overhead a 747 banked low, preparing to land at Miami International. Graffiti rushed by, spray painted on the metal guardrail in the median: SNOWBIRDS GO HOME. DOLPHINS ROCK. JULIO + ANA (TRULY).

The white Impala picked up speed, almost sideswiping a Mack truck. Rick jammed his foot down on the accelerator, raced past a school bus, barked out his location to Wally on the phone.

What happened next went down fast. The Impala, traveling an estimated hundred miles an hour in the passing lane, swerved to the right for a few seconds, almost clipping a red Mustang. When the Impala arced back into the passing lane, it skidded left into the grassy median.

Steer into the skid, Rick thought. He had a moment of jubilation when Martine appeared to be doing just that, but before he could draw another breath, the Impala's tires bounced off the pavement so that the car slewed sideways into the median again. Miraculously, it straightened. Then it struck the metal barrier, sending up a plume of sparks.

For one heart-stopping, surreal moment, the Impala seemed frozen in midair, no longer a car but a graceful white wingless flying machine. Rick's brain struggled to make sense of the scene as the car with his wife inside proceeded to land on its roof with a deafening crash, immediately bursting into flames.

Rick ran toward the twisted wreckage, heart thudding against his ribs. Other motorists stopped, and cars slowed on the highway as drivers craned their heads in curiosity. The blaze made it impossible to see anything but the outline of the car, and the heat drove him backward. Then he spotted a patch of pale green in his peripheral vision, Martine's dress, and he changed direction, dreading what he would find when he reached her.

He knelt beside her, appalled by all the blood. Soon, sirens were keening all around as pulsing multicolored lights illuminated a nightmare scene of fire engines and police cars. Martine was unconscious, but she was alive. He let the paramedics push him aside, their brief, urgent words mere babble in his ears as they strapped Martine onto a stretcher and slid it into the ambulance.

He'd supervised a hundred emergency scenes in the course of his work, but all of them had been marked by his own detachment and his ability to function well under stress. As one of the paramedics slammed the ambulance door, he tried to bring that same sense of focus into this situation but failed. The horror of the images and the engagement of his own emotions made it impossible.

He was in his car, hitting his cell phone's speed dial, before the ambulance pulled off the median with him following behind. The phone on the other end seemed to ring for an interminably long time, and he started muttering, "Pick up, pick *up*." He imagined his sister-in-law in her condominium in Columbia, South Carolina. She'd have recently arrived home from work at WCIC, where she was coanchor of the evening news. Or maybe she was staying late at the station tonight, but he prayed that wasn't the case. Due to her coolness under pressure, Martine's identical twin was the person of choice to call in crisis situations.

"Hello?"

He'd planned to cushion the blow of his news, but when he heard Trista's voice, he blurted it out.

"Tris, there's been an accident. It's Martine."

A sharp intake of breath. Then, in a rush, "Is she all right?"

"She's alive. We're on the way to the hospital."

"What happened?"

Keeping the ambulance in sight as he drove one-handed, he told her, his words tense and measured.

"I'll be there as soon as I can," Trista said, and he imagined her heading for her closet, phone still pressed to her ear as she grabbed a duffel and started tossing clothes into it. He was approaching the hospital by this time, speeding into the curve leading to the emergency entrance, and he didn't know what he said after that, only that they hung up.

He bolted from his car, stood jittery and on edge as the ambulance crew wheeled Martine into a curtained cubicle where he was not permitted to go. He paced the waiting room, thought about calling Trista again, but was reluctant because she'd be busy lining up airline reservations. Two officers from the department showed up and informed him that Padrón had died in the fiery crash, but Rick was too crazed with worry to derive any satisfaction from that.

The next few hours would be forever blurred in his memory. Long after Martine disappeared, a doctor summoned him to a small bare room. Rick swallowed, prepared to hear the worst.

"Your wife will recover," said the doctor, someone Rick had never seen before. His name tag pegged him as Ethan D. Stillwater, M.D.

Rick's knees went weak with relief, but the doctor didn't notice. He consulted his clipboard. "She's suffered three broken ribs, concussion, a fractured collarbone and assorted abrasions and contusions. She'll soon be as good as new."

Completely numb by this time, all Rick could do was try to pay attention as Dr. Stillwater rattled on about length of hospital stay and rehab. By now the issues Rick had with Martine before the accident seemed moot; he felt overwhelmingly guilty for what had happened to her. She'd never approved of his going into police work and had always resented the time he gave to his job. Maybe, in the long run, she'd been right.

"Sir, your wife has been placed in room 432," said a nurse, briefly and comfortingly touching his arm.

"Thanks," Rick said automatically. He took an interminable ride to the fourth floor on a jolting elevator whose mirrored walls revealed that his face was as white and pinched as those of his fellow passengers, all of whom must have urgent reasons for being there in the middle of the night just as he did.

He wouldn't have recognized Martine if her name hadn't been printed on a placard beside the door. A tightness gripped his heart when he first saw her, a heavy mantle of self-reproach pressing him down. Her face was bruised and swollen, her head bandaged so that only a few tendrils of hair escaped. She wore a hospital gown, its institutional print faded from many washings. When she first opened her eyes, she stared as if she wasn't quite sure who he was, her eyes drifting closed almost immediately after registering recognition but no emotion at all.

Rick settled himself on the uncomfortable plastic-covered chair and caught a couple of hours' sleep, waking when an aide delivered a breakfast tray. Martine was still asleep, so he forced down what he could from the tray—gummy oatmeal, a wedge of toast soaked with margarine.

After that he phoned a friend of his from the department and asked him to stop by the house. Charlie rang him back a couple of hours later and told him that Padrón had entered by disarming the security system and breaking a back window. "I'll take care of it," Charlie said, and Rick left it to him, knowing that he would.

Martine dozed most of the day, and Rick tried unsuccessfully to do the same. When the door swung open late in the afternoon, he glanced up sharply, expecting yet another nurse or an aide. Instead, Martine walked in, her eyes frantic. But no. His befogged brain cleared in a moment to realize that it was Trista.

Overwhelmingly relieved to see her, Rick stood immediately and pulled Trista into a hug, taking comfort from her warmth. Her bones felt fragile and her pale hair smelled of the almond-scented shampoo she'd favored for as long as he could remember. He released her reluctantly when she pulled away.

Trista turned immediately toward the figure in the bed. "I got here as soon as I could," she said, noting the monitors and machines crowding the small space. "How is she?" She wore little makeup and a white T-shirt with jeans and a navy blazer. The back of her hair was crushed, as if she'd rested her head on the back of the airplane seat and forgotten to fluff it afterward.

Rick filled her in as best he could, though he had the feeling he was leaving a lot out. Trista nodded, looking worried and upset as she slung her shoulder bag on the nightstand and slipped out of her jacket. "I called Mom. She's not well enough to come," she said. A sense of calm radiated from her, and Rick drew sustenance from it. He was desperately in need of support, someone to care about him, and Trista was the closest member of their family. His parents, fulfilling a lifelong dream to teach English in China, were living in faraway Nanchung, and he seldom saw his brother, Hal, whose prissy, uptight wife, Nadia, vaguely disapproved of him.

As Trista's glance took in his beard stubble and rumpled clothes, she moved to the side of the bed and caressed her twin's hand.

"I can't imagine how awful it must have been," she murmured sympathetically. "For both of you."

"I couldn't stop Padrón. I tried." As long as he lived, Rick would never forget those moments of watching helplessly as the man forced Martine into the car.

Trista's hand reached backward for his so that the three of them were linked as they'd been so many times when they were children growing up together. Her grasp was warm, familiar, and he should have completed the circle by clasping Martine's free hand. He didn't. The gesture was preempted by the IV needle.

"Why don't you take a break, Rick," Trista said quietly and sensibly. "Grab some sleep. I'll stay here."

He refused. He didn't want to leave Martine, even though Trista was more than capable of looking after her. But after he slumped over a few times in the chair and realized that he was viewing Trista's caring face as if through a heavy fog, Rick finally admitted to himself that he'd been wiped out by an ordeal that had begun with that unwelcome discovery in Martine's dresser drawer.

"I think I will go home for a while," he told Trista, who had pulled a second chair close to the bedside and was still holding her twin's hand.

"Go on," she said. "You're a walking zombie."

You don't know the half of it, he thought, but he didn't say it. His anguish over the rift between Martine and him was coming back, invisible and unknown to everyone. Certainly, he'd feel less raw and vulnerable after a good night's sleep.

"Go on," Trista urged gently.

"Call me if there's any change."

"I will." She smiled up at him.

It was eleven o'clock at night when Rick left the hospital. With Miami's streets almost deserted at this late hour, he didn't have to concentrate on his driving, only on staying awake. He pulled the car into the garage in Kendall and sat for a moment after the door descended behind him. Returning home was hitting him hard in his gut, and he had to force himself to go inside.

The house was neat and clean, thanks to Esmelda, their Guatemalan housekeeper, who cheerfully whooshed in and out twice a week bearing vacuum cleaners, solvents and a multitude of rags. The master bedroom was as he'd left it, and Charlie had already repaired the broken window in the utility room.

He showered, shaved, phoned Trista at the hospital.

"Anything new?" Rick asked.

"Martine's resting," Trista told him. "She's opened her eyes a couple of times, and she took a drink of water about half an hour ago."

Rick wanted to say, *Has she asked for me?* But his mouth wouldn't shape the words and he couldn't have forced the air out of his lungs even if it had.

And so he hung up. Even though he was exhausted, he lay awake for a long time, staring at the ceiling. He kept thinking of the first time he'd seen Trista and Martine, long ago at Eugene Field Elementary School. How they'd become fast friends immediately, and where they'd gone from there. How until recently the future had always seemed just around the corner, bright and shining as the sun.

If Rick had learned anything in his thirty-two years, it was that life had a way of rearing up in your face or skidding along in unexpected twists and turns, like now. And the worst of it was that you couldn't go back and change any of it afterward.

Chapter 2: Rick

2004

After Martine's accident, Trista and Rick alternated shifts at the hospital, and Rick was thankful that Trista could stay on in Miami to help him out. They didn't see each other often, mostly brief hellos and goodbyes as one left Martine's bedside and the other arrived.

Though Martine was more alert by the third day after the accident, she didn't talk to him much. The nurses told him that she needed her rest while her body healed. Rick suspected that Martine was more forthcoming with Trista, and he considered whether she might be filling her sister in on their personal situation during the long hours when Trista sat at her bedside. Even if that was what was going on, he knew that Trista would respect Martine's confidence and that she would never speak of their marriage difficulties with him.

Rick returned to work in Homicide, but his heart wasn't in it. More than anything, he wanted to patch things up with his wife, but he was reluctant to broach the subject while she was recovering. He was still wallowing in guilt. In his heart, he believed that the kidnapping would never have happened if he hadn't gone against Martine's wishes by choosing police work as a career.

Five days after the accident, Rick was sitting in the backyard of their house, watching the light from the moon dancing in the dense tropical shrubbery and thinking things over. Not that he got very far with it—his mind kept playing back the scenes with Padrón and the horror of watching the car roll over and explode into flames. When he heard the glass door behind him slide open on its track, he snapped out of his reverie and swiveled quickly in alarm. Since the break-in, he'd remained jittery and on edge. He sagged in relief when he saw that it was only Trista advancing toward him through the shadows.

"Hi, Rick. Martine practically pushed me out of her room and told me to get lost," she said.

It struck him how pretty she was, and though her features were the same as Martine's, Trista's were softer somehow, as if they were the same picture captured by a more flattering lens.

"She seems to be feeling better today," Rick said. He'd been encouraged by the color in Martine's cheeks and the fading of her bruises.

"So what are you doing out here all by yourself?" Trista asked.

"Thinking," he said.

She paused, skewering him with a glance. "About?"

He sighed. "A lot of things."

"Do I have to drag it out of you?" she asked with an impish grin, but he wasn't in the mood to be teased.

"I need to figure out where to go from here. I thought I could do a lot of good by working in law enforcement, and yet I endangered Martine. I can't forgive myself for that."

Trista's expression changed, became serious. "You didn't cause Padrón to do what he did. He's responsible for his own actions."

"Tris, I've learned the hard way that when you're dealing with the criminal element, you open yourself to things that should never happen." He was more than serious. Somber, even.

"We both figured that out a long time ago, didn't we?" Trista said, and he knew she was remembering her father, a prominent South Carolina attorney. Seven years ago, Roger Barrineau had been murdered by a former client, gunned down in cold blood on the steps of the Richland County Courthouse.

He nodded. His father-in-law had been Rick's friend and role model, and the shock and grief of his murder had never completely gone away. Now, years later, to be faced with nearly losing his wife in a similar situation had not only been terrifying, it had brought him up short. He didn't want to live his life like this anymore. He wanted things to be peaceful, calm, *nice*.

Of course, the case could be made that Rick had lost his wife before Padrón ever forced her into his car, but he wasn't about to discuss that with Trista unless she brought it up first.

Thankfully, she didn't. She stretched, smiled at him and stood. "That chair in Martine's hospital room has put a permanent kink in my spine. I could use a glass of wine to start the unwinding process. How about you?"

"I'll get it." He started to rise, but she stayed him with a light hand on his arm.

"No, let me. I'm going inside to change shoes, anyway. I'm ready to kick back some."

He looked at her feet, small for such a tall woman. She wore espadrilles with cork wedge heels that made her ankles seem impossibly slim.

"All right, if you insist. I like the Delicato chardonnay. It's in the refrigerator."

"I'll try it," she said.

When Trista returned wearing bedroom slippers, which were incongruously fuzzy and pink, she carried two glasses on a narrow tray. "I couldn't find any crackers or cheese. Maybe I should stop by the store on my way back from the hospital tomorrow." She sat down beside him and eased the back of her patio chair down a notch.

"I don't expect you to do the shopping. I'll be happy to pick up some food tomorrow. You've helped so much with Martine, and I'm grateful you're here, believe me."

She regarded him over the top of her wineglass. "Where else would I be?" she asked. "I belong with you and Martine at a time like this."

"I appreciate everything you're doing," he said, thinking back to all the other occasions when he and Martine had depended on Trista. The time they'd won a Caribbean cruise in a raffle and she'd house-sat, overseeing the building of their new Florida room while they were gone. Trista had rearranged her vacation days in order to accommodate them. And a few years ago when Martine had injured her knee while skiing, Trista had uncomplainingly occupied their guest room for two weeks, doing all the cooking and keeping Martine company. Martine declared that she would have gone stark raving mad sitting around the house by herself all that time.

"So what do you think of the Carolina Panthers' chances when they play the Dolphins next season?" Trista asked, and since this was something on which Rick held a well-thought-out opinion, he gratefully entered into a discussion. It amazed him that he was capable of this when he was hurting so much inside, but it had become second nature to pretend everything was okay when it wasn't.

The conversation progressed to updating her about his parents and their work in China and inquiries about Virginia Barrineau, who now lived with her sister in Macon, Georgia. It was easy talk, unchallenging and comforting because it required no thinking, no decision making.

"I like this chardonnay," Trista said when the conversation began to wane. She swirled the pale liquid in her glass, studying it. "You have good taste in wine."

"You used to be disappointed that wine didn't taste like Kool-Aid," Rick reminded her, recalling their first foray into alcohol together. When they were high-school juniors, he'd snitched a bottle of pinot grigio from his parents' bar at Sweetwater Cottage, and they'd drunk every last drop from paper cups on the beach. The wine had given them only a mild buzz, and Martine had declared that she liked beer better, so what was all the fuss about?

He and Trista had jumped all over Martine, demanding that she tell them when she'd had occasion to drink beer, and she'd laughingly informed them that she and her current steady date customarily downed a six-pack every weekend; they'd park in the lover's lane overlooking the lake behind their subdivision in Columbia and chugalug until the beer was gone. Then they'd make out.

If Trista recalled that long-ago discussion, she gave no indication of it now. She smiled. "Not much can beat cherry Kool-Aid, even today. I've considered adopting a kid so people won't tease me about having it in the refrigerator."

He cut a sideways glance in her direction. "You really mean that? About adopting a child?"

Trista shrugged, almost too casually, and avoided his eyes. "I've thought about it, usually when I've overwound my biological clock. Then I get sane again and realize that with my job, I wouldn't be a great single parent." She sounded sad or perhaps reflective, and he could only imagine what was running through her mind.

He infused his voice with what he hoped was encouragement. "You've got a great job. Don't knock it." After he said it, he realized that refocusing the conversation on her job rather than her wish to adopt could be construed as unfeeling, but it was too late to take back his words.

Trista pushed a strand of cornsilk-pale hair back from her forehead and adroitly changed the subject. "Martine's getting out of the hospital on Sunday. I'm planning to leave that morning," she said in a matter-of-fact tone.

He was surprised at the disappointment that washed over him when he thought of her leaving. "Don't you want to be here when she comes home?"

"I did, but Martine insists that she won't need someone around the house 24–7. And let's face it, I've got a job I should be tending. Anyway, Martine said she'd call Esmelda if she can't handle being by herself." Esmelda had been angling for more working time due to the fact that she was expecting her fourth child and could use the money.

Rick didn't say anything. He supposed he couldn't ask Trista to stay in Miami any longer, considering that she had her own life. For a few brief seconds, he wondered if it was a satisfying one. Her talk about adopting a baby seemed to indicate that she wasn't completely happy.

But she was already off on another tack. "Have you eaten?" she asked.

"Not yet." In fact, it hadn't even crossed his mind. He'd lost his appetite after the accident and it still hadn't returned.

"I picked up some Chinese food at lunchtime, and there's plenty left. I'll heat it in the microwave and we can eat out here." Trista set aside her empty wineglass before heading for the house.

"Need some help?" he called after her.

"No, it's just a matter of dishing it out," she called back. She disappeared inside, leaving him with his thoughts, not to mention regrets. Miami was a long way from Columbia, South Carolina, and he was a long way from the person he had been while he was growing up there. While *they* were growing up, he and Trista and Martine.

"Hey, Rick, can you get the door for me?"

Trista emerged carrying a tray loaded with plates of General Tso's chicken, moo goo gai pan and fried rice, and he hurried to pull their chairs over to the round patio table.

"I haven't had Chinese for a while," he said, watching her. She'd donned a loose cardigan over her top, but it didn't obscure her curves. Trista had the well-honed figure of an athlete, thanks to her habit of running before breakfast. Back in high school and whenever they were home from college, the three of them had liked to run together.

"Spicy for you," Trista said as she spooned a helping of General Tso onto his plate, "and bland for me." She dished out a small portion of moo goo gai pan for herself. She didn't like anything hot, but he and Martine did.

Tabasco sauce on eggs, hot red pepper flakes on almost everything else.

Rick was hungrier than he expected. It didn't take him long to devour all his food, after which Trista went back inside the house to get the rest of the moo goo gai pan, which he ate, as well.

"That was delicious," he said, smiling at her across the table. She'd brought a candle outside and lit it, and its sweet vanilla scent combined with the fragrance of night-blooming jasmine from the surrounding shrubbery. For the first time in days, he wasn't thinking about all he had to consider—his marriage, Martine's injuries, neglecting work.

"There's ice cream in the freezer," Trista said. "I peeked."

"What kind?"

She shot him a conspiratorial smile. "Our favorite. Mint chocolate chip."

The three of them must have eaten gallons of the stuff in the course of their childhood. Trista had laughingly pointed out that it should be their official ice cream, comparing Rick to the mint, Martine to the chocolate chips and herself to the ice cream itself. This was because, she said, Rick provided the spark, the excitement to the synergy that the three of them generated. Martine was the richness, and Trista was the no-nonsense person, the base of everything.

That was certainly true, he reflected as he gathered up the plates. Trista was the one that both he and Martine consulted before they made a move, the reliable anchor in their lives. Which was probably why she'd been promoted so quickly to her position at WCIC–TV; her crisp but serious reporting of the news gave it weight and meaning for the thousands of viewers who regularly tuned in.

Trista took cut-glass bowls from the cabinet, and he

scooped the ice cream. They sat at the kitchen counter to eat it.

"You'll be glad to have Martine back home," Trista said as she concentrated on scraping chocolate chips off the side of her dish.

What could he reply but, "Of course," but he averted his face so that Trista wouldn't read anything into his expression.

"I'll change the bed linens tomorrow, and—"

"Don't bother," he interrupted much too sharply. "Esmelda will do it."

"I'll leave a casserole in the freezer for you. Martine won't want to cook once she gets home. Did you like the chicken tetrazzini I made at the cottage last summer?"

"The best. Better than your mom's chicken and noodles."

"That's saying quite a lot," Trista offered with a smile. She got up and rinsed her bowl off in the sink. "I believe I'll turn in early," she said, but he couldn't help wishing she'd stay in the kitchen and talk awhile. He hadn't realized how starved he was for human companionship.

"Hey," he said. "How about a walk around the block?"

Trista shook her head. "Not tonight," she replied offhandedly. "Catch you in the morning." She touched his shoulder briefly before retreating down the hall and closing the guest-room door.

Words sprang unbidden to his mind: *Such a shame that Trista has stayed single so long.* She'd make a fine wife, a good mother. He entertained the fleeting notion that it might be partly his fault that she'd never married, his and Martine's, but he didn't linger on it. There was no point in allowing even more regrets to enter his consciousness; no sense in twisting this situation into something it wasn't.

Still, he minded that Trista couldn't stay for a few more

days. On the other hand, if she were here, neither he nor Martine would be likely to initiate a discussion of the intimate details of their marriage. For the life of him, he couldn't figure out if that would be good or bad.

He stared down at the melting ice cream in his dish. For a moment, it seemed like a metaphor for his life at present. Melting away, becoming something he didn't recognize anymore.

In the morning, he expected Trista to show up in the kitchen for breakfast and intended to suggest running together before she headed for the hospital. But she'd already left in Martine's car, so he gulped two cups of high-octane coffee, scribbled a note saying he was sorry he'd missed her and went to work.

He only saw Trista briefly on Sunday morning before she left for the airport. He would have driven her himself, but she'd already summoned a cab before he woke up. She seemed subdued, worried, but this scarcely registered with him. All his thoughts were focused on springing Martine from the hospital.

The night before, Martine had quizzed him thoroughly on the phone about what time he'd be there to pick her up. She'd remained all too quiet on his previous visits, barely replying when he spoke to her, but now he entertained the tentative hope that Martine was willing to give their marriage another chance. Maybe a couple of weeks at Sweetwater Cottage, just the two of them, would smooth things over.

As soon as Trista's taxi disappeared around the corner, Rick started for the hospital. He bought a bouquet of flowers from a roadside vendor, and when he reached Martine's floor at the hospital, he bounded off the elevator, smiling at the nurses and aides at the nurses' station. Martine's room was only a couple of doors down the hall, and he rounded the corner prepared to kiss her hello.

The bed was empty.

A cold hand clenched his heart. Of course he thought the worst. Visions of emergencies straight from TV dramas sprang to mind, all punctuated by doctors running down the hall, their lab coats flying, and someone yelling, "Stat! Hurry, she's coding!"

He rushed back to the nurses' station, losing a couple of daisies in the process. The flowers skidded across the highly polished tile floor as they scattered. Oblivious to his panic, one of the aides, a young girl named Kitty, glanced up from her coffee and doughnut. A scrim of powdered sugar trailed unheeded across her upper lip.

"Where's my wife? Is she all right?"

"Yes, Mr. McCulloch, she checked out about an hour ago."

This stopped him in his tracks. "She did?" He was incredulous. They'd discussed on the phone last night how he would be there to pick her up as soon as Trista left. He'd told Martine jokingly that he'd drive her directly to Starbucks for a chai tea latte because she claimed that she was going through withdrawal; she usually treated herself to one every day.

"A man came to get her." Kitty took another bite of her doughnut.

"A man—?" For one horrifying moment, a new picture of Padrón forcing Martine out of the hospital at gunpoint flashed through his mind. But Padrón was dead.

As this irrational vision faded, one of the nurses sitting behind the counter extended her hand, and in it was a white envelope. His name was scribbled on the front. It was

Martine's handwriting, distinctive and easily recognizable by its wide lower loops.

"Mrs. McCulloch left this for you," she said.

He accepted the envelope, slitted it open and walked slowly to the waiting area in a nearby alcove, where he sank onto one of the chairs to read the message.

Rick,
I'm sorry, but I can't go home with you. Steve is taking me to his apartment for now, and I'll send someone to our house to get my things as soon as I can. I want out of the marriage, and we'll have to talk about it. I can't face hashing things over now. I need to heal first, and then I'll be in touch.
Martine

Steve Lifkin, an attorney in the law office where Martine worked as a paralegal, was the guy who had written Martine those love notes. The letters had left no doubt in Rick's mind that Martine and Steve enjoyed an intimate, ongoing relationship of almost a year.

He glanced up when Kitty passed by. "Mr. McCulloch? Are you all right? You're so pale."

"I'll be fine," he said tonelessly. He stood, pulled his cell phone out of his pocket, but shoved it back in again. His first instinct was to call Martine and ask her what the hell she was doing. If she was with Steve, though, she wouldn't talk to him anyway. He wondered how she could have gone from joking about chai tea lattes last night to moving in with Steve today. He wondered what he was going to do with himself for the rest of his life, and he wondered why he cared.

★ ★ ★

In the days that followed, Martine's belongings disappeared mysteriously, piece by piece, from their Kendall home, as well as furniture that she'd brought into the marriage. The grandfather clock that had always stood in the foyer of her family's Columbia house, the engraved crystal wineglasses that were her mother's. Blank spaces on the walls appeared where Martine's beautiful watercolor paintings had been; the stained-glass window that she'd crafted so carefully was missing from where it hung on the screened porch. Every day when he arrived home from work, Rick would amble around the house, glumly taking note of the things that were newly missing, then sit down to a tasteless frozen dinner heated in the microwave.

At first he'd thought that before she left Miami, Trista must have known Martine wasn't going to come home from the hospital with him, but when she called two days after Martine left the hospital, she seemed astonished when he told her that Martine was living at Steve's place.

"Oh, Rick, I'm sorry," Trista said, her voice low. Other women shrilled when they were upset, but not Trista. If anything, she became more centered.

He greeted this with silence. Though Trista and Martine had grown apart in recent years, he couldn't imagine Martine's embarking on such a course without running it past Trista first.

Trista sighed. "Rick, she told me on Saturday that she was going to file for divorce. She mentioned that you'd had a fight before Padrón forced her into the car, and she said she wanted to leave you. I couldn't talk her out of it. I tried. She never mentioned that another man was involved."

"She and Steve have been having an affair for almost a year. Maybe she'll fill you in on what's happened," he said.

"She doesn't talk to me," Trista replied despairingly. "And I don't understand her or the things she does sometimes."

"Ditto for me."

After they hung up, Rick buried his face in his hands. Through his pain, he was furious with Martine for putting them through this and angry with himself because his wife had felt a need to include another man in her life. He was well aware that it was too late to go back and change the way things were, and he didn't much like the way they were going to be, either.

Shortly after this conversation, Rick descended into a depression the likes of which he had never experienced. As always when things got tough, he began to ruminate over his life as it was before things got so complicated. Before he had a job that was becoming increasingly difficult to perform.

Maybe that was because he was drinking too much, staying out later and later at one bar or another and avoiding one-on-one social situations of any kind. Still, he believed that he was performing his job to the best of his ability until his boss called him into his office late one Friday in early March.

"Rick," Shorty said, walking around his desk and perching on the edge of it as he was wont to do when attempting to establish rapport. "You've been through a lot, and I think you need a break. I hope you don't take this as a put-down, and I have great respect for your ability, but I'm going to put you on an extended leave starting today."

Rick hadn't seen this coming at all. "Extended leave?"

"Don't worry, we'll welcome you back after a few months. We're giving you time to pull yourself back together, that's all. I'll keep in touch, and—"

"What have I done wrong?" Rick was in a state of bewildered disbelief; how could this be happening? On top of everything else?

Shorty sighed and stared out the window for a long moment. "Son, you're not playing at the top of your game. People complain that you don't call them back, you forgot an important meeting last week, and I suspect that your mind's not focused on your work. I'm doing this for your sake as much as the department's. I don't want you finding yourself in an edgy situation and getting into trouble."

I'm already in trouble, it looks like. "My divorce will be final this week. After that—"

"Please don't argue, Rick. What's the name of that place in South Carolina you go to every summer? Where your family has a vacation cottage?"

"Tappany Island," Rick said in a low tone.

"Take a break—that's all I'm asking." Shorty paused at the door and appeared to be thinking something over for a moment, before abruptly leaving the room. Rick sensed that the conversation had been almost as hard on his boss as it had been on him.

Numb after this dismissal, still scarcely believing it, Rick cleaned out his desk and set about getting roaring drunk as soon as he got home. When he emerged on the other side of this binge with a nasty hangover, he tossed some things into a suitcase in preparation for leaving.

He'd planned to head for Sweetwater Cottage anyway. He just hadn't expected to be going alone.

Chapter 3: Trista

1981

Click: Class picture of Miss Davison's third grade, Class 3-A, Eugene Field Elementary School, Columbia, South Carolina. Rick, the new boy in class, stands in the back row because he's tall. I'm grinning, Martine is biting her lip, and we're holding hands.

The first picture of Rick, Martine and me was snapped on his second day in Miss Davison's third grade. There he is, standing in the back row with the other big boys, grinning widely and completely at home.

In the picture, Martine and I sit in the front row, two skinny nine-year-old girls missing various front teeth. We were the twins. Our names were always scrunched together—TristanMartine. If you're not a twin, you probably have a hard time imagining how we were never separate identities but a collective noun, not to mention that people could hardly tell us apart, though we are mirror twins. I'm left-handed, Martine is right-handed. I part my hair on the left, and Martine parts hers on the right.

Rick was a transfer student who arrived in the middle of the semester, and we were drawn to him as soon as we spotted him shuffling his feet beside the teacher's desk on that first morning. He had sandy hair shading toward brown and blue eyes tending more toward gray than ours, which were on the violet side. Freckles. A strong, straight nose. High cheekbones that were to become craggy in adolescence and a ready smile that would become his trademark.

I can't explain it, but it was as if the three of us were instantly connected on sight, as if someone somewhere had thrown a master switch and we were three instead of two plus one. Soon we were no longer TristanMartine; we were Trista, Martine and Rick. Three names were more difficult to run together than two.

By Rick's second week in our class, we'd formed a secret club we called the ILTs. This came about when the school cafeteria served tacos and we discovered that we all loved them more than any other lunch food at Field School. For some reason, Rick felt compelled to trade his prized red-and-blue Richard Petty Matchbox car for Goose Fraser's unwanted taco and chivalrously presented it to us. We showed our appreciation by sharing it with him, after which the three of us raced through the wide halls back to the classroom in spite of the No Running rule, screaming, "I love tacos!"

Even today I can almost smell the chalk dust in the air as I remember how, under Miss Davison's stern eye, we laboriously wrote "I will not run in the hall" a hundred times on wrinkled notebook paper with our stubby pencils. In the back of the school bus on the way home, we unanimously agreed that ILT was our shorthand for I Love Tacos. On the reverse side of one of the "I will not run in the hall" papers, the three of us added our first initials to ILT so we'd have names that rhymed. Rick became Rilt, Martine was Milt and I was Tilt. The password to our secret club was "Burrito," and that was what we also named the club goldfish, which belonged to Rick.

I was the introvert, my nose always stuck in a book. Rick was outgoing, the kind of guy everyone liked. And Martine—well, she was artistic and creative, mercurial, flighty and fun. It wasn't long before we discovered that we worked well together. Never a dull moment, Dad would always say, but it was clear that he doted on Rick, and soon, he considered Rick to be the son he'd always wanted.

By the time summer arrived, the three of us were inseparable and our parents had become good friends. We all lived in a new country-club subdivision grandiosely named Windsor Manor and populated with big two-story brick houses where professional people like my dad, a criminal lawyer, and my mother, a volunteer in local charities, lived and reared their families.

Windsor Manor abounded in vacant lots lushly shaded by tall and fragrant loblolly pines as well as a goodly number of oak trees cloaked in wisteria vine. The three of us claimed these lots for our own. Our tree house, erected in the low fork of an oak in the woods not far from our house, was the neighborhood gathering spot for all the kids.

Martine and I were raised Southern, my parents' families both having settled South Carolina before the American Revolution; Barrineaus and Woods fought for the Confederacy in what we were taught to call the War of Northern Aggression. Our grandmother, Claire Dawson Barrineau, signed Martine and me up for the Daughters of the American Revolution the day after we were born, and Rick's father's most prized possession was a copy of the Order of Secession, signed by one of his ancestors. He hung it over his desk at Carolina Gas and Energy, of which he was president.

That summer after Rick arrived was the first year that we three spent time together at Tappany Island, an unspoiled barrier island off the South Carolina coast reachable only by a picturesque side-swinging drawbridge. Rick's mother usually spent the whole summer there with Rick and his elder brother, Hal. Boyd McCulloch, Rick's father, drove down on weekends, and the first time we were invited to the cottage, Martine, our parents and I accompanied him in his big Roadmaster station wagon.

After a wonderful weekend, Mom and Dad departed on Sunday night with Boyd, but Martine and I stayed for the rest of the week. We settled happily into a guest room connected to another by a bath. Our room was decorated with antiques, heirloom quilts and hand-crocheted dresser scarves. We loved the ornate iron bedsteads, delighted in the wispy, drifting curtains that could be looped back to expose the view of the dunes with a slice of blue ocean beyond. Ever after, that was our room when we stayed at the cottage.

I mean to tell you, Sweetwater Cottage was no palace. It was an unpretentious old grande dame of a house, built high off the ground but not spiked up on stilts like the ones they build in flood zones today. The cottage was surrounded by a veranda, which we always called the porch because,

Rick's father said, *veranda* sounded much too granda for a blowsy old lady like the cottage.

Rick's grandfather, Harold McCulloch, built the house on several oceanfront lots back in the 1940s when land was cheap, and the cottage sat far away from its neighbors. Over many years, the original three rooms were expanded into the present L-shaped structure with the Lighthouse room on top. The shingles on the outside have been painted many colors and were, in my childhood, a milky blue. Lilah Rose, Rick's mom, who delighted in decorating and redecorating both the cottage and her house in Windsor Manor, had the shingles painted yellow some years back, and she's the one who skirted the space under the house with white lattice.

Spreading oak trees shrouded in wispy curtains of gray moss shaded the house; dried fronds of palmettos at the edge of the dense woods across the road clattered in the breeze. The island abounded in roads of white sand, fine as sifted sugar; glistening salt marshes sheltered all manner of wildlife; tidal creeks wended their pristine, unspoiled way through the island. And best of all, we had the wide majestic ocean with its many moods.

Across the road was the river and the marsh, home to a variety of creatures both large and small. I loved to watch the birds—dapper little crested kingfishers, diving from tree limbs to catch their dinner, ospreys soaring and wheeling against the brilliant blue sky, graceful white ibis stalking the shallows. But we saw lots of animals, too, raccoons and otters and turtles. Even a couple of alligators.

I guess you've figured out that Tappany Island was a kids' paradise. Our primary playmates on the island were the innumerable nieces and nephews of Queen, who cooked and cleaned for Rick's family during the summer. Queen invariably arrived for work accompanied by a gaggle of beautiful brown-skinned children. When these happy denizens of the island weren't available to fish with us or play tag or join us in pestering Queen to whip up a batch of her wonderful featherlight waffles, the three of us, Rick, Martine and I, often rode bikes to Jeter's Market at the crossroads of Bridge Road and Center Street.

The store was fragrant with the smoky scent of the barbecued pork that the Jeters made in the wooden shed out back and with whatever fresh fish local fishermen brought in that day from the nearby public docks. Old toothless Mr. Jeter never minded if we kids read comic books without buying them, perhaps because while reading, we consumed great quantities of boiled peanuts and Gummi Bears, which he charged to the McCullochs' account.

We walked every one of those winding roads. We yanked untold numbers of blue crabs out of the marsh and poked curiously at jellyfish stranded on the wide sandy beach by the tide. So happy were we during our first summer there that we vowed on both spit and blood to meet on Tappany Island every single summer of our lives as long as we lived.

Making such a promise exhilarated us, gave the stamp of permanency to our extraordinary friendship, and was the occasion for Lilah Rose to snap a picture. We're nine years old, arms flung around each other, eyes squinting into the bright sunshine and wearing T-shirts with our club names Rilt, Milt and Tilt emblazoned across the front. Martine is sticking out her tongue at the camera, and Rick's fingers are forked behind my head, giving me devil's horns.

That's how it started for Rick and Martine and me. Later, after I read *The Three Musketeers* and we watched the movie video together at my insistence, we adopted "all for one, one for all" as our motto. It was unthinkable that anything would ever come between us.

Unthinkable—but inevitable. What we didn't know is that it would be one of us.

As I said, we were all best friends, but I first felt something special for Rick over and above friendship the day of our class picnic when were in sixth grade.

Our middle school was located across the street from a city park, and at the end of the school year, the room mothers brought fried chicken, potato salad and brownies and spread the food out on the picnic tables there. After we ate lunch, we ran wild, playing Crack the Whip and Red Rover while the mothers chatted with the teacher nearby. The boundaries were impressed upon us: no leaving the picnic area, and a buddy system was strongly enforced.

For some reason I'd worn strappy white sandals instead of my usual Nikes. It was a foolish decision because they weren't the proper shoes for playing such lively games, and eventually one of the straps broke. I retrieved my shoe in dismay as the hubbub swirled around me, limping over to a bench partly screened from the picnic area by a bush. I'd been having a great time whooping and hollering with the rest of the kids, and those sandals were my favorite shoes. I was so disappointed at being sidelined that tears gathered in the corners of my eyes and one slid slowly down my cheek.

I sat there for a while before Rick spotted me and left the others to come over and kneel at my side. "Tris?" he said. "What's wrong?" He tilted his head sideways, and his eyes reflected concern. For the first time, I noticed that the lashes were gold-tipped, bleached by the sun.

Wordlessly, I held out my shoe. "Look at this. My mom's

going to be so mad that I wore these today." I wondered if I could talk her into buying me another pair. I wondered if the store would still have that particular style.

"Oh, that's too bad," Rick said. He was studying the broken strap.

"Uh-huh." I wiped the tears from my face with the back of my hand.

"Listen, Tris, give it to me."

"What?"

He took the shoe from my hands and stood. "Stay there, I'll be right back." He loped toward the street.

"Rick, wait," I called after him, though I didn't want to get him in trouble by attracting attention. He disappeared around a magnolia tree, and all I could think of was that he'd better hurry back before we had buddy check, because they'd surely find out he was missing then.

I sat. I waited. The other kids eddied by, and once someone said, "Tris, what's wrong?"

"Nothing," I said, my unshod foot tucked beneath me on the bench. "Just resting."

Though it seemed like much longer, it was probably only twenty minutes or so before Rick returned.

"Here," he said. "Your shoe's fixed." He tossed it in my direction. Sure enough, the strap was newly attached by means of heavy white stitching.

"But how?" I whispered, turning it over in my hands.

"There's a shoe repair place right up the street. I've been there with my mom before." The sunshine glinted on the lighter strands of his hair, and he smiled at me.

"Thanks," I said. "I mean, really. Why, if they found out you left the park, you could get detention until school's out. Or maybe even suspended."

"It was worth it if you can enjoy the rest of the picnic," he said gruffly and as if embarrassed by my gratitude. I aimed a sharp glance up at him and noticed something different shimmering in the air between us, a tentative knowing, a recognition of important things left unsaid. Surprised, I blinked, and it was gone, like a burst soap bubble.

"Hey, Rick," called one of the boys over by the water fountain. "Let's play some ball."

Rick touched my hand so briefly it might not have really happened, and then he ran away to join the game. I never mentioned Rick's thoughtfulness or daring to Martine, mostly because I wasn't sure what to make of it. The complexity of the look that had passed between us that day became a secret between Rick and me, one of the many that we were to share during our lives.

It would be romantic if Rick was the first boy I kissed or the first one I dated, but that wasn't what happened. That day in the park when we were eleven was very special, but it wasn't the precursor to something more, at least not then. It was as if we both tucked the memory away for future reference, for taking out at a later date when something might come of it. As it turned out, that date was a long time coming.

We progressed through our teenage years making new friends and branching out in our interests, though the three of us, Rick, Martine and me, remained special to one another. We were still best friends. We were buddies. All for one and one for all.

In the middle of April during our senior year at John C. Calhoun High School when we were eighteen, Rick dropped Martine and me off at home. He drove a spiffy red Camaro in those days, a birthday gift from his parents, and we rode back and forth to school with him every day, the windows wide open, stereo speakers blaring full blast. On this occasion when we arrived home, two white envelopes were displayed prominently on the dining-room table. Martine spotted the envelopes first as she dropped her backpack on the nearest chair. "They're here!" she shouted gleefully, and her yell brought me running from the kitchen, where I was already digging the container of our favorite mint chocolate-chip ice cream out of the freezer.

The envelopes bore the return address of the University of South Carolina. True, it was our hometown school, but it was also first choice for all three of us. We'd grown up cheering the Gamecocks at football games in Williams-Brice Stadium, and graduating from USC seemed as natural as spending weekends at Sweetwater Cottage or eating the traditional black-eyed-peas-and-rice dish known as hoppin' john every New Year's Day for luck. As natural as being Southerners, for that matter.

Martine and I ripped open the envelopes and read the acceptance letters within. It wasn't five minutes before Rick phoned to say he'd received his letter, too.

"All for one, one for all, and all for USC!" we exclaimed gleefully, hanging up right away so we could call our friends to find out if they would be at USC, too.

It wasn't until my acceptance from Furman arrived a week later that any of us had an inkling that our plans could change. Furman offered me a scholarship that, according to my guidance counselor, merited serious consideration.

"Do you realize what you've got here?" asked Mrs. Huff, eyeing me sternly through her bifocals after cornering me near the snack machines in the school hallway. "They don't hand out this kind of money for nothing, un-huh. Your excellent scholastic record and your performance on the SAT went a long way toward getting you this scholarship award. I can't believe you'd consider turning it down."

I didn't hesitate. "I'm going to the University of South Carolina with my sister and Rick," I said firmly, whereupon Mrs. Huff yanked me none too gently into her cramped cubicle and sat me down for a serious talking-to.

"Listen up, honey. Furman is a small, private college. Here in the South, a Furman education is comparable to one from Princeton or Yale. Trista, you need to consider this. You really do."

I'd applied to Furman only because earlier in the year Mrs. Huff had badgered me until I relented and filled out the forms. The spring before, I'd sleepwalked through a Furman-campus tour, bored because Martine and Rick had refused to accompany me. Martine wasn't a Furman candidate, nor was Rick. Martine's grades weren't nearly as good as either Rick's or mine, and Rick had no intention of going anywhere but USC; his brother played football for the Gamecocks, and besides, he planned to join the same fraternity.

"I don't want to go to Furman," I told Mrs. Huff that day, but she wouldn't allow me to exit the room until I'd promised to consider it. I always suspected that Mrs. Huff put a bug in my parents' ears, because when I arrived home from school that day, they were both waiting in the living room to speak to me.

"Honey, a scholarship to Furman is a huge honor," Mom said gently, her brow wrinkled in concern. The formal education of my mother, Virginia Wood Barrineau, had ended abruptly after two years at Columbia College when her parents lost everything they owned in a securities scam. As a result, Mom had had to support herself from the time she turned twenty. She'd worked as a file clerk in a law office until she married her boss, my dad. Mom regretted skipping her last two years of college, mostly because she'd always felt educationally, though not intellectually, inferior to the wives of Dad's friends. To her credit, Mom wanted the best for her daughters, and if that meant shipping me off to Greenville a hundred miles away, well, so be it.

"Of course you'll miss Martine and Rick, but Furman is a great opportunity," my father added. "Maybe it would be good for the three of you to split up. You might enjoy exploring your independence in the next few years."

The idea of that opportunity, at least, did resonate with me. I'd never hurt Martine's feelings by telling her so, but wearing the same outfits, which we'd continued even after we became teenagers, was getting old. Martine was sensitive; Martine didn't like change. Normally, I didn't mind coddling her, and Rick catered to Martine, too. It was an unspoken pact of benevolent complicity: Martine was the weakest of the three, and the two of us compensated for that.

"I'll think about it," I sighed, intending no such thing. Mom smiled, and Dad chucked me under the chin the way he used to do when I was a little kid. He still harbored the hope that I would join the rapidly expanding family law firm someday, and Rick and I had often planned to do just that. When we were younger, a career in law sounded exciting to us, but lately I'd been doubting that I really wanted to be a lawyer.

Martine had already declared that she wasn't going to sign up for three extra years of education after getting her B.A. Worse, as far as our parents were concerned, Martine was bent on pursuing an art degree, which Dad said would prepare her for nothing except flipping burgers at a local

Hardee's. I hadn't yet told them that I was thinking about working in TV. Writing for the school newspaper had sparked an interest in journalism, and the insightful analysis of current events appealed to me. Moreover, I longed to be involved in something compelling and immediate, like television. If I'd mentioned this to my parents, they both would have gone ballistic.

The thing that finally tipped the scales toward Furman for me started out, ironically enough, as a small argument over who was going to bathe the dog. Bungie, our cockapoo, had ventured into the creek behind the house and tracked mud all over the back porch before being discovered. It was afternoon on a school holiday, and our parents stopped by the house for a few minutes before going on to a steering-committee meeting at the church.

I'd just come downstairs after getting ready to go to the mall with a group of friends, and Martine was lolling on the couch in the family room, watching TV. Our parents' appearance set off a spate of delighted barking from Bungie, who took anybody's arrival or departure as an occasion to initiate noise.

Barking drove my mother crazy. So did that peculiar deranged jumping up and down that Bungie always did when excited, kind of like a bucking bronco, over and over and over. We'd tried obedience training once, but Bungie flunked out.

"For heaven's sake," Mom chided from the kitchen over the sound of running water. "Somebody give that fool dog a bath."

"Do it right now before she tracks mud into the house. You know how your mother feels about that," and Dad glowered menacingly, only to grin and waggle his eyebrows when Mom turned her back. "Hurry up, Virginia," he called over his shoulder. "We're going to be late."

"Trista, you can take off my new hoop earrings right now," Martine said.

I'd worn them without asking, true, but what were sisters for if not to borrow things? While Martine and I were engaging in a heated altercation that resulted in my forking over the earrings, Dad wandered back into the kitchen, and soon we heard the Lincoln backing out of the driveway.

Martine glanced around at me. "Your turn to give Bungie a bath," she said in a blithe singsong that always set my teeth on edge. "I did it last time."

I knew what was behind Martine's attitude, other than the borrowed earrings, that is. I'd been invited to tag along on an outing with friends from Spanish class, and Martine was jealous because she wasn't included. Why should she be? She'd opted out of Spanish for French, airily pointing out that she needed to know French so she could converse with future lovers.

I rubbed my earringless lobes and kept a watchful eye on Bungie, who had tired of bouncing and was no doubt dreaming up her next mischief. "Get real, Martine," I said. "We both bathed her last time, and Rick helped."

"Well, I'm watching *The Young and the Restless*. I want to find out what Nikki will do if Victor hires the thug who made the indecent comment to her."

I had little patience for soap operas, or, for that matter, Martine at the moment. "I'm all dressed and ready to go. I don't care to get dirty." I stalked over to the bookcase, where I'd left yesterday's earrings after removing them last night. I slid them into the holes in my ears and squinted critically at my image in the mirror over the couch.

"So?" Martine flounced back around and gave her full attention to the drama unfolding on the TV screen.

Outside, Bungie began to whimper and paw at the door.

"We could do it together," I suggested. "You hold her and I'll squirt the water."

Martine shook her head. "Uh-uh. You've got the wr-o-o-ng number."

"Come on, Martine," I wheedled in desperation. It was almost time for my ride.

"No way."

I tried reasoning. "If Bungie pokes a hole in the screen, Mom will start talking about how we ought to give her to the people next door." This had been a constant refrain from our mother, who said the neighbors would provide a better place for Bungie, seeing as they had no kids and stayed home all the time, and we would be going away to college in the fall, anyway, and then who would take care of that dog? Mom, that's who, and she'd never even wanted a pet. You may have figured out by this time that our mother was anything but an animal lover.

Martine got up, and at first I thought she was giving in. Instead, she walked to the back door and held it open. The ecstatic Bungie immediately began to race in frantic circles around the kitchen, tracking muddy smudges wherever she stepped. With a triumphant smirk, Martine went back to her TV program, ignoring my outraged shrieks.

Past experience had taught me that there was no point in further arguing, so I grabbed Bungie and hustled her outside, where I washed her as best I could without hog-tying her. Of course, Bungie shook water all over me, and of course I ended up a mess, after which I went back inside and cleaned up the footprints in the kitchen. By the time I'd finished, I was so angry that I could have throttled Martine.

Which was why, when the gang stopped by, I told them to go on to the mall without me. Then I went upstairs and composed a letter informing Furman University that I was accepting their kind offer of financial aid and would enter as a freshman in the fall.

When she found out, Martine was shocked. Rick was surprised but cautiously supportive. My parents were ecstatic.

During the frequent periods of doubt that ensued after I made this momentous decision, I reminded myself that my father could be right. It was time for me to stop being the person I'd always been and to start creating the woman I wanted to be. The ideal way to do that, in my estimation, was to sever my identity with Martine and Rick once and for all.

The only thing was, I'd miss my soul mates, the two most important people in the world to me. I'd miss them so very much.

And they, of course, would miss me.

Chapter 4: Trista

1990

Click: Prom night in our senior year at John C. Calhoun High, Columbia, South Carolina. The three of us are posed in a latticed gazebo. Rick is standing between Martine and me, one arm around each. We're wearing identical black dresses, strapless and slinky, with a wide white band circling the top of the bodice and identical chrysanthemum corsages on our wrists. I'm smiling up at Rick, whose expression is serious. There's something spacey about the way Martine is grinning into the camera, though I didn't notice it at the time.

The fact that I wouldn't be at the University of South Carolina the following year made senior-prom night—our last big blast together—even more poignant and important. Rick insisted on squiring both Martine and me to the dance, declaring that he'd have the two prettiest dates there. We were more than agreeable, since Martine had broken up with her boyfriend a couple of months before, and I wasn't dating anyone special.

It should have been perfect—the limo, our corsages, everything. Our class had chosen to hold the prom the Saturday night at the beginning of spring break at the biggest hotel in downtown Columbia. The theme was Summertime, like the song from Gershwin's *Porgy and Bess*. Martine and I shopped for two months, checking out boutiques and department stores in Greenville and Charleston before we found the perfect dresses, which were excruciatingly expensive. Dad sprang for them anyway, remarking that when you were a man blessed with two beautiful daughters, it was your responsibility to keep them looking good. Martine and I giggled at that; we were tall and blond and attracted more than our share of attention because there were two of us, but lots of other girls at our school were just as pretty and every bit as pampered by their fathers.

Trouble started to brew a couple of weeks before the big event when I casually mentioned at the dinner table one night that Rick and one of his friends were going to chip in to rent a room at the hotel on prom night. Adjourning to hotel rooms after the dance had become standard procedure at our school, and I was sure that our parents would fall into line. We'd heard lots of chatter about other kids' parents paying for the rooms, the rationale being that they didn't want the kids driving home drunk, and they were good kids, never any problems, so why tempt fate? Safe at the hotel, kids could hang with their friends, watch TV, and if they were going to sneak a few drinks, so what? I'd heard stories of people puking their guts out at last year's prom, of a girl who'd called her parents at three in the morning begging them to come to the hotel and get her, but I'd discarded them as exaggerations. Besides, in every group of teenagers, you'd find guys who considered it cool to drink until they barfed and girls who got scared when their dates became too familiar.

After I innocently dropped the information over dinner one evening that Rick was planning to get a hotel room and that Martine and I intended to stay there overnight, my father slid his chair back from the table and drew his brows in the way that usually preceded a lecture. Martine darted a covert warning glance in my direction.

"And I suppose Rick will be bringing you home in the morning?"

"Sure," I said, already sorry I'd floated the idea.

"How? I doubt that the limo driver is going to stick around waiting that long." Renting a limousine for prom night was the norm, and Rick had already paid the deposit.

"Maybe Rick will leave his car at the hotel earlier and drive us home in the morning," I said, definitely on shaky ground.

"Sometimes guys do that, leave their cars there the afternoon before the dance," Martine chimed in.

"Hunh. So let me get this straight. After the prom, everyone sits around a hotel room in their prom finery? On the beds?" my father asked, a scowl spreading across his handsome face.

"Usually, kids dress for the prom at the hotel beforehand, and afterward they wear the same clothes they had on when they checked in. Then everyone watches TV and maybe orders room service," Martine said. "And they have tables in the rooms. Sometimes a couch to sit on."

"But there are beds," Dad said ominously.

"It's not a big deal, Dad," I said. "Anyhow, you don't have to have beds to do what you're thinking." This seemed like common sense to me, knowing as I did two or three girls who'd had babies, and not by stumbling across them in a collard patch, either.

He glowered across the table. "My daughters do not spend the night in a hotel room with a guy." Have I mentioned that as a defense lawyer, our father excelled at the art of logical argument and enjoyed sparring with us?

"Dad—" I said, not too worried at this point. His resistance might be no more than part of his training program; Dad still cherished the possibility that Martine and I might join his law firm someday.

"Daddy—" Martine said at the same time.

"Roger," Mom said hastily, "maybe we should talk this over later."

"It's only Rick, Dad," I reminded him patiently. "He's not just 'a guy.'"

"Roger, there *will* be three of them," Mom added. "It's hard to imagine that anything, um, bad could happen. Rick's parents gave him permission."

Dad slapped his hands on the table, palms down. A vein throbbed in his neck. "Rick is a fine young man, but Trista and Martine are not spending the night at a hotel with him or any other boy. Stuff happens. Bad stuff. And don't give me 'Daddy, please,' or 'Dad, all the kids are doing it.' Just because everyone else decides to jump off a cliff, does that mean I have to let my daughters do it?" This, of course, was a rhetorical question, and one that we'd heard often enough as we were growing up.

"But if you don't let us stay at the hotel all night, we'll have to come home after the prom is over," Martine wailed.

"Nothing wrong with that," my father stated firmly, tossing his napkin onto the table and stalking out of the room.

Okay, so Dad's abandonment of the argument meant that his decision was final. The master of our fates had spoken. I was smart enough not to push it, at least not then.

I gazed down at my lap, my mother emitted sounds of distress and Martine burst into tears.

Martine and I spent the next few days commiserating with each other. Our friends added fuel to the fire by declaring that *their* parents were allowing *them* to stay at the hotel overnight, and how could *our* parents be so mean? To which we replied sorrowfully that it was beyond us, our father was hopelessly old-fashioned and *just didn't understand*. Keep in mind that this was the year that Martine and I alternated between loving our parents to death and being sure they were out to ruin our lives.

A few days before the prom, our mother, her blue eyes sparkling with excitement, walked into our room and perched on the edge of my bed. She'd just had her hair trimmed, and it swung across her cheeks in a shiny arc as she told us she had a wonderfully exciting secret to reveal.

"It's about prom night," she said, barely able to contain her glee. "The Finnerans are having an all-night party at their house and you two are invited!"

I was folding socks to put in my drawer, and Martine sat at her desk producing a pen-and-ink cartoon for the school paper, where we both were on staff. My face fell, and Martine let out a groan. "Alec Finneran is the biggest dork in our school, and I wouldn't spend prom night at his house for anything in the world, not even a date with Keanu." This announcement was major, since Martine had been in love with the movie star Keanu Reeves for over a year. She even blotted her lipstick on a mini poster of him that she'd taped on the inside of her school-locker door.

Mom plowed ahead. "Both Gail and John Finneran intend to stay up all night to monitor the party. They'll set up tables around their swimming pool, and they're planning to order an eight-foot-long sub." I had to hand it to poor Mom; she was trying to make the idea sound attractive.

"I told you Alec was dorky," Martine said with conviction. "Otherwise he wouldn't agree to an eight-foot-long sub." Her words oozed sarcasm.

We waited in stony silence for Mom to say the next word, and of course she did.

"Your dad said it would be okay if you stayed out at the Finnerans' after the prom."

"Auurgh! I hate my life," Martine said, flopping onto her twin bed and burying her head under the pillow.

"Me, too," I agreed. I crossed my arms over my chest and avoided Mom's eyes.

Our mother heaved a sigh, stood and headed for the door. "Mine isn't so great right now, either. You twins didn't arrive with an instruction manual." She was still smiling, forced though it was. "I worry about you."

"We're eighteen, Mom," I reminded her with growing impatience. "We can take care of ourselves."

"You don't even know what to watch out for," she said with considerable conviction, and Martine and I exchanged a baffled glance. This was another parental declaration that made little sense to us.

As Mom's footsteps faded down the stairs, Martine spoke up, her words still muffled by the pillow, "You'd better call Rick and tell him the fantastic news about Alec Dork's party. And don't forget the eight-foot sub, which we'll be eating by the romantic blue light of the Finnerans' humongous bug zapper."

When we told him about the party, Rick tossed off a good-natured comment along the lines of "Let's roll with the punches." As a result, by the time prom night trundled around, we were psyched up for the dance and resigned to Alec's party. A few other kids in the neighborhood would be there, and one of them was bringing his guitar. If the weather was warm enough, we'd go for a moonlight swim in the Finnerans' pool. None of that would be so bad, really, and Rick even talked Alec out of the sub in favor of grilling hamburgers.

When Rick arrived at our house on prom night, we oohed and aahed over him in his rented tux. He'd chosen black, like our dresses, and the white tucked shirt had a cool wing collar and cuffs fastened with links borrowed from his dad. He wore a red cummerbund and shiny black shoes. He looked fantastic and said the same about us.

Of course, we had to troop out to the backyard and have our pictures taken in front of Mom's prize camellias. Another snapshot, another milestone in our lives.

When the three of us walked under the bower of fresh flowers into the ballroom at the hotel, we were a showstopper. Heads literally snapped around in midconversation, jaws dropped and Mr. Helms, the principal, favored us with one of his toothy smiles. He clapped Rick on the shoulder, shook Martine's and my hands and directed us to the refreshment table, where Mrs. Huff was ladling out syrupy pink punch.

"What is this stuff—antifreeze?" Martine murmured, smiling sweetly at a bevy of chaperones all the while.

"Flop sweat," I told her, having recently heard the term

and thinking it appropriate, though I had no idea what flop sweat might be.

Martine snickered, and Rick grinned. "Which one of you would like to dance first?" he asked as the band ground out a heavy rock beat. They were a local newbie outfit called Hootie and the Blowfish, whose popularity was growing with the college crowd.

"I'll dance," Martine said offhandedly. She set her cup down on a nearby table and accompanied Rick out on the floor.

After that, guys asked me to dance, putting both arms around my waist, and I looped my hands behind their necks. It was the classic prom waddle, nothing fancy. I'd known a lot of the boys from kindergarten—Dave Barnhill, Shaz Gainey, Chris Funderburk. They all had dates, but their dates were my friends, and we had no illusions of exclusivity.

Things got a little crazier as the evening wore on, and the dancing became less inhibited as more people arrived. Girls exclaimed over one another's dresses, the guys joked, the chaperones beamed approvingly the way they always do as long as things remain calm. The stays from my long-line strapless bra dug into my ribs, and I was glad to dance with Rick after a while because I could be honest about my agony.

"You should be wearing a choke collar like this one." With a grimace of distaste, he removed his hand from my waist and ran a forefinger inside the offending object. "But—" and he gazed down at me with a twinkle in his eyes, just managing not to ogle my cleavage "—I'm awfully glad you're dressed the way you are. You're gorgeous, Trista."

"Martine, too," I replied automatically as she swooped into the periphery of my vision. Shaz was dipping her, and her laughter verged on the manic. I tried to catch her eye, but Rick twirled me too fast. When I remembered to look for Martine again, I didn't see her.

I was having such a good time that it didn't matter. Martine and I weren't joined at the hip, after all. Kids began to drift out of the ballroom toward the end of the evening, heading upstairs to their rooms, and I admit to a pang of frustration as I watched them leave. I was eager that night to leave my childhood behind. Senior prom marked a rite of passage, and I was heady with the promise of the future and all the wonderful new experiences that would soon open to me.

Before the last dance, Mr. Helms climbed the steps to the bandstand. He intoned something into the microphone about the revels at the hotel being over, that mumble mumble we were a fine group of young people, that he harbored great mumble hopes as he loosed us on the rest of the world. He also said, his voice lowering on a note of seriousness, that none of the gatherings at the hotel after midnight were school-sanctioned. He'd sent flyers home stating that very fact, much to the satisfaction of my father.

The last dance was slow and dreamy, and Rick appeared as if by magic and took me in his arms. This time, unlike during our other dances, he rested his cheek against my temple, making me conscious of how well we fit together. For a few minutes, I imagined how it would be if Rick were really someone I dated. I'd had boyfriends, a few that I liked a lot. I never fell in love with any of them, and to the guys I went out with, I was just a date who had a few interesting things to say and knew how to shag really well. No, that doesn't mean what you're thinking. The shag is what we call our South Carolina official dance, and I'd learned it from my parents, the 1970 shag champions of Myrtle Beach.

Okay, okay, I can't help it if that's what they call the sex act in England. A shag can also be either a rug or a haircut, take your pick.

Anyway, as the band wound the song to a close, Rick held me close for a moment. Then it was over, and everyone started calling out their good-nights. One boy stumbled over the edge of the dance floor, and Rick pulled me back in case the guy fell in our direction.

"That's Bill Kryzalic," Rick whispered. "Drunk as a skunk."

"What did he do—bring booze in a flask?" The chaperones were keeping a sharp eye out for any flouting of the rules, which were clear: we catch you drinking at the prom and you get a stern lecture, plus we deliver you in disgrace to your parents. Serious infractions were penalized by school suspension, and with final exams in the offing, this could jeopardize a student's graduation.

"Some guys had flasks in the restroom," Rick acknowledged. "Pretty stupid, if you ask me."

"Have you seen Martine lately?" I asked, frowning.

"She was dancing with Hugh Barfield about twenty minutes ago." A lightning streak of alarm rippled through me, a warning, an alert. A glance passed between Rick and me, an instant communication of alarm. We each knew what the other was thinking, as we so often did.

I kept my voice calm. "Think I should check out the ladies' room?"

"Sure. We don't want to be late for Alec's party," Rick said, devilishly trying to distract me from worrying about Martine.

Exasperated, I punched him in the arm and left. He leaned against a column, hands in pockets, to wait.

The ladies' room was not as crowded as it had been earlier. "Martine?" I called as I entered the anteroom, where a couple of girls were applying lipstick or tucking stray wisps of hair into their elaborate hairdos.

"She's not in here," drawled Kaytee Blackmon, one of the girls from Spanish class. "Are you two heading up to the sixth floor for the parties?"

I didn't feel like launching into the poor-pitiful-us explanation. "Not sure yet," I said, pretending that everything was normal and breezing out of there as quickly as I could.

Rick was still leaning against the pillar where I'd left him, but he had loosened his tie so it hung around his collar. He lifted his eyebrows. "So where is she?"

"I haven't a clue. Rick, I'm worried."

"Let's check the ballroom," he said.

The only people still around were members of the hotel cleanup crew, our principal and Mrs. Huff, who was packing up the punch bowl.

"Do you know," she said, smiling as we approached, "this is my aunt's Waterford that she willed to me? Aunt Eulalie would be so pleased that I've put it to good use."

"Mrs. Huff, do you know where Martine is?"

"Oh, she was out dancing the boogaloo with some John Travolta look-alike a few minutes ago," Mrs. Huff said.

Rick and I exchanged grins. Boogaloo? John Travolta? What century was Mrs. Huff living in, anyway?

Still, I couldn't shake the sense that something was wrong, terribly wrong, with Martine. My concern mounted as we pressed into the lobby behind a couple of football players who were friends of Rick's. We asked them if anyone had seen her.

"Didn't she go upstairs with some of the other kids?" asked one of the guys.

"I doubt it," I replied.

"I'm sure she got on the elevator," said one of the others.

"Oh, shit," Rick muttered. "What the hell is she up to?"

I rested a hand on Rick's sleeve. "Rick, she could have gone up for a while and meant to be back but lost track of the time."

"You're right," Rick said, a line of worry appearing between his eyes. He knew as well as I did that Martine had no business being on the sixth floor.

We crowded into the elevator, and the exchange among the other kids was loud and jocular. When the doors opened and we all tumbled out, someone behind us yelled, "Party!" at the top of his lungs.

Most of the doors to the rooms lining the corridor were open, and music blared from several. Shannon Sottile, one of my colleagues on the school newspaper, lounged in a doorway, sipping from a paper cup.

"Hiya, Trista. Whassup?"

"We can't find Martine," I told her. Shannon had changed into hip-huggers so tight that she must have slithered them on.

"She's not in my room," she said, "but come in anyway. We've got a bunch of food that my mother sent over, Triscuits and cream cheese with hot-pepper jelly. Half a ham."

"Later," Rick said, pushing past her.

The next room's door was closed, a discarded bow tie draped across the doorknob in a not-so-subtle signal that the occupants wanted privacy. I wondered who was in there doing the deed; I wondered whether I'd be having sex, too, if I had a boyfriend. I had never let anyone get past second base, though I was curious about how I'd feel if I ever did. Happy? Scared? In love? Who knew?

Rick's hand in the small of my back guided me to the next door, behind which a raucous gathering was in progress. Sam Gambrell, wearing a pair of wrinkled Bermudas and nothing else, staggered into the hall. In the room behind him, the cheerleaders' captain danced on one of the beds to an MTV video playing loudly on the television set behind her. She was bouncing up and down, her hair loose and unruly, a group of onlookers egging her on.

"Has Martine been around here?" Rick asked Sam.

"Ummmm, yeah. A while back. She went through there."

Something was wrong with Martine, I felt it in my bones. I slipped my hand into Rick's as we craned our heads far enough inside the door that we could see where Sam was pointing. A corridor in the room led past a bank of closets on one side, and an open door adjoined this room and the next. Rick stepped into the murky gloom inside and pulled me in after him.

The closets in the hall between the two rooms faced a bathroom, where someone was washing her face.

"Hi, Rick," said Kim Yarbrough. "Hi, Trista." She was stuffed into a royal blue satin dress like a sausage into a casing.

"We're trying to find Martine," I said, standing on tiptoe to peer over Rick's shoulder.

"She was with Hugh Barfield," Kim said in a confidential tone. "They went in there." She angled her head over her shoulder toward the other room.

"Hugh had a date with Abigail, didn't he?"

"They were fighting, and she ran down the hall crying," Kim said.

Just then we heard someone vomiting in the bathroom next door. I was right behind Rick when he rounded the corner into the brightly lit vanity alcove. The open door to the tub and toilet area revealed a pale Martine leaning over the white porcelain john and retching miserably.

My heart sank. Somehow Rick and I had to get Martine out of there, and it didn't look as if she'd be in any shape to leave for quite a while.

Chapter 5: Trista

1990

"Martine!" I said, brushing past Rick, who stood frozen in the doorway.

"Tris, oh Tris. I'm so-o-o-o-o sick."

I knelt beside her and held her head, murmuring to her. When she leaned back against the bathtub, I stood, rinsed a clean washcloth in cool water and passed it to her so she could wipe her face.

She handed the washcloth back, eyes sunken, cheeks hollow.

"Are you going to be okay?" I asked, not at all happy with the state she was in. We'd have some explaining to do if we didn't manage to remove the stain down the front of her dress before Mom saw it.

Martine nodded wearily. "Hugh gave me something to drink. I had too much. Or maybe it was because I mixed it with all that sickening punch—" She clutched her stomach but managed to get her nausea under control.

"You're going to be just fine," Rick said from behind me. "Let me help you up."

"Where's your purse?" I asked.

Martine only moaned, and I went into the other room. Unlike the room we'd passed through earlier, this one was dark and quiet. I groped for a light switch, my eyes unaccustomed to the darkness after the glaring brightness of the bathroom. Someone reached out and grabbed my wrist.

"Where've you been, Martine?" asked Hugh Barfield, looming out of the darkness. I recoiled at his boozy breath.

"I'm not—"

"They have names for girls like you. I'd never have pegged you for a tease. Now, come on and I'll show you the fun I promised." Behind him I saw a king-size bed with its bedspread flung back and the sheets all rumpled.

"I'm Trista, not Martine," I said. "She's in the bathroom, throwing up her guts. Let me *go*." I wrenched away from him, but he was too quick for me, also very strong. He played guard on the football team and was built like a Hummer on steroids.

"You're Martine. You can't fool me," he said, and in horror I felt him fumbling with the top of my dress. I said, "No!", but he lurched against me and before I knew it, I was on the bed and he was lying on top of me.

I was terrified. Sure, there were other kids nearby, but now this guy was yanking my dress up. My futile struggles only incited him more.

"Stop," I said, but the word was muffled by his chest pressing against my face so I could hardly breathe. I turned my head aside and tried to scream, but all I managed was a grunt.

And then Hugh's weight suddenly lifted off. Rick yelled something and tossed Hugh across the room, where he landed on a table and yelped. Hugh was up in an instant, slamming Rick into the wall. Out of the corners of my eye, I saw classmates crowding around both doors.

Martine was wailing, but Rick kept his cool. Pinned against the wall as he was, the only thing he could do was crack his head against Hugh's. It worked. Hugh loosened his grip, and Rick twisted away. Blood ran down his cheek, staining his white shirt.

Hugh staggered backward, but Rick wasn't through with him yet. He grabbed a handful of Hugh's shirt and unleashed a punch that connected with Hugh's jaw. Rick would have kept hitting him except that Sam, Shaz and some of the others inserted themselves between them. Hugh, his nose bleeding copiously, struggled to lurch to his feet.

I ran to Rick, collapsing against him, and Martine joined us, hugging us both. Martine and I were sobbing, me with considerable relief.

"Hurry," Rick said. "Let's get out of here." We broke apart, Martine and I linking arms around each other as Rick aimed us toward the door. Which was where we encountered a couple of stern hotel security guards, who took a dim view of the situation, though they eased off when we told them we were going home. Shaz was tending to Hugh, and everyone stood silently aside while the security guards escorted us from the room and then out of the hotel, where the limo driver was waiting patiently under the front portico.

I'd managed to pull myself together, to be strong for

Martine and Rick because that was what they expected of me, but apart from my indignation and anger, I was just plain scared. Even so, damage control was uppermost in my mind. I was already thinking ahead to how to keep Mom and Dad from finding out what had transpired that night. Finally I understood the dire looks that had passed between my parents when we'd all sat around the dining-room table the night Martine and I had asked permission to stay at the hotel. "Stuff happens" is the way Dad had put it, and now I understood what kind of stuff he meant.

On the way home in the limo, Martine lay with her head cradled in my lap. Beside me, Rick dabbed silently at the cut on his forehead, which was still bleeding. We sped away from downtown Columbia, leaving its bright lights and nightlife behind. Commercial buildings gave way to residential neighborhoods, and soon we reached the suburbs with their neat houses and quiet streets. Before long I spotted a white H on a blue road sign. We were near the hospital where Mom had gone to have her broken foot X-rayed some years ago.

"Should we stop by the emergency room? See if you need stitches?" I asked Rick.

"No," he said. "It's nothing much."

Martine groaned. She'd be feeling the aftereffects tomorrow morning, I was sure. Part of me sympathized with what she'd done—I'd wanted to go to the party on the sixth floor, too. Still, I was furious with her for getting Rick and me in such a mess.

As we climbed out of the limo in front of our house, a gentle breeze soughed through the oak trees. I curved my arm around Martine's shoulders while Rick tipped the driver. Above us a myriad of stars spun through the sky, gleaming points of white. You think the stars will always be there, yet they blaze into life and then drift away, eventually burning themselves out. Like people, I thought. Like us.

"You sure you kids are going to be all right?" our driver asked. He'd waited patiently outside the hotel, expressed concern about Rick's cut and given him a handkerchief with which to blot up the blood.

Rick's gesture encompassed the cul-de-sac. "We all live here. We're okay. Thanks, man."

The driver nodded but didn't leave until we'd gone into the house.

Only the dignified ticking of the grandfather clock punctuated the silence inside. Mom and Dad had left a night-light burning in the hall as they always did when Martine and I were out in the evening.

I peeked into the garage to check on the Lincoln. It was in its usual spot, so I hurried back to the hall, where Martine was leaning with her forehead against the wall and Rick was awkwardly patting her shoulder.

"Wait here," I whispered.

I made my way up the stairs as quietly as I could. My parents' bedroom door was open and the room was dark, the red digital display of the alarm clock glowing beside the bed. A board creaked under my light footsteps.

"Martine?" my mother said sleepily.

"Trista," I corrected her. I stopped at the door. Dad was snoring; nothing ever woke him, but Mom was a light sleeper.

"Did you enjoy the dance, honey?"

"Uh-huh."

"That's wonderful. Have a good time at Alec's party. You can tell us all about the prom tomorrow morning. Dad's going to cook one of his belly-buster breakfasts, so be sure to invite Rick." Every once in a while, Dad outdid himself on Sunday morning—eggs, ham, grits and flaky batter biscuits made from scratch the way his mother taught him.

"That's good. G'night, Mom." I moved toward our room.

"Have fun, Trissy." I heard her roll over and sigh.

After a minute or so, I tiptoed back downstairs. By this time, Martine and Rick had moved to the kitchen, Martine pale and sitting in a chair, Rick's cut still bleeding a good bit.

"Go on up and get into bed," I directed Martine. "If she hears you, Mom will assume we're changing clothes for Alec's party. Dad's not going to wake up—he's dead to the world."

"What about the party?"

I glared at my sister, disheveled and clutching her stomach. "I'd say that's out, Martine. You can't show up at the Finnerans' like this, and there'd be too many questions if I went without you."

"Okay," Martine said weakly. "You'll be up to bed soon, right?"

"Yeah, but I suggest you take a few Tums. Dad's planning a belly buster for tomorrow."

I pushed Martine toward the hall. "Go *on*. Before Mom decides to wake up again and get chatty because she can't go back to sleep. And hide the dress. We'll drop it off at the dry cleaner's Monday."

Martine went.

"Now you," I said to Rick. "I'm afraid you're going to resemble a piece of raw hamburger tomorrow."

"I guess, considering where the cut is, I can't pass it off as a shaving nick," Rick said.

"There's always running into a door."

"Or falling downstairs," he said.

We kept a well-stocked first-aid kit in the hall bathroom,

and I made Rick sit on the toilet lid while I washed out his wound with peroxide. He winced but didn't complain.

"This is deeper than I thought," I said as I studied it. "No wonder it bled so much."

"The shirt is ruined," he said, gazing down ruefully at the blood-spattered tucks and pleats.

"I'll handle that," I said. "Take it off."

As he shrugged out of the shirt, I peered at the cut on his head again. I didn't like the way it splayed from the center. Stitches might be required, and I said so.

While I ran cold water into the sink, Rick stood and inspected his reflection in the bathroom mirror. "It could be worse. Just stick a Band-Aid on it."

He sat back down, and I pressed the bloody shirt into the water before rummaging in the first-aid kit. I remembered how, when Dad cut his hand while sharpening a lawn-mower blade, he'd refused to go to a doctor. Mom had positioned the two sides of flesh together before securing them with a butterfly bandage, and I was lucky enough to find such a bandage in the kit.

I squirted a liberal dose of Bacitracin on Rick's wound, padded the cut with gauze and applied the butterfly. I did a pretty good job, and I was sure that when Rick washed his hair and it fell in its natural pattern over his forehead, the cut would be barely noticeable.

"There," I said. "We're finished." I turned my attention to the sink, where the blood had colored the water bright pink. I swished it, rinsed it, squeezed some of the water out and studied it. "The bloodstains are fading," I said.

"Are you going to tell your parents that we went to Alec's party?" Rick asked as he followed me into the kitchen, where I rolled up the shirt and shoved it into a plastic bag.

I shook my head. "No point in lying if we don't have to. I'll invent some reason we didn't go." I handed the bag to Rick, who squished it smaller and stuffed it into his pocket. He picked up the tux jacket and slung it over his arm.

"Like what? Let's coordinate our stories."

"Cramps. One of us had cramps and had to come home, so the rest of us skipped the party, too." I'd let Martine have the cramps, I figured. That way Dad might exempt her from his belly buster in the morning.

"Okay. That'll work." I felt no embarrassment talking about something as intimate as menstrual cramps with Rick. He'd heard many discussions of female topics over the years.

"I might stop by the party after I change," Rick said. "I could explain to Alec that you're staying home. That way no one will call here to find out why we haven't shown up."

I certainly didn't want anyone calling us. Any unusual activity at this hour or later had the potential for raising our parents' suspicions, and if either of them woke up and found Martine soused, both of us would be grounded for weeks.

"Not a bad idea," I agreed.

I preceded Rick into the kitchen, switching out lights as we went. Rick walked to the door, and I followed him onto the porch. A sweet breeze whispered through the dogwoods, trembling the blossoms on their stems. A mist of petals drifted through the air, sinking to join those that already blanketed the grass. The moon was a pale crescent floating through the night. The sky seemed not only alive with stars but with possibilities, promise and the excitement of being. I shivered, but not from a chill.

Rick grinned down at me, and I recalled how we had danced and how being held in his arms had touched something magical inside me.

"Quite a night, huh?" he said.

"It was supposed to be one of the happiest nights of our lives," I replied wistfully.

"That's the usual PR on proms."

"It's all hype," I retorted.

"At least this one will be memorable."

"Unfortunately. Rick, thanks for what you did at the hotel. It was awful. I—I was scared. If it hadn't been for you—" I stopped, tears filling my eyes.

"All for one and one for all," he reminded me. His eyes were dark, his face silvered in moonlight.

The three of us had an unwritten rule that we didn't make moves on one another, but without realizing it, I'd been leaning toward him. Suddenly, I felt a kind of magnetic pull. A tug, an impetus so strong that I couldn't resist, and as if he read my mind, Rick swayed toward me. My arms went around him, embracing bare skin. His enfolded me, and, as I had back in the hotel room, I felt protected by their strength.

It was as if a dam broke inside me then, releasing all the terror I'd felt when Hugh had tried to rape me. I'm not sure what emotion was uppermost in my mind as I gave vent to my tears—grief for the loss of innocence? A new and inescapable knowledge of my own vulnerability in the adult world that I'd been so eager to join?

"Tris?" Rick said uncertainly, touching my face. "Trista?" His hand dropped away and he stared down at his damp fingers. I lowered my head and sobbed against his bare chest.

His embrace tightened around me, and I clung to him, drawing on his strength, his support, his caring. Afterward, I couldn't name the moment when my misery turned from pain to pleasure, when his comforting caresses became sexual in nature. I remember Rick's heart beating beneath my palms, the roughness of his cheek against my temple, my astonishment at my own arousal. As my sobs stilled, my head angled back, and when my eyes met Rick's, all the world was concentrated in his gaze.

Our lips met tentatively at first, gentle, soft, tender, flavored by the salt of my tears. I'd kissed a lot of boys, but never one who awakened a longing in me. Kissing was just kissing, done for kissing's sake, but not this time. Not with Rick. When our kisses deepened, when I realized that I wanted him to touch me in a way that no other boy ever had, I was truly shaken. But not shaken enough to call a halt.

Instead, I moved even closer, pressing my hips against his, feeling his erection against the front of my dress. It was so different than with Hugh. That had disgusted me, but the sheer unexpected pleasure of this made up for that ugly scene in the hotel room. Being held by Rick cleansed me of any lingering distaste for an act that I knew in my heart should be beautiful, and in those moments, I wanted to make love with him. Wanted Rick to be the first. Wanted, more than anything, to give him something that I'd never given anyone else.

His hand molded my cheek. Slowly, I raised my own and laid it over his, threading our fingers together. Then I guided his hand down along the curve of my throat to the warm hollow just above my bodice.

He breathed in deeply, and his fingers tightened under mine. I wasn't sure how we'd manage to do what was supposed to happen next with my parents asleep upstairs and Martine apt to waken at any moment. It didn't matter. I wanted to do it. Maybe a blanket of dogwood blossoms would be our bed. Or—or—

"We shouldn't," Rick said, his mouth still close to mine. "We can't."

I disagreed. His hand clasped in mine, I urged him down the steps. He was willing—oh, yes. Our footsteps thudded in cadence with our heartbeats as we ran together through the backyard and into the woods, stopping to kiss and touch more than once, then breaking away and slipping through the shadows as if we were shadows ourselves.

I hadn't visited our old tree house in a while, but I knew Rick and his buddies used it for a gathering place where they could drink beer or smoke cigarettes away from the watchful eyes of parents, and I'd long suspected that some of them met girls there. When we reached it, I turned, wanting to remember always the way Rick looked—hair rumpled, eyes heavy lidded, the rest of him a dark outline against the moon-dappled forest.

Rick circled his arms around me. He backed me against the tree trunk and we kissed lingeringly, passionately, lost in the sense of doing something forbidden. For the first time in my life I felt voluptuous, wanton, with the power to make a man desire me. From the direction of the Finnerans' house came the sound of laughter and the smell of charcoal smoke, but it seemed far away and in a different world.

It wasn't much of a climb to the platform, which was only five feet above the ground, and I shimmied my dress up over my hips before I started up the ladder. Rick followed, and, standing there in the place where we'd spent so many good times together, I went tremulously into his embrace. Slowly and ceremoniously, he unzipped my dress in the back. Unhooking my strapless bra, he released me from those dreadful stays, and I looked down wonderingly to see my breasts cupped perfectly in his hands.

He bent and kissed one, then the other, and I could have swooned with the heady excitement of it. Together we moved beneath the roof, lost in our mutual desire, kneeling to face each other on a thin mattress that someone had put there, exploring each other's bodies with reverence and a remarkable lack of self-consciousness. In a way, it seemed as if every single moment of our childhood and the abiding faithfulness of our friendship had led us to where we were at that moment.

The mattress smelled musty, but there was a clean blanket over it. Someone had camped there recently and left not only the blanket but some towels and a few empty beer cans, which glimmered like gold in the moonlight. The leaves rustled above us, allowing light to shimmer across our bodies. Our kisses deepened, lengthened, and it was as if I'd always known the taste of Rick, the texture of hard muscles braided beneath his skin. I shifted into a mindless absorption, a state where sensation was all. When he settled himself between my thighs, I was overcome with gladness. I wrapped my arms around him and took him into me easily and as painlessly as if he had always belonged there. In those moments, I felt wrapped in his love, and I loved him in return.

When it was over and we lay quietly in each other's arms, I touched Rick's eyes, traced his lips with my fingertips and contentedly fitted my head to the hollow of his shoulder, sure that nothing could have been more moving. As we listened to the plaintive music of a lone guitar drifting from the Finnerans' backyard, Rick stroked my hair, lost in his own thoughts, which I could barely imagine. I hoped he felt what I felt. How could he not? An act so earthshaking and so fulfilling couldn't have failed to complete him in the same way it had me.

"Hey," he said after a while. "We'd better go." He dropped a kiss on my cheek, caressed my breast one last time.

I sat up, loath to leave him. "I wish we didn't have to." His eyes were dark, the outline of his face limned in moonlight. Rick had been my friend for half my life. He'd inhabited my days and nights since I was nine years old, but now I felt as if I'd never seen him—*really* seen him—before.

"Martine may wake up and wonder where you went."

I ignored his comment. Suddenly shy about my nakedness, I clutched the blanket around me. Rick pulled on his clothes and bent to gather mine before I preceded him down the ladder, and then we wordlessly picked our way through the woods to the dark and somnolent house.

At my back door, I raised my lips for his kiss, which he gave freely. I accepted the bundle of my prom gown from him and said, "Don't forget Dad's breakfast tomorrow. You're invited."

He shook his head. "I don't think so, Trista. Not after—" And he gestured toward the woods. "I can't." For a moment, he looked stricken, but he quickly masked the expression and I didn't think anything of it.

"Are you going to the party?"

He shook his head. "I'll say I didn't go because you and Martine didn't. That'll work, I guess."

"All right. Good night, Rick." I touched his cheek, and he smiled briefly.

"Good night."

Rick waited while I went inside, and I watched from the kitchen window as he angled off through the hedge and disappeared in the direction of his house. I stopped in the downstairs bathroom and flipped on the light, staring at my reflection in the mirror. Recognition of our new status as lovers burned through me, but I marveled that I didn't appear any different except for my lips, which were swollen from

Rick's kisses. This was a disappointment. I wanted to be marked by an experience that had irrevocably changed me.

Upstairs, Martine lay sound asleep, breathing audibly with her mouth open. I shoved the blanket into the back of the closet for washing in secret later and tossed my dress and underwear on the desk chair. Then I crawled into bed and slept, oblivious to the possible consequences of what Rick and I had done.

The next day I was surprised when I heard from some of the kids that Rick had driven down to Tappany Island early that morning with his brother. I didn't understand how he could have left now that we were lovers, and I could hardly wait to see him again. Afire with a new urgency, I walked around in a trance of desire, obsessed with my own sensuality. My body seemed heavy and ripe, my breasts pendulous and sensitive to the chafing of my clothes. Love songs on the radio acquired a special significance. Mom or Dad would speak to me, and I wouldn't hear. Martine would suggest something fun to do, and I'd forget about it.

When finally Lilah Rose called and suggested that Martine and I join her family at Sweetwater Cottage, I was so eager to get there that I counted the hours until it was time to leave. I was sure that once we were together, Rick and I would renew our passion for each other. I planned how and where Rick and I would rendezvous—in the woods on a blanket, and on the beach at night, and even during stolen moments in the house in the afternoons when everyone else was on the beach.

In midweek, with Martine behind the wheel, we drove to the island in Mom's BMW convertible. My sister knew nothing about what had happened between Rick and me, and I wasn't eager to enlighten her.

Rick wasn't at the cottage when we arrived, and showed up barely in time for dinner. He was unexpectedly gruff, though he did tease Martine about the decals on her fingernails and asked me if I'd lined up a job for the summer. As usual on our first night there, we went for our ritual walk on the beach. Rick kept his distance, which was easy enough since his brother had invited a group of college friends who were boisterous as we drifted along the shore. I'd work toward Rick as we walked, only to have him shy away, and then someone would jostle between us and I'd have to start all over again. I kept sending Rick meaningful glances, which he pointedly ignored. *Touch me,* I thought. *Just touch me, and we can go back to where we were that night when everything seemed so clear, when life took a turn for the wonderful.*

But Rick didn't touch me. Didn't even talk to me beyond the necessary. We all went back to Columbia at the end of the weekend, sat for our final exams and graduated in the middle of May. During that whole time, I hardly saw Rick. He was always busy after school, claiming to be studying for exams or running errands, and due to his unpredictability, Martine and I began to ride home from school with our friend Kaytee, who lived two streets over.

It didn't take a whole lot of smarts to figure out that Rick wanted nothing to do with me. Of course, his parents invited us to the cottage for the week after our graduation, but while we were there, it seemed that Rick was always one giant step ahead of me, that step positioning him out of my immediate vicinity. He was lifeguarding at a pool on the mainland, not on the public beach on the island as he had for the past two summers, and this meant that he worked longer hours. As a result, Rick and I were seldom together and certainly never without others around. I was heartbroken. Needy. Lost.

I suppose I could have been more proactive. I could have thrown myself at Rick, though I believe I had too much pride for that. And as the days wore on, I began to be more insecure and afraid of rejection. What if I overstepped my bounds and Rick laughed at me? What if our friendship broke down completely as a result of my pursuing him? That was something I didn't want to risk.

To anyone else's eye, our last summer together before college appeared to proceed as planned. Martine signed on as a file clerk in Dad's office, and I was hired to babysit for a neighbor who was recovering from major surgery. Our jobs sharply curtailed the time available to spend on the island, though we still managed a weekend here and there. To stay away would have been unthinkable.

Fortunately, our Tappany Island traditions eased the tension between Rick and me and made my short visits bearable. The three of us caught crabs off the dock; we carried on our usual running banter with Queen. At night, if we weren't building bonfires on the beach, we met friends at the outside pavilion of the Purple Pelican, the island's only hangout, where we perfected our shag and openly defied Lilah Rose's spurious curfew. As was her custom, she always left a key for us in the kitchen window box.

Sometimes, and in various places, I caught Rick watching me steadily, a long searching gaze. When I noticed, an unreadable expression would shutter his eyes and he'd immediately glance away or sometimes leave the room. That summer, he didn't date anyone as far as I knew, but I became the life of every party, flirting and laughing with all the available guys, some of them college boys. This did not make Rick jealous, as I hoped it would. If anything, such displays made him even more remote.

By the end of the summer, I was stoically resigned to the way it was. I resolutely told myself that what had happened after the prom was a mistake. Rick and I had made no promises that night or at any other time, nor should I have any expectations. That one sexual experience, after all was said and done, was nothing more than part of growing up. I was lying to myself, but so what? Lots of other people hid their hurt, and I could do it too.

By the time we had to leave for college, my pain had made me even more determined to lay claim to my own future, separate and distinct from Rick's. Once I was at Furman, I wouldn't have to encounter Rick on any sort of regular basis. Or think about him. Or anything.

Chapter 6: Rick

2004

The scent of the sea washed over Rick like a balm as soon as he crossed the new, high-tech Cooper River Bridge connecting the city of Charleston with Mount Pleasant before heading north on U.S. 17, the coastal highway. The previous night, he had closed the Kendall house and tossed everything he needed into the trunk of his sedan before heading out of town.

Along the way, the road was dotted with open-air stands where Gullah women sold the beautiful braided baskets that they wove from sweetgrass gathered in the marsh. Now, in early March, the tawny marsh grass rippling into the distance was greening again after the brief Low Country winter, and the air held the promise of summer, of soft breezes and warm sunshine and pure bliss.

Homecoming. That was what this was, and Rick felt an inexplicable catch in his throat. When he'd moved to Miami, he'd settled in and learned to converse passably well in Spanish. He'd drawn energy from the throbbing Latin beat of the city, flourished under the relentless sun beating down on blindingly white buildings. But the gentle Carolina Low Country was where he belonged, where he was born and bred. The enchantment of the place never failed to infuse him with hope.

By the time he crossed the antiquated bridge to Tappany Island, Rick was warbling the beer-bottle song at the top of his lungs. It was silly, but he and his brother had always started singing as soon as they left Columbia, starting at a thousand bottles and working their way down.

This had the effect of driving their mother crazy. "I'm getting pure-tee annoyed," she'd say in her flat Alabama accent, flicking on her blinker to pass a truck on I-26. Or, "Can't you boys sing something else? Like Boy Scout songs?"

The year he and Martine and Trista had competed in the high-school talent show, they'd practiced their favorite song all the way from St. Matthews to the Tappany Island causeway. It was a hit by Concrete Blonde called "Joey," and by the time they reached the island, Lilah Rose had declared that she never wanted to hear one word of that song again as long as she lived.

Today Rick stopped singing on the causeway and inhaled deeply of the fresh salt air. The bridge over the Intracoastal, one of the few remaining that swiveled sideways, closed after letting a tall-masted sailboat pass, and ahead he saw the ocean, reduced to a few glimmery shreds of blue interspersed with rows of beach cottages. For a moment he caught a glimpse of the neighboring island, a ragged spit of land that was home to a herd of sturdy marsh ponies, wild and untamable.

The ramshackle old white-painted building that housed

Jeter's Market hadn't changed much over the years; a Nehi sign still swung from a bracket over the door, and a few drab guinea hens pecked in the dirt in the side yard.

"Don't I know you?" asked the man at the counter, shoving a frayed toothpick to the other side of his mouth. He wore a tattered baseball cap with a Panthers logo back to front and was reading the latest issue of the *Island Gazette*.

Rick grabbed a six-pack out of the cooler and shoved a twenty across the scarred counter. "Rick McCulloch," he said. "Been here a lot. Aren't you Jolly?"

"Yup, sure am. Jolly Jeter. I remember you coming in here all the time."

"How's business?" Rick asked.

"Can't complain. PawPaw passed on, Dad's retired and me and my brother Goz took over the store." It seemed like only a few summers ago that Jolly had been a little kid scrambling around after a pack of nondescript dogs in the dust outside.

Jolly jerked his head back over his shoulder toward a shed in the backyard. "Goz makes the barbecue."

"Yeah, it's the best damn barbecue in the South," Rick said. "If you've got some handy, I'll take a quart. A pack of boiled peanuts, too." It reassured him that a jar of Gummi Bears stood on the counter exactly where old Mr. Jeter used to keep it.

As Rick popped the top on a beer can, Jolly disappeared into the back room and returned with a chilled container packed to the brim with pulled pork. The large pot steaming on a hot plate in back of the counter yielded a ladleful of peanuts that he sealed into a plastic bag.

"Thanks, catch you later," Rick told Jolly, who gave him a casual salute.

In the car, Rick nestled the beer can between the barbecue and peanuts on the seat beside him. He took a sip now and then, feeling a modicum of guilt about drinking and driving as he headed toward Sweetwater Cottage. He slowed when he passed the oceanfront park where he'd learned to fly a kite, and in a few minutes the tower surmounting the gabled roof of Sweetwater Cottage hove into view above the trees.

Dubbed the Lighthouse by Rick and his brother, the tower had always been Rick's favorite spot as a kid, and he'd spent long hours hunkered down on the widow's walk, pretending he was a pirate on the lookout for ships. Later, he and Martine and Trista had sat out there and smoked their first forbidden cigarettes unbeknownst to Lilah Rose or the ever-vigilant Queen.

The rutted oyster-shell driveway leading to the cottage curved through a paltry stand of pine trees and a lush population of palmettos with rough, wind-bent trunks. When the car emerged from the woods and underbrush, he was, as always, heartened by the vista of white dunes fringed with sea oats and the blue, blue ocean beyond.

He parked beneath the massive and twisted live oak that had sheltered each of his cars in turn. The old place needed some work, he realized as he unfolded himself from the front seat and inhaled a long breath of the soft sea air. Several shutters hung loose, and the windowpanes were cloudy with salt spray, but Sweetwater Cottage was home. Comfortable. Easy. A place to renew his soul.

Which he started by hooking the frayed Pawleys Island rope hammock between two porch posts and sagging gratefully into it, after which he feasted greedily on barbecue and boiled peanuts and drank the beers one by one until he fell asleep.

★ ★ ★

The cold wind from the ocean nearly tipped Rick out of the hammock at approximately three in the morning. March was not a time that anyone would want to camp out in the Low Country unless well shrouded in blankets or a sleeping bag, and Rick had neither. Woozily, he flexed his stiff joints and stumbled inside, but he didn't bother to climb the stairs to the tower room. He crashed on the bed in the guest room Trista usually stayed in, off the hall beside the dining room and the kitchen. No sheets on the bed, so he upped the thermostat and wrapped himself in the bedspread, where he stayed cocooned until well into the morning.

He woke up to rain rattling against the windows and made his bleary-eyed way through the living room to the porch on the front of the house. Wind-driven waves surged on the shore, hesitated in swirls of silvery foam, then drew back to join the pewter sea. The palmetto trees near the path shivered with a water glaze, and whether it was rain or sea spray, Rick couldn't tell.

You took your chances here in the spring. One day could be mild, the sun shedding its golden benevolence on the shore, the cries of small seabirds punctuating the gentle rise and fall of the waves. Or it could be like this, cold and forbidding, damp and even hostile. As a veil of fog began to advance across the water, he felt a chill and went back inside. He should call his brother, tell him he was at the cottage and to plan for necessary repairs. Their parents had left Hal in charge when they left for China.

But right now, Rick didn't want to talk to Hal. His gaze fell across the bookcase in the living room, where, many years ago, his mother had put a framed snapshot of him with Trista and Martine.

Lilah Rose had taken their picture just before they'd climbed into their father's old aluminum johnboat to go fishing in the marsh. Trista and Martine sat on the dock, arms around each other and Trista holding a bamboo pole. He crouched behind them with a hand placed casually on each of their shoulders. Martine was blowing a huge pink bubble from gum they'd bought that morning at Jeter's. Trista was laughing up at him, and he was crossing his eyes. Their hair was still slightly green from dyeing it with food coloring for St. Patrick's Day a month or so earlier, much to the disgust of both sets of parents.

Rick couldn't have said why his mother had chosen that particular picture to frame. It certainly wasn't that good of any of them. It captured the immediacy of the moment, and that was about all. Maybe that was enough.

Suddenly, he wanted to talk to Trista. Not that he had anything in particular to say to her. He just wanted to hear her voice. He dialed her on his cell phone's speed dial, waiting impatiently for her to answer.

"Hello?" She sounded groggy with sleep.

"Tris—did I wake you?" It was ten o'clock in the morning, and Trista wasn't usually a late sleeper.

"I worked late last night at the station, anchoring news coverage of a big tanker-truck snafu on I-20. What's up? Is everything okay?"

"Uh—" He imagined her smiling as she rolled over in bed and propped herself up on a pillow.

"Dumb question," she said, sounding more awake. "Let's start over. What's new with you? Or is that another dumb question?"

"I'm at Sweetwater Cottage. Seems strange that I'm the only one here."

"Is Martine…?"

"Has she told you the divorce is final?" He wondered how much time would elapse before saying the words didn't hurt anymore.

"I haven't talked with her for a couple of weeks," Trista said slowly, as if trying to gauge his reaction.

"She's still living with Steve," he said.

"I'm sorry, Rick."

"Yeah, well." By sheer force of will, he adopted a matter-of-fact tone. "Shorty put me on leave from the department. He says he's giving me time to get my act together."

A long silence ensued. "What can I do to help?" Trista asked somberly.

"Console a new bachelor by coming down here to play strip poker?" He didn't really mean it. It was just a quip to fill the silence when nothing else came to mind, and he hoped it would make her laugh. It brought an image to his mind of Trista on that one occasion so long ago when they'd made love. It had been his first time, and he was sure it had been hers, as well. For years he hadn't allowed himself to think about that.

"Very funny, Rick. With this cold front passing through, and wearing layers of clothes, it would take a while to get to the objective," Trista said, and he heard the smile in her voice. She sounded fully awake now. "On the other hand, Easter's only a few weeks away. Maybe I could talk Lindsay and Peter into a short vacation from their kids that weekend, and we could pay you a visit." Lindsay and Peter Tolson were college friends who had been the most frequent visitors during spring and summer vacations on the island.

Rick really didn't like the idea of Trista and the Tolsons overrunning the cottage, imposing their ideas on him.

Laughing. Being cheerful. Trying to boost him out of his doldrums. "I'll give it some thought," he said.

Trista pretended to be offended. "Well, I like that, Rick McCulloch. Besides, aren't Lindsay, Peter and I welcome anytime, strip poker or no?"

"Of course, but—"

Her tone, now that she was wide awake, became teasing. "Don't put me off. We'll be there even if I have to pay for a babysitter for Lindsay and Peter's kids myself. We'll walk on the beach and find sand dollars. We'll pig out on barbecue. We'll go crabbing."

"How am I going to get my head together that way?" he asked in exasperation, belatedly realizing that Trista wasn't going to back off.

"We're good at jigsaw puzzles. We'll help you fit all the pieces in place," she said soothingly.

He groaned inwardly and told himself that he never should have called her.

She was still talking. "I'm way behind on taking my vacation days. I've got some left over from last year that will expire if I don't use them soon, so I'll add them to the back end of the week."

He groped for words that would dissuade her. He wondered if she planned to bring a guy this time. He hadn't much liked the last one, whose first name was Armistead, last name something he couldn't recall. Armistead had worn the same pair of green plaid Bermudas the whole weekend and nicknamed everybody, male and female, "Sport."

"If you're planning to come," and he emphasized the *if,* "let me know when."

"We've got to find you something fun to do. It's not good

to sit around getting overly introspective. Listen, how about if I supply details in a few days."

"Sure thing," Rick said, eyeing the liquor cabinet in the bar, which was kept fully stocked. It was a bit early to start drinking, but as one of the old sots retired from the department was fond of saying, the sun was over the yardarm somewhere.

They hung up, and Rick sauntered into the bathroom, where he eyed his beard stubble and decided not to bother shaving. He dressed before he poured the first shot of scotch, unpacked his clothes before he drank the second. By the time he downed the third shot, he didn't care about anything.

Thus ensued the next couple of weeks, during which Rick slept a lot, drank a lot and ate too little. He grew a beard. He didn't do laundry but let the clothes pile up until he wore shorts and underwear two, then three times. Often he didn't shower for days.

In the mornings, he often felt as if his head had caved in and usually wished it had. He gulped water to soothe his unnaturally dry throat, then pop a few Alka-Seltzers for his rebellious stomach. After a while, he scarcely recalled how he'd felt on ordinary days in his past life.

Mostly he'd wish he hadn't had so much to drink and sometimes denied how much it had been, though the stack of beer cans in the living room was an ongoing reminder. As for the liquor bottles, he lined them up on the stone hearth, occasionally taking aim at one of them with a crumpled beer can and knocking it over. One finally broke, and he left the pieces lying on the floor, grim symbol of his shattered life.

Somewhere along the way, Rick lost track of what he did and when, which didn't seem to matter now that he'd also lost himself.

Chapter 7: Trista

1994

Click: Rick, Martine and I are lined up in front of Sweetwater Cottage with our friends Lindsay and Peter. The mood is joyous, excited, happy, and our arms are entwined. Even so, we three are clustered together, slightly apart from the other two. A shadow falls across our faces; it belongs to Graham Oliver, my fiancé, who snapped the picture shortly after we arrived.

In recent years, the South Carolina Low Country, popularized in books and movies, has become fashionable, but when Martine and I first started visiting Rick and his family there, it was a well-kept secret.

The three of us stayed true to our promise to meet at Tappany Island every summer, even when we were in college. Often, in those days, we'd bring friends, none of those relationships as enduring as ours with each other. But

Sweetwater Cottage was a kind of beacon, always beckoning us back, lighting up our lives.

After working on the Furman University TV station for three years, I headed for a communications career. When WCIC, the TV station with the highest viewership in Columbia, offered me an internship in my senior year, I snapped it up. I was no more than a glorified gofer, but I learned a lot and found that I enjoyed being in Columbia again. The worst thing was being away from Graham, my fiancé, who had to stay in Greenville to finish school while I lived with my parents.

Graham had a great job offer with a brokerage firm in Raleigh. I intended to study for my master's degree in communications at the University of North Carolina in Chapel Hill the following year and had already been accepted into the program. Even though Martine and Rick had met Graham at Thanksgiving, they hadn't been around him much, and I was eagerly anticipating all of us spending time together at the cottage during spring break. Lindsay Coe and Peter Tolson, friends of Rick and Martine's from USC, would be there, as well.

Graham was a Yankee from Pennsylvania, who had come south to college. He was the physical opposite of Rick. Instead of being tall, he was of medium height and tended toward thickness around the waist. His dark hair curled when he let it get too long, and he chuckled rather than laughed outright, which I considered an engaging trait.

It's true that when I first met him, Graham's honking accent grated harshly on my ears, and he had abrupt ways of asking questions instead of working around to things circuitously as we do in the South. Still, as I grew closer to Graham, I'd ceased being startled by his Northern ways and learned to accept him as he was. He openly adored me, and I was ready to settle down.

By the time I became engaged to Graham, I had schooled myself to regard that sexual encounter with Rick after the prom as a reaction to the other things that had happened that night, understandable under the circumstances. What Rick thought about it, I never knew. It was something we'd not discussed in the intervening years. Over time we'd managed to fall back into a comfortable easy friendship without much effort, and I was thankful for that and for Rick's presence in my life. What was important was that our friendship had endured, and I hoped it always would.

When Graham and I arrived at Sweetwater Cottage on that sparkling blue March day, the sky scoured clean by a broad swish of mare's tail clouds, Martine and Rick ran out to meet us on the path, Lindsay and Peter close behind. A flurry of introductions ensued, and then we trooped inside to eat a fragrant and hearty oyster stew that Rick and Martine had made before we arrived. The meal was meant to be a chance for all of us to get to know one another better, and I was eager for Graham to learn our Low Country ways. I expected him to adopt them for his own. After all, now he was part of us.

We sat around the well-worn kitchen table, dipping up the rich buttery stew and washing it down with cold sweet tea. I was thinking how delicious everything was and how happy I was to be there, when suddenly, Graham said, "Where I come from, we eat oysters raw on the half shell. It's the only way to eat them." I glanced up in surprise at this declaration, thinking he couldn't possibly be serious and must be making a joke, the meaning of which wasn't quite clear. Across the table, Martine narrowed her eyes.

Rick jumped to the rescue. "We do that sometimes," he

said easily. "A squeeze of lemon, pour on the Tabasco sauce, and you've got yourself a treat." His attempt to defuse the situation was transparent, and I smiled my hesitant thanks.

Graham frowned. "Tabasco? Last year in Jamaica, I bought a hot sauce that'll knock your socks off. Devil's Thunderbolt, it's called. Hardly anyone could eat that stuff, believe me."

"As far as we're concerned, Tabasco sauce is the be-all and end-all," Martine said, exaggerating her drawl as she stood and flounced over to the refrigerator, where she opened the door and took out a pitcher. "Anyone want more tea? It's sweetened, of course. Not like you drink it up North."

I warned Martine with a lift of my brows, but she was hell-bent on playing the part of exaggerated Southern belle to the hilt.

"I'll have water," Graham said, sounding anything but polite, and Lindsay shrugged slightly. I understood why. The way one of us would have replied to Martine's offer could have been to say, *Thank-you, but I don't believe I care for tea right now, and a glass of water would be fine if it's not too much trouble.* You might wonder why we'd use all those words. Well, as a communications major, I've considered this, and I suspect it's because we Southerners believe in allowing others to save face. The longer we stretch out our regrets, the more time the other person has to school his or her facial expression and frame a reply. Oh, we Southerners are subtle, all right.

Martine, ever gracious in her gesture, poured water from the refrigerator jug and handed it to Graham with a smile. Only I detected the smug superiority she exhibited now that she'd given Graham the opportunity to display his bad manners. He'd been one-upped and didn't even realize it.

Nudged into a change in subject by Peter, who asked if any of us had ever been to Africa and what did we know about Uganda, the conversation moved on. However, the gauntlet had been tossed, and over the next couple of days, the sparring between Martine and Graham increased. My sister's goading of Graham became downright merciless, and I was at a loss to stop her. Due to the unpleasantness of it, Lindsay and Peter quickly adopted the principle of avoidance, which meant they disappeared on long beach walks and minimized their exposure to the rest of us. They were newly in love, and, unlike Graham and me, dragging their feet about making the final commitment.

But Rick, bless his heart, lost no time in playing the peacemaker between Martine and Graham. He asked Graham intelligent questions about growing up in a Philadelphia suburb, pointed out the similarities between his early life and ours, and when Jeter's ran out of Corona, he invited both Graham and Martine to go on a beer run to the supermarket on the mainland. When I later asked Graham what the three of them had talked about, he merely said that Rick told a couple of funny jokes. Well, by the third day, Martine stopped her constant gibing. Much to my relief, after the beer run she contented herself with mild jabs now and then, such as on the afternoon when we all ate barbecue.

"You don't have barbecue like this in Philly, do you, Graham?" Martine asked, all interested innocence. I knew what she was up to, and so did Rick. We exchanged a glance while I tried to figure out some way to head this off.

Meanwhile, Graham, his fingers greasy from nibbling on

tender baby ribs, shook his head. "Nah, but we've got steak sandwiches like you wouldn't believe."

"Why, a steak sandwich couldn't possibly compare with Jeter's barbecue, could it, Trista?" asked Martine.

Caught in the middle, I mumbled something diplomatic, and Lindsay jumped to the rescue by telling us that her relatives in Texas barbecued beef, for Pete's sake, and who ever heard of such a barbaric custom? When everyone knew that pork was the only thing worth lighting a charcoal fire to, and besides, what about all that awful red tomato sauce Texans slather on their food?

While this was going on, Graham kept gnawing on ribs, oblivious to everyone, and Peter got up to get a drink of water. Only Rick noticed my discomfort, and his smile was kind. It was another one of those times we didn't have to speak to know each other's thoughts.

During the days ahead, we discussed our futures. Lindsay and Peter had signed up for a stint in the Peace Corps, although they hadn't decided whether it would be together or apart. Martine was going to work again in our father's law office in the summer. Dad was delighted, since he still hoped that at least one of his daughters would go to law school, but I sensed a caginess when Martine talked about her plans, and besides, I understood that the main thing Martine liked about the law office was that she got to dress up and wear high heels every day. This, as far as I was concerned, was only another sign of my sister's innate flakiness, with which I was well acquainted.

That summer, I was totally wrapped up in my newfound bliss at being one-half of a couple. At night, Graham and I snuggled in his creaky narrow bunk in the house's bachelor quarters, which he occupied alone. It was a dormitory-style room, ranging along the older north wing of the house. Rick slept upstairs in the Lighthouse tower room, which was reached by a spiral staircase from the living room, and Martine and I occupied our customary digs off the hall by the dining room. Lindsay and Peter, who lived together in a cramped student apartment in Columbia, were openly sharing the guest room connecting to Martine's and mine via a bathroom; sometimes at night I heard them making love through the thin walls.

Usually I'd wait until the enthusiastic sounds from their room ceased, then slip from between the soft percale sheets and tiptoe out the door. Before I left, I always made sure that Martine was breathing evenly, indicating that she was asleep. I was certain that everyone else understood that I sneaked into the bachelor quarters sometimes.

I'd sleep all night curled comfortably against Graham's warm body, reveling in the knowledge that this was the way it would be the rest of my life. A strong man snoring softly beside me, the certainty that one of the important questions in my life had been settled. We would have beautiful, intelligent children and grow old together. We would flourish and prosper like my parents, only better.

In the morning, as the pearly dawn was beginning to glow on the horizon, I'd leave Graham's bed and tiptoe barefoot through the obstacle course of table and chairs in the kitchen. After several days, I became proficient at navigating my passage back to my room without stubbing a toe. I could have done it with my eyes closed, but fortunately I didn't, because one night a few days before we were to leave, I spotted someone cautiously descending the staircase from the Lighthouse in the dark.

I hugged the wall, hiding. Rick was probably hungry and

headed for the kitchen to grab a few of the cookies that Lindsay had baked that afternoon. But as I shrank into the shadows, I realized that it wasn't Rick. It was Martine.

My sister was wearing only her thin batiste nightgown, and her hair was tousled, her footsteps stealthy. I could have been gazing into a mirror; I knew exactly how I would look to her if she saw me.

At first the wild notion occurred to me that Martine had thought of something she wanted to tell Rick in the middle of the night and had gone up to his room to speak her mind. Almost at once I realized what a preposterous theory it was. Martine had visited Rick, all right, but as she unheedingly glided past the place where I stood concealed in the darkness and continued into our room, I understood what she had really been doing upstairs. Martine and Rick were lovers.

My head reeled with this new information, and a rare and stunning clarity swept over me. Martine and Rick, cozily ensconced next to each other last night when we indulged in one of our cutthroat games of dirty-word Scrabble; the way Rick's gaze had followed Martine the other day as she ran down the stairs to the sand wearing a thin turtleneck that outlined her breasts; Martine's solicitousness of Rick when she made sure he was allotted the last ribs on the platter the day we got the takeout from Jeter's.

To say that this was unexpected was an understatement. I felt deceived. It dawned on me that I'd become so absorbed in my own life that I hadn't been paying attention to Rick and Martine. My job at the TV station, living at home with my parents—these things combined with my burgeoning interest in all things Graham to block out any clues about what was happening between my sister and Rick.

My bewilderment was accompanied by guilt over my engagement. Why this should be, I had no earthly idea. I was happy, maybe the happiest I'd been in my whole life, and planning a future with a man I loved. The fact that Rick and my sister were sleeping together shouldn't affect me in any negative way. I should be neutral about what was going on between them, whatever it was. They were two consenting adults. Considering my own adventurous nocturnal activities, especially taking into account what had happened between Rick and me in the tree house all those years ago, I had no business judging them.

I examined these arguments one by one in the hours that followed. Martine, dead to the world, slept in her nearby bed, but I couldn't drift off. I wanted to talk with her about my discovery, I wanted to ask Rick what was going on, I wanted—but I didn't know what I wanted, and that was the problem.

The next day, Graham realized that something was upsetting me, and in his brash Yankee way, he kept pushing me to tell him what it was. Have you missed your period? he asked. Are you catching cold? But I could no more tell him what was wrong than I could confront Rick or Martine.

In the afternoon, when we all went to the beach, I had little patience for the frequent smoldering eye contact now so obvious between Martine and Rick. I felt like the odd man out. Grumpily, without saying anything to anyone, I got up and ran lightly to the water.

The air was hot and humid, but that didn't stop my skin from turning to goose bumps at the first splash of waves on my feet. I eased into the water bit by bit but finally decided that I might as well get it over with and plunged in. I burst to the surface well beyond the breaking waves and gulped a long draft of sea air.

Back on the beach, Rick and Lindsay were deep in conversation. Martine had settled on her stomach, and as I watched, she scooped a hand under her hair and twisted it up off her neck. Rick smiled indulgently, all eyes. I could imagine how Martine appeared to him, all pink and white and gold in the bright hot sunshine, and how eager he would be to have her all to himself at night in the Lighthouse.

I felt an immediate frenzied need to strike out and away, to put them far behind me. I began to swim toward the horizon, with its limitless possibilities; or at least, that was what the line smudged between sea and sky represented to me in those moments.

The ocean had been calm when we arrived, but now there was a rolling-wave action that I found soothing. That only added to my desire to swim and swim until I was exhausted, and I kept paddling in a kind of mindless state, concentrating on my stroke and my kick. I was an excellent swimmer; Rick, Martine and I had all lettered on the swim team in high school. But I no longer swam regularly, and I wasn't any match for the undertow I soon encountered.

The waves became stronger, something I first noticed when they slapped me in the face every time I turned my head to breathe. I stopped to tread water for a moment, surprised at how far out I was. The waves were cresting so high that I could barely see the others on the beach. It didn't take long to figure out that I was being swept far out instead of being propelled toward land.

At first I fought it, but it was no use. I made myself recall all I knew about surviving rip currents—swim parallel to shore, float until carried into deeper water, then try to work back toward land. I heard a loud shout—Martine—and

Rick's answering call, and that was when I understood that they'd seen me foundering and were coming to my rescue.

Don't, I tried to say, but saltwater splashed into my mouth, and the word became a gargle that didn't project past my own nose. Staying afloat was now a full-time occupation. And through it all, I was concerned about Martine and Rick, not wanting them to put themselves in harm's way in order to save me.

The sun spiraled into a brassy hot orb, burning itself upon my retinas. It hurt to keep my eyes open. I closed them, opened them again, felt myself slip underwater into the clear, cool depths. I heard Rick shouting my name, and Martine, too, as I struggled to reach them. My lungs were bursting, my arms refused to obey my commands and I couldn't feel my legs. I wondered if there were any sharks around, wondered if they kept a sharp eye out for swimmers in trouble who might be easy prey. The saltwater invaded my eyes, my throat, stinging so much that I thought I'd rather drown in fresh water because maybe it wouldn't hurt so much.

Drowning? I thought with a sense of disbelief. How could this be happening to me?

Chapter 8: Trista

1994

Strong arms lifted me out of the water, and my cheek pressed against a firm, hard surface. Rick and Martine had paddled out with a surfboard that they'd borrowed from a kid on the beach, and after they shoved me onto it, I vomited and gagged on saltwater and bile until my throat was raw.

"Take it easy, Tris. You're going to be okay," Martine said close to my ear. When we reached land, the two of them pulled me off the surfboard while I coughed and coughed, my sides heaving like those of a beached fish. They made sure I was breathing normally, hugged me until I was warmer, then wrapped me in Martine's beach jacket and walked me back to the cottage.

"Y'all saved my life," I said weakly when they had sat me

down in the kitchen and were plying me with hot tea. Graham held my hand, Lindsay rubbed my feet and Peter hovered in the background, all but wringing his hands. Rick stood in a corner of the room, arms crossed and a white line around his tight lips.

Martine scooped another spoonful of sugar into my tea. "I couldn't believe it when I saw your head bobbing around in the water. I said, 'Rick, Trista's in trouble!'"

"What in the world were you thinking?" Rick asked explosively, and I cringed at his tone.

"I wasn't," I said, but I didn't add that driving myself to my limit so I wouldn't have to face the reality of their relationship was the whole point of swimming so far out.

Much chastened, I went to bed early that night. I was exhausted and didn't wake up if Martine crept out and went to the Lighthouse to be with Rick. As for Graham, he didn't expect me to honor his bed after my ordeal and kissed me a chaste good-night at the door to my room before heading for his bachelor bunk.

Even though I still felt weak the day after my disastrous brush with death, I trooped with the others down to the dock on the marsh to catch blue crabs for dinner. We carried a sack of chicken necks for crab bait, several short poles to which were fastened lines with hooks at the end, a bucket to contain the crabs once we'd caught them and a cooler of beer. After we settled on the dock, the others proceeded to lower the chicken necks into the water. I begged off, citing my ordeal the day before.

It was hot. I forced a beer down a throat still sore from throwing up saltwater and wished forlornly that I'd worn a hat to protect my fair skin from the sun. By the time the bucket was almost full with the catch of the day, Martine and I were turning pink.

I fanned myself in a desultory fashion. Besides not being in the mood for crabbing, I wasn't soothed by the rhythmic lap of water against the pilings, and in my stomach lodged a cold, hard stone, placed there by my anxiety and doubt. Out in the marsh, cord grass rippled green and gold, but on the dock, no breeze stirred. A mullet jumped in the distance, and far away, hummocks of pine and palmetto rose out of the marsh, their outlines blurred by the shimmering heat.

Martine leaned close to Rick, helping him bait his line. Her breast brushed his arm. All at once, the weight of the sunshine on my shoulders seemed too heavy to bear.

"I do believe I'll start back to the cottage," I said.

Graham glanced back over his shoulder with a smile but quickly returned his attention to his bobbing line. I stood and shook out my legs, which tingled from sitting all folded up on the hard dock.

"Wait, I'll go with you," Martine volunteered, jumping up from her place beside Rick.

I'd rather have left alone but gritted my teeth and didn't object. Martine and I traipsed up the dock, the uneven boards creaking beneath our feet, to the oyster-shell path, where Martine abruptly halted in her tracks.

"Let's not go back to the house," she said. "Let's stop in the shade of that palmetto tree and wait for the others."

Katydids chirred in the underbrush, lending a dissonance to the still air. "Someone should set out hammers and nut-crackers on the kitchen table for cleaning the crabs," I reminded her.

"Later," Martine said, sliding her arm companionably through mine.

I allowed Martine to lead me to the bench beneath the tree, keeping an eye on the others. The palmetto and the forest behind it created cool, soothing shade, such a relief after the relentless heat on the dock.

"I'm pretty sure Lindsay and Peter are going to get hitched," Martine said suddenly. "They can't count on their Peace Corps assignment keeping them together unless they sign up as a married couple."

"That's nice," I said. From what I could tell, they were well suited.

"Unfortunately, Lindsay's mom had her mind set on medical school for her only daughter."

"Oh well, that's something like Dad wanting us to go to law school," I said, pulling a face.

"You still could," Martine said seriously, swiveling toward me. "As you and Rick always planned."

"We were such kids back then," I retorted. "Lots of things were different."

I must have infused my tone with multiple shades of meaning, because Martine's eyebrows shot up.

"Like what exactly?" she asked mildly.

Still out of sorts, I blinked at her, unable to contain myself any longer. "I saw you leaving Rick's room," I blurted. I looked down at my hands, folded in my lap, where Graham's engagement ring, a round brilliant-cut diamond with two trillions, glinted on my finger.

At first Martine glanced away, and the flush working its way from her neck to her cheeks had nothing to do with the effects of the sun.

"We were going to tell you this week," she said. "We never got around to it, what with Lindsay and Peter here and what happened to you yesterday and all."

Some remote part of me had clung to the hope that there was another reasonable explanation for Martine's late-night ramblings, and I felt a sharp deflation of spirit.

"Rick and I," Martine began, and the words now implied an exclusivity that hit me hard in the gut. "We've been seeing each other for a few months now." She turned troubled eyes on me. "You don't mind, do you? Because you have Graham?"

My gaze sought out Graham's stocky shape on the dock. Usually when I spotted him from a distance, a warm glow of recognition settled across me, a protective mantle of belonging and comfort. *Graham,* I would think, and I'd be glad that one major question in my life had been answered in such a reassuring way. But in the past few moments, I hadn't even thought of him.

"How did this get by me?" I asked.

Martine shrugged. "You're busy with your internship, and Rick and I have stuck close to campus this semester. All the parties and everything. And studying. The three of us haven't spent much time with one another lately."

She was right. Since I'd moved back home, they'd been over for Sunday dinner a few times, and Martine brought her laundry to the house to wash occasionally, visiting with Mom and me over coffee. I had been blind to signs of attachment, if there'd actually been any.

"I wish you'd told me," I said unhappily. The rest of the group had gathered up the crabbing gear and began to drift up the dock toward us.

Martine swung around, a hint of defiance sparking in her eyes. "I should have, but I wasn't sure how you'd take it. Rick and I are going to get married, Tris."

Married. Married. *Married?* The word resounded like a

drum inside my head, beat against my brain in rhythm with the thrumming of the katydids, and my knees went wobbly. I'd barely learned that Martine and Rick were lovers. How could I accept that they were to marry?

Like all girls brought up to be Southern ladies, I'd been taught to offer genteel congratulations upon the delivery of good news. Such news didn't have to be in any way felicitous in our own minds; it was only necessary that the person delivering it believed in its worth. I felt my teeth clenching but pried them apart long enough to say, "I—I'm happy for you." Rick and Graham had almost reached us, toting the big bucket full of crabs between them.

"I'm glad," Martine said with the hint of a wishful grin. "Maybe we could have a double wedding. In August before Rick starts law school and you go to grad school."

I was too shaken to reply. Since I was planning on grad school in the fall and Graham was starting a new job, we hadn't come close to setting a date, nor had we discussed it with any real seriousness.

"How about it, Tris? Wouldn't that be a kick?"

"This summer," I said when I'd regained my voice. "Isn't that a mite soon?"

"I want to be with Rick at law school," Martine said.

My heart iced over at the familiarity with which she spoke. "Have you told Mom and Dad?" I asked.

"Mom may suspect. She remarked the other day that Rick and I seemed to be hanging out a lot."

Graham and Rick drew nearer, snickering about something as men do when they share a camaraderie.

"Rick, I've just told Trista the happy news," Martine called out. She sounded pleased and relieved, and she was smiling broadly.

Rick's gaze met mine as a fleeting expression of resignation passed over his features. In that moment, all my uncertainties were mirrored in his eyes.

"Congratulations," I said, hoping I didn't sound halfhearted. I must have, though, because Graham treated me to a skeptical quirk of the brows as he and Rick set down the bucket.

"What news?" he asked.

"Rick and I are going to be married," Martine said, smiling beatifically. She stepped into position beside Rick, forcing him to curve his arm around her.

I schooled my expression to become blank. Graham, in the manner of men who are buddies, slapped Rick on the back, and I don't recall what was said after that. I was too numb to join in the lighthearted chatter about when and where their wedding would take place. Rick put up a good front and said all the right things in response to Graham's enthusiasm, but he avoided looking at me.

Finally, we all strolled back to Sweetwater Cottage, our voices ringing out in the fresh air. Peter pulled a six-pack out of the refrigerator, and Lindsay served benne-seed wafers she'd bought on her shopping expedition to the Old City Market in Charleston. We ate our rich bounty of blue crab with three-bean salad that I'd made that morning, and later we walked on the beach, the stars spinning overhead in patterns that suddenly seemed too fragile.

After our walk, we all went our separate ways, me to the room I shared with Martine, who didn't appear even after I crawled between the sheets, Graham to his bachelor quarters, and Lindsay and Peter to the front porch, where I heard them murmuring and occasionally laughing.

When I couldn't sleep, I slipped on a robe for a trek to

the kitchen. There I poured myself a glass of milk and stood at the door to drink it. Moonlight etched the house and the forest beyond in silverpoint, and I caught a glimpse of movement under the tree where the cars were parked.

I recognized Martine's laugh, and then it was quiet. Rick and Martine were kissing, and after a time, she tugged at his hand and drew him toward the grove of oaks. Together they glided into the shadowy depths.

It was almost as if I were watching Rick and me as we slipped into the woods together all those years ago. Sick at heart, I crept back to bed, reminding myself that I had successfully overcome my love for Rick. I'd found someone else who was part of the life I lived now. And yet I knew in my heart that I still wanted Rick, wanted him all the more for not being able to have him. It was beyond reason, such wanting. Irrational, even. Poison.

The next day I pleaded a headache and upset stomach, staying in my room while the others went on an expedition to Charleston. That evening, while everyone was putting together what was supposed to be our last meal on Tappany Island, Graham opened the door and was silhouetted in the shaft of light from the hall.

"Are you feeling well enough to join us?" he asked, keeping his voice low. He sat on the edge of the bed, so that I rolled slightly toward him. Idly, he picked up the tassel on the cord that closed the hood of my sweatshirt and fiddled with it for a moment while I prepared an excuse.

"My stomach's still upset," I said. "Maybe it's from swallowing all that saltwater."

"I'm sorry, sweetheart. Can I bring you anything?"

I shook my head. "I'm going to get some sleep, since we'll be leaving early tomorrow."

Graham accepted the excuse and left me alone with my head pillowed on my hands. There was no time for sleep before the phone call from my boss, Keisha Tyner, at WCIC. Graham handed me the phone through the door of my room, his forehead knotted in anxiety. I sat up on the bed cross-legged; Graham wandered off again, leaving the door open. I heard the others exclaiming over the Frogmore stew they'd made and Lindsay laughing her long throaty laugh.

Keisha wasted no time on small talk. She understood that I was planning to go to graduate school, she said. But would I consider postponing my education and taking a job as her assistant at the station? For some time, the powers that be at WCIC had been casting around for ways to develop new on-screen talent, and she'd pointed out that I was right under their noses—photogenic, intelligent and above all eager. I had a good chance of eventually becoming a news anchor, and they were planning to groom me for the job.

Keisha named a salary that was far beyond any expectations I might have had, and while she was talking, possible scenes from the near future—next year—zoomed through my consciousness on fast-forward. According to our present plan, Graham and I would be living in Raleigh, though not together, and Rick would be enrolled in law school in nearby Durham, by that time married to my sister. The four of us would be expected to mingle on weekends, to socialize with the same people, to attend football games together as a foursome. And new rules would apply.

I have a reputation as the steadfast twin, the firm and determined one. But every once in a while—for instance, when I accepted that scholarship to Furman—I zig when people expect me to zag.

"I'll take the job," I said in a rush. This statement was met with stunned silence on the other end of the line.

"You will?" Keisha said, her voice rising to a shriek. She was incredulous.

"I absolutely will."

Not one to dally, Keisha got straight to the point. "I'll have the papers prepared, and we'll get you on the payroll right after graduation," she said, all but gushing.

"Great," I said. "That's wonderful." Then I went in the bathroom and threw up.

And so that's how I came to move back in with Mom and Dad after graduation while Graham went to Raleigh without me. I wrapped myself in a blanket of numbness, shielding myself against the pain that threatened to overwhelm my emotional life.

Before they even graduated from USC, Martine and Rick began to plan their August wedding, and naturally, she invited me to be her maid of honor. We'd always eagerly anticipated being in each other's weddings, but under the circumstances, I did not rejoice. No one suspected that I approached the task with hesitation, uncertainty and a marked lack of enthusiasm. With everyone focused on her choice of gown, whether she should wear her hair up or down, if she should have four bridesmaids or six, Martine was the center of attention. And that, for once, was okay with me.

I quickly nixed the idea of a double wedding with the excuse that Graham and I first needed to figure out how to manage our careers with each of us living in a different city. Mom took my decision in stride, though she regretted the chance to mount an extravaganza the likes of which Columbia, South Carolina, had never seen. As for Dad, he liked to joke that it would have saved him a whole lot of money to marry off two daughters in one day, but he was only teasing. I wasn't sure if he actually liked Graham much, but he was delighted that Rick was to be his son-in-law.

Now that Graham and I lived so far apart, the way I related to him slowly began to change. When I visited him in Raleigh, little things started to annoy me, such as his reluctance to try new experiences. Once, on impulse, I suggested that we attend a state park lecture on the upcoming Perseid meteor shower, and he refused. Another time I was excited that we had a chance to participate in a progressive dinner with people from his firm, but he derided the idea, with the result that we sat home and watched something tedious on TV that night.

As time wore on, I found it hard to imagine a life in which nothing new was allowed to be added to the mix; I suspected I'd be bored out of my mind. I must tell you that Graham had no idea that things were cooling off between us, and to me his obliviousness was indicative of the whole problem. I wanted—needed—him to be more aware of me, of what I expected from a life partner.

On the night before Martine's wedding, after the rehearsal dinner given by Rick's parents at the Windsor Manor Country Club, I couldn't sleep. Martine had fallen into bed, declaring that her feet hurt from all that standing around at the rehearsal, and wasn't the minister, Dr. Stith, getting kind of deaf in his old age, and tomorrow she'd be Mrs. Rick McCulloch, could I believe it? I didn't have much to say about that.

Curry Anne Dawes and Tottie Newsome, Martine's out-of-town bridesmaids, occupied the guest room next door, and I heard them murmuring and laughing long after Martine fell asleep. Despite the house's central air-conditioning, our second-floor room seemed stifling, and I longed for the steady breeze given out by the ceiling fans at Sweetwater Cottage, where I'd spent an uneasy weekend with Martine and the McCullochs about a month before.

After a while, I got out of bed and sat on the window seat overlooking the garage roof and the backyard, remembering all the times that Martine and I, unbeknownst to our parents, had climbed out that very window and slid down the slope of the roof to the lattice trellis, from which we could drop to the driveway below. Acting on a whim, I grabbed a couple of Little Debbie fudge rounds from the dresser where Martine had left them earlier after designating them emergency rations for the rigors of her wedding week. Then I yanked a pair of shorts over my nightshirt, pulled on a pair of laceless canvas sneakers and threw open the window.

After baking all day in the hot sun, the roof shingles were warm to the touch. I scraped one knee in my progress toward the trellis and fought for a grip on the ivy before I tumbled too far. I noted that the trellis was a bit shakier these days, but then so was I. It had been awhile since I'd chosen this way to exit the house.

The night was rife with sound; crickets sent up a raucous chorus from the shrubbery. There was no breeze, and the humid air enfolded me like a warm, damp quilt. I had no idea what I was going to do after escaping the house, but after a moment, I circled the extra cars in the driveway belonging to Curry Anne and Tottie, striking out toward the old tree house.

I knew the way, could have found it blindfolded. I followed the twisting rabbit trail that was the path, and soon I was climbing up the rough, weather-beaten old ladder.

As I reached the platform, I inhaled the delicious fragrance of pine straw, resin and a faint whiff of—Drakkar Noir? It was the aftershave scent that Rick always wore.

"What took you so long?" From under the shelter of the roof, Rick's white teeth gleamed in a shaft of moonlight, and soon the rest of him materialized like the Cheshire cat.

I knew I should turn and run back home as fast as I could, but I was caught up in a web of memories. "What are you doing here?" I blurted. "You're supposed to be home in bed resting up for the wedding."

He shrugged. "Couldn't sleep. Same for you?"

I nodded and sat down with my back against the tree trunk. Rick was dressed as I was—baggy shirt, shorts, sneakers. His hair was mussed, giving him an appealing little-boy look.

"Curry Anne and Tottie are gossiping and giggling in the guest room, and even if I joined them, I'd be bored," I said. The scaly tree bark bit into my back, and I eased the discomfort by scooting forward a bit.

"Those two annoy me, too. Don't tell Martine I said that," he added hastily.

"I can't tell Martine anything," I replied. "You know that." I handed him a fudge round and tore the cellophane from my own.

"Are Lindsay and Peter here yet?" I asked. During the wedding festivities, they planned to stay with Rick's family. They, also, would be married soon in a low-key ceremony at Kalmia Gardens in Hartsville, where Lindsay had grown up, after which they'd head out to their Peace Corps assignment.

"They're driving over first thing in the morning," Rick said.

"It's neat that they can go to Uganda together," I said. "Though I can't quite imagine either of them living in a grass hut and helping people install toilets."

Rick laughed. "Peter said he prefers toilets to torts any day," he said wryly.

"Are you all set for law school?" I asked.

"Martine told you about our apartment, I guess."

"One bedroom and a bath on the second floor of an old house with a sunporch facing east," I said, repeating what Martine had said. "It sounds wonderful."

"Once we get our things moved in, it will be awesome. I'm grateful to your dad for helping Martine find a job in his ex-roommate's law office in Durham. Her salary will be a big help."

"Dad thinks Martine will do well at that paralegals' course."

"Three years, and I'll be working for Barrineau, Dubose and Linder. That's a long time."

"The law-school years pass very fast," I said. "Everyone says so."

"I wish you were going with me, Trista, the way we always planned."

"Yeah, well," and I made a vague gesture that I quickly realized wouldn't be visible in the dark. "I like my job. My goal is to coanchor the noon news in two years."

"That's what Martine said," and I felt a twinge of sadness that communications between Rick and me were filtered through my sister these days. I'd better get used to it, I told myself. It would be that way for us from now on.

We didn't speak for a long time. Then, "It bothers me, too," Rick said softly, and I wished I could see him clearly. "I'd never hurt Martine for the world. Never."

As always, Rick knew what I was thinking before I even voiced the words. I swallowed past the lump in my throat. "Neither would I."

"I value your friendship, Tris, just as I always have. Now

that I'm going to marry Martine, I've had to adjust the two of you in my mind and in my heart." He paused, and I sensed that he was trying to frame his next words as kindly as possible.

"I love you both," he said, and the breath stopped in my chest as he spoke. "I love Martine as my wife, you as my sister. It's the way it's worked out, the way it should have worked out, and I hope you understand it as I do."

He'd said he loved me. That had never happened before, though once I'd desperately longed to hear it. The night stilled around us, and I couldn't speak past the lump in my throat.

"Trista?"

"Thanks for telling me that," I whispered. Something twisted inside me, wrapped itself around my heart. I hugged my knees and willed the pain to go away.

"I hope you and Graham will be very happy," Rick said, sounding rather formal. "As happy as Martine and I will be."

Tears welled in my eyes. "I—"

"I mean it, Tris. I hope you wish us well."

"Yes," I said. I paused, unsuccessfully fighting for composure. "I've got to go now, Rick." I lurched to my feet and made for the ladder, but before my shoe struck the first rung, Rick grabbed my arm.

"Hey, you're upset," he said.

I shook my head vigorously.

"Oh, Tris," he said. "If I've hurt you, please forgive me, but after you and Graham became engaged, I didn't think there was any hope for us."

"Us?" I said unbelievingly. "You never let me think—you never allowed any indication that there was an *us*."

"I was so ashamed that I took advantage of you," he said,

the words tumbling out one after another. "Right here, in the tree house, on a night when you were the most vulnerable."

I couldn't believe what I was hearing. I stared at him, the darkness all around us seeping into my soul. "I was crazy in love with you that summer, and you wouldn't pay one bit of attention to me," I blurted.

"My God, Trista," he said feelingly. "We were kids. The whole world was opening to us. Neither of us was ready for commitment, but I hoped that maybe later…" He trailed off into a shrug.

"I can't talk about this," I said, wrenching away from the full blaze of his eyes upon me. My feet fumbled for the rungs, and I scrambled down the ladder as quickly as I could. I ran along the trail as fast as the topography would allow, my tears drying on my face. The old oaks crowded close, tendrils of the encroaching vines dragging at my clothes; the pungent scent of leaf mold stung my nostrils. I stumbled a couple of times but didn't go sprawling, thank goodness, and soon I had reached our own driveway.

Curry Anne's car was unlocked, and I slipped into the back seat to collect myself for a few minutes. I didn't want to encounter anyone in the house before I had a chance to mop my face and blow my nose. My chest heaved, and I felt dizzy.

After I calmed down, I emerged from the car. The night was quiet and still. I dug in the wood box beside the back door for the spare key and let myself inside.

I wished I hadn't encountered Rick at the tree house, and yet our conversation had left me sure of something I'd been considering for over a month. I was going to break my engagement to Graham, the sooner, the better. That would be tomorrow after the wedding, and he would be heartbroken.

My mind raced: What if I had told Rick tonight that I wasn't going to marry Graham? Would that have made any difference?

No. He loved Martine. He'd said so. He'd put me firmly in my place—sister, not lover, and certainly not wife.

When I'd found Rick in the tree house, I briefly entertained the foolish hope that a talk would clear the air between us. Too late I realized that the words that we'd spoken had only stirred it into a whirlwind.

On the morning of the wedding, Mom was in a tizzy and depending on me to iron out last-minute glitches with the caterer and the musicians. Curry Anne and Tottie were driving Martine crazy with suggestions about her makeup, so by the time Dad left for the airport to pick up Aunt Cynthia, I was the only sane female in the house, which wasn't saying much.

When Graham arrived late that morning, I met him at the car. Girlish laughter pealed from the house, and since it was August, the crepe myrtle trees were shedding all around, their blood-red blossoms littering the grass.

"Hi," I said as Graham offered his lips for our usual kiss.

"You smell so good," he said. I'd recently showered and was ready to dress in my maid-of-honor finery, a stiff taffeta nightmare that Martine had chosen over my objections.

"I brought you some baklava," he said, handing me a square white box tied with string.

I was touched by Graham's thoughtfulness. When I visited him in Raleigh, we often dined at a small Greek restaurant around the corner from his apartment. His gift made it even more difficult for me to steel myself for the inevitable speech I planned for later in the day—the one where I told him it was my fault that our relationship hadn't worked, not his, and that I hoped we would always be friends. Standard Breakup Speech Number One, Martine and I always called it.

While I was staring down at the little white box containing the pastries, Graham pulled me inside the garage through the open door to the utility area and kicked the door shut after us. Dad's workbench occupied one wall, and a rusty wheelbarrow was propped against another. From the shelves at the end of the space came the distasteful smell of fertilizer and insecticide.

He kissed me long and hard. We hadn't seen each other for two weeks due to my duties as maid of honor; I'd had to remain in Columbia for the bridesmaids' shower last weekend and the final fitting of my maid-of-honor gown the week before that. My reluctance must have come across, and anyway, the baklava box was between us. He eased back, regarding me quizzically.

"Hey, what's the matter?" he asked.

"Just prewedding jitters," I said, trying to joke with him. Outside, I heard another car wheel into the driveway, and the driver got out and slammed the door even as Graham slid his hand under my T-shirt. His fingers closed around my breast.

I jumped when Rick called out, "Is anyone home? Martine asked me to pick up her shoes from the department store, and here they are."

Curry Anne must have been stationed near the back door. She giggled. "Tottie, turn off that TV. You're going to drive us all crazy with that awful jewelry channel."

"I'm shopping for my engagement ring," Tottie retorted. "Now that Martine is getting married, we're all going to have to follow suit. I'm hoping for a diamond as big as one of those gardenias on that bush in the front yard." This statement was met by laughter from Curry Anne.

The back door slammed, indicating that Rick had entered, and the laughter stopped.

After that, all I heard was the girls' high fluting voices superimposed over Rick's deep one, their actual words lost to me because Graham was speaking close to my ear.

"Set the date for our own wedding, Trista. It's time," he urged. "I'll put in a formal request for a transfer to the firm's Columbia office. How about it?"

"Not now, Graham." I pushed him away. *Not ever,* I was thinking. I was more attuned to the starting of Rick's car engine than to what Graham was saying.

"What could I do to change your mind?"

"Graham," I said, twisting out of his embrace. I inadvertently stepped on the business end of a rake and the handle jumped up, nearly swatting me in the eye.

Impatiently, Graham shoved the rake aside and reached for me again.

I shook my head to clear it. "This is really bad timing," I said. "I have to hurry back inside, get dressed, see if Martine needs anything."

"I've missed you. I lie awake every night wishing you were beside me."

Rick's Toyota stuttered off into the distance. My knees were wobbly, my tongue tied. And certainly I had no more patience.

"Graham, you and I have to talk," I said as a means of preparing him.

"Talk?"

"About—about our relationship."

"This sounds like bad news," he said jovially, though there was a thread of tension drawing the words tight.

I drew a deep breath. "Come on, let's walk down to the park."

"You're supposed to be helping Martine," he said.

"Yes, but—oh, Graham, can't you make this easier for me?" I blurted the words and was not surprised when Graham's face turned white.

I brushed past him, charged out of the utility room and down the driveway. It was all Graham could do to keep up with me.

I don't want to go over the terrible scene with Graham that day. It's enough to tell you that I broke it off as kindly as I could, and he reacted with anguish and more in-your-face belligerence than I thought he was capable of displaying to me or anyone else. I considered myself fortunate to have learned about his tendency toward out-of-control anger before I married him. In the end, I ripped his ring from my finger, and he jumped back in his car and roared back to Raleigh, leaving me stony-faced but unrepentant. I was convinced I'd done the right thing for both of us, but just between you and me, I haven't been able to stomach baklava ever since.

At the church a few hours later, my bouquet of roses and baby's breath gave off a sickening-sweet fragrance and created a headache that two hastily swallowed aspirins would not cure. Before I started my march down the aisle, I had to wait for Curry Anne, Tottie and the two other bridesmaids to reach the altar and turn to face the assembled guests. Then, feeling faint from the combination of flower fumes and emotional tension, I preceded Martine to the altar and assumed my place to the left of her. I avoided looking at Rick.

When Dr. Stith indicated with a nod that it was time for the ring ceremony, things began to get crazy. Hal, Rick's best man, was so nervous that he dropped Martine's ring, setting off a Keystone Kops scramble. One of the groomsmen dropped to his knees to grab the ring as it rolled merrily past him, and I tried to stop it with the toe of my shoe. The ring jumped down the altar steps, and Rick chased it, setting off amused murmuring and a snicker or two from the wedding guests. Finally, in front of the first pew, Rick pounced on the ring and slowly rose, waving it overhead as if in victory. Then everyone broke into laughter.

While the guests were settling down, Rick walked up the steps and turned his head to stare at me, a panoply of emotions flitting across his features. And then he spoke to me in a terse whisper.

"Why didn't you tell me you were going to break off with Graham?"

No one else heard what Rick said to me, and if anyone noticed that he spoke, they would have merely attributed it to a comment about the dropping of the ring. Old Dr. Stith was almost deaf, and no other attendant stood near.

Martine was the only one whose attention was focused on us, but her expression was serene. She probably hadn't heard. Probably.

"Because it wouldn't have made any difference," I said fiercely, and Rick recoiled as if I'd slapped him in the face.

Dr. Stith cleared his throat. "Shall we proceed?" he asked mildly as we all resumed our places.

I know I must have looked faint as I returned to my position beside Martine. Beside me, Tottie steadied me with a hand to my elbow.

"Now, Richard, repeat after me…"

The rest of the ceremony is lost to my memory except for the very end. When the minister said benevolently, "And now you may kiss the bride," I handed Martine her bouquet and threw back her veil.

Turning to Rick, Martine lifted her lips and closed her eyes. And it was in that brief moment, that tiny space in time, that Rick's gaze met mine. In his expression I read reproach and mute anguish. It stabbed through me like the coldest, sharpest icicle, and I swayed with the pain.

Tottie asked in a low tone, "Are you okay?"

I nodded as Rick kissed my sister with a passion that I believed driven by an emotion more profound than I had ever witnessed between them, the sight of which pierced me to the heart.

Chapter 9: Trista

2004

I was overcome with a giddy feeling of expectation as I anticipated spending the first Easter after Rick and Martine's divorce at Sweetwater Cottage. Lindsay and Peter planned to come also; they'd settled in Aiken, where Peter ran an alcohol and drug rehab center. Since returning from Uganda, they'd become the parents of a four-year-old boy, Adam, and a two-year-old girl, Ainsley, who closely resembled Lindsay.

In our phone conversation a couple of weeks before, Martine had been vague about her holiday plans. Naturally, I had refrained from mentioning the cottage because it was an awkward subject now that she and Rick were divorced. I felt somewhat uneasy that Martine wouldn't be there, but under the circumstances, I didn't expect her to be welcome, nor, I was sure, would she. The rest of us would be a comfort to Rick, and we all agreed that we were exactly what he needed.

I set out from Columbia early one morning after a difficult week at work, during which I'd lost all confidence in my relationship with my coanchor, Byron Stott. I'd recently learned that Byron was making a play to cut me out of the evening news, and I was still smarting over it because I'd considered him my friend. The stress of our differences had made me weary, and I was happily anticipating a week at the beach.

As always, the gentle rise and fall of the country roads soothed me, and soon my sporty little Miata was rolling through glimmering marshes and lush, flat woodlands. By the time I reached Berkeley County I was hungry, so I stopped and grabbed a plastic-wrapped sandwich out of the glass case at a convenience store and munched it along the way. Later, at Jeter's Market, I wheeled into the parking lot and bought serious food—shrimp, fat and freshly caught; Little Debbie fudge rounds; a case of Cheerwine, our Carolinas soft drink of choice.

As I left the market, my tires stirring up a cloud of white dust, Jolly Jeter, who was emptying garbage out back, lifted a hand to wave, though it was more like the gesture he'd use to brush one of the Low Country's pesky gnats away. No wasted motion in that wave, no sirree. I could imagine him saying that in his native drawl, which is something I'd worked hard to excise from my speech. Native South Carolinian or not, I was expected to speak like a Midwesterner when I read the news. People say that I still talk like a Southerner, though. It's in the inflection.

The air presented a veritable feast of scents—the marshy smell of estuarial mud freshened by the flow of brackish water, a salt breeze carrying with it the inevitable suggestion of fish and spiced by a pungent pine fragrance from the woods. I realized that my palms were perspiring and that I was actually nervous at the prospect of seeing Rick again.

Sweetwater Cottage was located down a jolting road that Boyd McCulloch had promised would never be paved. "All that would do is bring a passel of tourists down heah," he'd said seriously. "Let them stay on the beach road when they invade in the summer. Sweetwater Cottage is not for gawkers."

Not that any of the Northerners who have recently discovered the barrier islands off the South Carolina coast would be interested in the cottage. Although genteel, the big rambling house is nothing like the modern glass-and-wood-siding abodes favored by newcomers. We South Carolinians prefer our beach houses slightly out of fashion, so shabby that they're chic. You can't get that gently softened effect until a property has been lived in and loved by a couple of generations.

As I slowed my car in approaching the house, I saw that Rick's Taurus was parked under the oak in its usual spot, and it was spattered with mud; dead bugs were encrusted on the windshield. Rick had always taken such pride in his cars, keeping them waxed, turning them over to a car detailer for a thorough cleaning a couple times a year. Stranger yet, there was no sign of him or of the Tolsons, either.

The house always seemed dormant when no one was in residence. It took people to wake it up. But now the curtains were drawn across every window, something I'd never seen before, and this was peculiar since Rick had been here for weeks. Shutters hung loose, and the shrubbery was leggy with neglect. In all the years I'd been visiting, I'd never seen the cottage in such a state of disrepair, and I felt a sudden shiver, as if a chill had settled over me.

Carrying the bags of groceries, I hurried up the back steps. "Rick?" I called. The door was open, and I peered through the screen into the kitchen. A mound of dirty dishes caught my attention first, followed by a trail of clothes on the sandy floor. I set the groceries on the porch swing, sending it into a wild little jig of protest, and knocked. No answer.

I cracked the door open and slipped inside, forgetting any attempt at stealth. "Rick?"

I skirted the blue picnic table in the kitchen, where we had all traced the outlines of our hands with white paint years ago. The *ticktock* of the old schoolhouse clock, a McCulloch family relic from the days when Rick's great-grandmother taught school on one of the neighboring islands, punctuated the silence.

I started down the hall, still wary but figuring that Rick would be out on the front porch, enjoying the sweet, balmy breeze. As I passed the room where I always slept, the one off the dining room to which Martine and I laid claim long ago, I did a double take.

Rick was sleeping sprawled across one of the beds, his mouth open. He snored softly, and a rank sour smell hung in the air. He was buck naked. I stopped dead in my tracks.

I started to shut the door between us, planning to flee outside and regroup, but the bracelet on my right wrist jingled against the metal of the doorknob. At the sound, one of Rick's eyes opened, then the other. Both locked into mine.

"Trista, what are you doing here?" he asked. Showing great presence of mind, Rick yanked the rumpled sheet over himself.

With my hand poised delicately on the doorknob and speaking as if I walked in on naked sleeping guys every day of my life, I said, "I drove over from Columbia today. I told you I was coming, and Lindsay and Peter, too. They're not here yet, so I'll just—"

"Damn! I thought it was tomorrow." Rick pushed himself up on his elbows. I was shocked at his appearance, at the reddened whites of his eyes, the pouched skin beneath, and his beard showing an unexpected touch of gray. This was a man who had always turned heads wherever he went, but I almost didn't recognize him.

Then, so help me, I yanked the door closed and fled, knocking a plant to the floor with a crash as the phone rang.

I hurried into the living room, taking note of the beer cans, the line of liquor bottles on the hearth. Lilah Rose, who was aided every summer by the meticulous Queen, had never been guilty of sloppy housekeeping. The cottage had always been kept obsessively clean and neat. Scooping up the phone beside the bar, I noticed absently that the plant I'd sent flying was a dead fern, its fronds brown and brittle. The condition of the fern fit in with the wisps of spiderwebs trailing from the light fixture and the dirty clothes covering every available surface.

"Hello?" I said.

"Trista, is that you?" Lindsay's voice crackled through a bad connection on her cell phone.

I sagged against the bar in relief. The image of Rick's naked body was burned into the inside of my eyelids, and I couldn't make it go away. I pinched the bridge of my nose between thumb and forefinger, not that this helped. "Lindsay, this is an emergency. When will you and Peter get here?"

Her tone was sharp. "What kind of emergency?"

"The worst. I can't talk about it right now." From behind the bedroom door emitted a series of muffled thumps that could possibly mean that Rick was getting dressed.

"Fine, because I have my own problems," said Lindsay, never one to mince words. "We're driving on the interstate about an hour away from you, but we're heading home to Aiken. We called home, and Adam's sick." Lindsay sounded more resigned than alarmed.

"Sick? What's wrong?"

"Peter's mother suspects the chicken pox. Adam's been vaccinated, but it was only a few weeks ago. He may have a mild case—no one can tell yet—and if Adam has it, Ainsley might come down with it, too. My mother-in-law is panicking."

I was sliding headlong into a panic attack of my own. "Lindsay," I said urgently, "you and Peter *have* to show up. I'm not sure I'm capable of dealing with Rick all by myself."

"I'm sorry, Trista. Is it bad?"

"It's certainly not good. For starters, the cottage looks run-down. And oh, the living room—damp towels ornamenting every chair, dirty dishes supporting unknown lifeforms on the coffee table, and if you stacked the beer cans end to end, they'd probably reach New Jersey. Rick—well, he was asleep," I said, lowering my voice and glancing back over my shoulder.

"Asleep? When he was expecting us?"

"Yes, and—I don't know. I'm not sure he'll react to me the same way he would if we were all here."

"I can't believe you're so negative, Trista. And Rick was supposed to be seeing to repairs around there."

"He was?" This was news to me.

"I talked with him a couple of weeks ago. Remember I told you about it?"

"Vaguely," I said.

"Well, he said that Hal had been neglecting the cottage

with their parents gone and hadn't been able to get down there much because they recently took in Nadia's father, who has Alzheimer's."

"That explains a lot," I said. "But not everything."

"Wait a minute, Trista. Here's Peter."

I heard the rustle of the phone being passed, and Peter said, "Trista, you've always been our cheerleader. You can pump Rick up better than Lindsay or me."

"Uh, right." I didn't add that Rick seemed in no mood to accept succor from me.

"Tell you what, Trista. Lindsay and I will go home, calm my mother and check on our sick kid. Once we get the situation squared away, we'll join you and Rick in a day or two. If it's at all possible, that is. Does that sound better?"

"Maybe," I said.

Peter chuckled. "Attagirl, Trista. Here's Lindsay."

Lindsay came back on the line, her tone apologetic. "It's been a long time since Peter's mom nursed sick children."

"I understand, Lindsay. Your place is with the kids." I considered Peter and Lindsay to be model parents, all too rare in my world, which was populated by people who made the news by breaking the law and who were generally not sterling examples of parenthood or anything else.

Lindsay became more concerned. "Trista, if it gets rough for you, maybe you should head back to Columbia."

"I didn't really want to be alone over Easter," I said, though I could have visited Mom and Aunt Cynthia in Macon. They'd have been thrilled if I'd showed up, but I was scheduled for a visit with them to celebrate Mom's birthday the first week in May.

Lindsay sighed. "How about if I call you tomorrow and find out how things are going?"

"I'll settle for that. Give the kids a big hug from me."

"I will. Bye, Trista."

"Goodbye."

I hung up and stood pensively gazing around the cottage. Even in the dim light, I recognized the sweetgrass basket of sand dollars on the mantel. The bookcase held books that we'd brought with us at various times, all lined up to greet me like the old friends they were.

The click of a door latch jarred me out of my reverie, and I whirled to see Rick sauntering out of the bedroom, hair mussed, khaki shorts pulled on in haste and the waistband left unsnapped.

"Trista," he said, his voice rusty from sleep. "I guess I should apologize. I must have lost track of the days."

I forced a smile. "I—well, there's no harm done. Other than to the plant, that is." I waved my hand in the direction of the upended fern. "I'm sorry about that."

"No problemo." He yanked the fern up by its crumbling fronds, marched to the back door and pitched the plant out. The unbroken pot met the same fate. He nudged at the dirt on the floor with one bare foot, as if that might make it disappear. It didn't.

Such a display made me uncomfortable. I'd expected Rick to be levelheaded, the way he'd always been, but clearly something in him had changed. He'd been through a lot, I'd grant that, but wasn't he grateful I was there?

Flustered, I turned toward the kitchen. "I'll put the food away," I said. I needed something to do, something to cover my awkwardness and confusion.

I went outside and retrieved the grocery bags from the porch swing. Inside, Rick had angled his frame against the doorjamb, from which vantage point he observed with heavy-lidded eyes as I slid the curtains open at the kitchen window to allow light into the room, then self-consciously busied myself stashing the packages of shrimp and collard greens in the refrigerator.

"Who was on the phone?"

I spoke briskly. "That was Lindsay, calling to say that she and Peter won't be here for a day or so. Adam may have chicken pox, but they didn't find out until they got more than halfway here, and Ainsley might be coming down with it, too. They're going home to check on them. I guess Peter's mom isn't comfortable staying with two sick kids."

Rick's trademark smile had always started in his eyes and worked its way down; there was no sign of it now. "Chicken pox. Sounds miserable."

I murmured something in agreement, making a giant effort to collect myself.

"Is your car unlocked?" Rick asked. "I'll get your suitcase."

Mutely, I dug the keys out of my pocket and tossed them to him.

"Be right back," he said with a curt nod.

Feeling more and more as if I should give Lindsay's suggestion that I go back to Columbia serious consideration, I threw open the draperies to admit more light into the living and dining rooms.

"All right," Rick said, entering through the front door and carrying my duffel. "I'm going to take your things up to the Lighthouse."

"You've always slept there," I protested in surprise.

"I've settled into your room," Rick said, his expression a little too blank to make me believe that he liked that room better. I followed him silently through the living room and up the spiral iron staircase.

At least no curtains were drawn in the circular tower, where window abutted window to provide a stunning, wide-angle view. As dusk crept up from the horizon, the sea was a sheet of silvery silk rippling gently to the shore, where it broke into a rim of white froth. From this high vantage point, I spotted a sailboat scudding south, and below, a couple walked hand in hand in the sand, their flop-eared spaniel gamboling in and out of the water ahead of them.

Rick set my suitcase on the plump blue-and-white-striped cushion of the window seat. "You know where everything is," he said, jerking his head in the direction of the built-in cabinets below the tall windows. "Drawers, TV, bathroom, bed."

Not that the bed would be easy to miss. It was a magnificent mahogany four-poster, its posts carved in representations of the rice plant, a Low Country crop that had been the staple of the region's economy before rice became too expensive to grow. Lilah Rose's deft decorating touch was evident in the blue waffle-knit eyelet-edged coverlet and the canopy of sheer white fabric that fell all the way to the floor and was tied to each post with a scrap of moiré ribbon.

"You'll find more blankets, pillows and so on in here," Rick said, indicating a sea trunk near the foot of the bed.

"Thanks, Rick," I said.

He ran a hand up the back of his neck. "What's for dinner?"

"Shrimp and cheese grits and a big mess of collards like Queen used to make, what else?" I replied in an attempt at lightness.

"Sounds great," he said. He turned and clattered down the metal stairs, whistling tunelessly between his teeth.

This new headed-for-dereliction Rick was a surprise to me. Clearly, Lindsay, Peter and I were going to have to confront him and make him understand that Martine's exit from his life didn't mean it was over. I did not for one minute believe that I could handle this task alone, since I was a bit too close to the problem for comfort. I felt in some way responsible for Martine's behavior. Logically, I knew I wasn't, but she remained my twin, my sister and my friend. However, she certainly wasn't confiding in me now.

After I cooked our dinner, I heaped sautéed shrimp into one side of a divided platter and spooned creamy cheese grits into the other. The collards went into a bright yellow bowl that Lilah Rose had always prized. We seldom used the dining room at the cottage, and the kitchen wasn't exactly neat after I finished with it, so Rick and I carried our plates and silverware onto the wide porch overlooking the beach and sat at the round patio table, where we'd eaten so many meals in the past. The weather was cool enough so that I needed to wear a sweater, a loose pullover almost the exact blue-gray shade as the ocean at this time of day. It was the color of Rick's eyes, as well.

Rick had disappeared into his room earlier and returned wearing a polo shirt and boat shoes with his shorts, and he'd somehow subdued his wild hair. I was relieved that he'd pulled himself together and, though still remarkably detached, was making an effort to converse. *If* you could call his short replies to my questions conversing, and by the time we reached the end of the meal, I wasn't sure I could.

Rick spoke in a series of grunts and indistinguishable syllables. I struggled for things to say, which had never been a problem before. Relating stories about my work that I considered humorous seemed like my best bet, though the telling of them fell flat. I consoled myself that I was trained to deliver the news, not engage in comedic entertainment of an audience of one, who, at the moment, couldn't have been more unresponsive.

When I started asking him questions about the deplorable condition of the house in the hope of sparking conversation, he did no better. Though I mentioned the porch's missing a couple of sections of railing, he merely mumbled something about having discussed it with Hal, and the rotten steps apparently caused him little concern.

"Nobody visits, anyway," he said, shrugging it off.

"It doesn't matter," I argued. "Hal's not going to like it when he sees this place."

"No need to dump more guilt on me," Rick snapped. "I've stockpiled plenty of it from other areas of my life."

"You feel guilty about Martine?" I asked skeptically. "When she's the one who left?" I didn't stop to think about what other guilt Rick might be feeling. I was only interested in his relationship with my sister, wanting his point of view. She'd clammed up about her reasons for their divorce and wasn't confiding in me at all about Steve Lifkin.

Rick regarded me morosely. "Stating the obvious," he said, "she left because I was a lousy husband. I wasn't providing what she needed in the marriage."

"Martine couldn't have asked for anyone better," I told him. I fervently believed this, but Rick only glowered at me for a moment and went back to eating.

The rest of our dinner dragged along in silence while I tried to reconcile the Rick I'd always known with the angry lost soul sitting across the table from me.

I wondered what he would have thought if I blurted that I'd had illicit dreams about him over the years, the kind that wake you up in the middle of the night and won't let you go back to sleep. I glanced over at him surreptitiously, trying to detect a glimmer of the boy I'd known. That boy was there, all right, in the planes of Rick's cheeks, the curve of his brow, but his man's face reflected wounds to the spirit. I felt a rush of tenderness toward him, a yearning for the simpler days of our youth. Right after that, I remembered that I'd come to the island to help Rick heal, and that was what I must do. It seemed a daunting task.

My appetite had disappeared by this time, and it was futile to try to eat any more. "Here, Rick," I urged, trying to return to some semblance of normality. "Finish off the shrimp." I shoved the platter toward him.

"Okay," he said as he dumped the rest of the shrimp onto his plate. End of topic. End of discussion.

Finally, Rick pushed his chair back from the table. "You cooked. I'll clean up," he said.

"I'll help."

"Whatever." Rick stood and started piling dishes on a tray.

I took my time gathering the extra silverware and salt and pepper shakers before following him inside. I adopted a brisk tone, the one that Martine used to complain was bossy. Never mind, it got the job done, and Rick was used to it, or had been once. "Tomorrow you and I can be our own cleaning crew," I said as I skirted the mess in the living room. "That way everything will be spiffy when Lindsay and Peter arrive."

"Why bother? Maybe they won't show," Rick said. He sounded as if he'd be happier if they dropped off the world somehow, and this surprised me. Rick had always been loyal to his friends.

"Oh, you can count on those two unless they absolutely can't make it," I said with more conviction than I felt. I was certainly ready for reinforcements.

"Uh, right." Rick began to stack dishes in the dishwasher.

"And Lindsay loves to bake, so we can probably count on her for some of those delicious snickerdoodle cookies she makes, oh, and maybe some fresh-baked bread that she'll bring from home. I was thinking of making chicken tetrazzini, since you like it, and—"

"You don't have to become a talking menu," Rick said, interrupting me. "It doesn't matter what we eat." He slammed the upper dishwasher rack in so hard that a spatula slipped through and bounced onto the floor.

I stared with my mouth open. I'd never known Rick to be deliberately rude, and I'd only wanted to help. Suddenly, I was tired of the whole charade that had commenced the moment I set foot in the cottage. "Personally," I said with equal snarkiness, "I think you should be interested in hanging out with your best friends, but hey, that's just me."

"Of course I'm interested," he shot back, though his stance, his attitude and lack of eye contact belied that statement.

"You could have fooled me," I retorted. When he didn't comment, I started passing dirty dishes to him, and he loaded them, the silence between us growing heavier with each moment. Every small sound was magnified—the clink of the dishes, the metallic clang of silverware as Rick chucked it into the basket, even the steady tick of the old schoolhouse clock on the wall. The tension continued to build. After I'd finished, I turned off the water and wearily dried my hands on a paper towel, wondering if I should just bolt toward the stairs to the Lighthouse or take the time to murmur a quiet good-night.

Just when I'd decided on bolting, Rick slammed the dishwasher door and leaned on the counter, effectively blocking my way out of the kitchen. For the first time all evening, he looked into my eyes.

"Listen, Trista," he said uncomfortably.

"I'm listening," I answered, though not without trepidations.

Rick tightened his lips, then gazed out the window, where the porch light illuminated the oleander hedge. "Things aren't the same now," he said, looking back.

"You didn't have to tell me that," I said quietly. "I'm aware of it."

"I mean, I'm different since...*since*. I can't be the same person I was before Martine left."

I truly couldn't summon a reply. Anything I could say seemed inadequate. I was treading on dangerous ground here, and my emotions made it a quagmire.

"I—understand," I said helplessly.

"I hope so." He appeared undecided for a moment, then heaved a giant sigh. "Tris, I know I haven't been good company, but why don't we go for a walk the way we always did on our first night here. Are you up for it?"

It struck me that no matter whether I wanted to go or not, if I didn't try to connect with Rick in a meaningful fashion, there was no point in being there at all.

"I'll put on my beach shoes," I said, and I fled to my room. Once there, I sat on the edge of the bed to buckle my sandals, taking my time about it. I reminded myself that I'd understood from the outset that Rick required careful handling, and I resolved to allow him a bit of leeway. I couldn't expect to put things to rights in a matter of hours. I needed to give him time and, apparently, a whole lot of patience.

Rick offered a tight smile when I descended the staircase. It wasn't his old smile, full of warmth, but it would do. "Let's go," he said, and I followed him through the French doors and down the outside stairs.

The beach was deserted at low tide, the shore adorned with shells, seaweed and bits of driftwood scattered at the high-water line. We wended our way through the clumps of sea grass on the dunes. Automatically, because it was always the preferred direction for our walks, we headed north into the soft evening wind, keeping a reasonable distance between us. Rick walked swiftly, hands stuffed deep into his pockets. From one of the houses floated the sound of reggae and a peal of laughter, and ahead of us I caught a glimpse of two people sitting on lounge chairs inside a portable cabana. The man spoke as we passed, and the woman murmured an inaudible reply as their shapes merged into one.

Rick plowed ahead, his long legs outdistancing mine. Masked as it was by facial hair, his expression was inscrutable. I wondered how I could get him to shave the beard, then decided that it wasn't an important issue.

"Hey, McCulloch," I called, striving for the old compatibility. "Wait for me!"

Rick slowed his pace. He turned and walked backward for a few steps as I jogged to close the space between us. "What's the matter? Can't keep up?"

I drew even with him. "After a few days, I'll be racing you down the beach."

"In your dreams," Rick scoffed, but I caught a foreshadowing of his familiar grin.

"Do you still run every day? Work out?" I asked.

"The only time I run these days is if someone's chasing me, which hasn't happened lately."

I slid a sideways glance at Rick's profile. I forced my eyes front again and wished I'd worn something heavier than a sweater. The wind had freshened, blowing a hint of chill along with it.

I wanted to keep Rick talking but not to chatter so much that I turned him off as I had earlier. Finally, I settled on picking up where we'd left off a few minutes ago. "Rick, if you don't socialize and you don't exercise here on the island, how do you occupy your time?"

His eyebrows lifted and he shrugged. "Doing whatever I damn please," he said as if to put an end to the matter.

"Which is what?" I prodded.

"You ask too many questions," he countered, sounding irritated.

"I'm only trying to—"

"I told you I'm different now, Trista. Get used to it." He bit off the words sharply.

I adopted a reasoning tone. "We've all changed over the years, Rick, including me. That doesn't mean our friends should give up on us."

This only angered him. "Wait a minute, Trista. *Life* gave up on *me*."

"I care about you, Rick." This was a bald statement of fact and one that should have been obvious, but Rick seemed so unlike himself that I wasn't at all embarrassed about pointing it out.

We walked on in silence. The sky above was a wide indigo bowl, pale tufts of clouds concealing the moon and drawing a curtain across the stars. I grew increasingly more troubled about my inadequacy in dealing with Rick. Furthermore, I couldn't shake the conviction that Rick didn't want me around.

In our ramblings, we seldom walked farther than a landmark gray clapboard house that was now being used as a bed-and-breakfast. When we reached it, we turned back by tacit agreement, this time with our backs to the wind.

As we drew within sight of Sweetwater Cottage, we veered to our right, away from the ocean. Light poured from the cottage's windows and Lighthouse tower, limning the gentle slopes of the dunes in gold. Unfortunately, the picture-perfect scene didn't make me feel any better.

Our steps slowed as we crossed the dunes, and because Rick's closed expression offered me little encouragement, I erased any urge I might have had of spending time watching TV with him or sitting out on the porch before we went to bed. It was sad, but we seemed to have nothing more to say to each other.

At the bottom of the steps, Rick unexpectedly swiveled toward me. His hands were still shoved deep in his pockets. "How about a beer, Trista?"

I busied myself tapping my sand-encrusted sandals against the bottom step.

I inhaled a deep breath. "I don't care for anything to drink, Rick. What I really want is to figure out what's inside your head."

"I'm not sure what you mean," he said.

In another person the words might have sounded evasive, but I recognized the perplexity in his tone. My words tumbled out in an impassioned torrent. "If you want me to leave, I will. Say the word and I'll drive back to Columbia tonight."

Bafflement washed over his features, and he rocked back as though I'd slapped him. "Is that what you think I want?"

"I have no idea, Rick. I only know that I'm uncomfortable being around you."

"I don't want you to go," he said, meeting my gaze unflinchingly. I believed him.

"All right," I said wearily. "How about if we start over?"

"From where?" he shot back. "Fourteen years ago? Ten? Or since this afternoon?"

I could only stare at him, speechless. It was, under the circumstances of our lives, a reasonable question. If we really could start the clock again, go back to a previous time, would either of us choose to begin again at age nine? At age eighteen? Or after?

While I was asking myself these questions, Rick turned abruptly, headed up the stairs, and disappeared into the house with a slam of the door.

One thing I learned long ago is that it's always easier to be the one who's leaving instead of the one who's been left. The leaver has the satisfaction of having made a considered decision, whereas the leavee is stuck with having had someone else choose his destiny. This holds true in almost every relationship situation, with almost every person.

I sank onto the bottom step and stared out across the dunes, wishing that I'd been the first one to walk away on this occasion. For a moment I considered tossing my suitcase into my car and roaring away into the night but then decided to sleep on it. It was a long drive back to Columbia, and the road was lonely and much too dark.

Chapter 10: Rick

2004

The next day Rick awoke before dawn. On previous days, his inclination would have been to lie staring listlessly at the revolving ceiling fan for a couple of hours, but today, because he'd pretty well screwed up last night with Trista, he forced himself to get up and into the bathroom. He listened but didn't hear her stirring upstairs in the Lighthouse, though it was a time-honored tradition in spring and summer for them to plunge into the surf for a sunrise swim on their first morning at the cottage.

Should he wake her? Maybe she was too tired to get up this early. He was ashamed of his churlish behavior the night before, though she'd shocked him out of it when she suggested leaving. Up until then, he didn't think he'd been *that* bad. While he uncomfortably confronted how his surly attitude was driving Trista away, he caught sight of his glum countenance in the mirror. Just for the heck of it, he practiced smiling. Hey, he still could. This was a momentous discovery.

He went into the kitchen and started the coffee, figuring that its aroma would bring her downstairs. Still, she didn't appear. After taking his time over his first cup, he stood irresolutely at the bottom of the spiral staircase, gazing up at her closed door. He finally concluded that maybe she didn't consider this the right time to continue the tradition of the first-morning swim, since Peter and Lindsay weren't here yet. And then there was the matter of last night, which hadn't gone well. Mostly thanks to him, of course.

After waiting a few more minutes for some sign of life in the Lighthouse, Rick gave up. He grabbed one of the gritty towels off the couch as he let himself out of the cottage, and a glance back at the upstairs windows revealed that the curtains were still pulled shut. He supposed he didn't blame Trista for sleeping in, considering that he'd made such an ass of himself yesterday.

He ran to the ocean and dived in, surfacing well beyond the breaking waves. The water was cold and bracing, and he struck out toward the gray clapboard house, his strokes strong and precise. There were no other swimmers around, only a man strolling at the edge of the surf. He rested for a few minutes on the beach before starting back.

As he strode out of the water, he was relieved to note that Trista was sitting on the porch. His heart gladdened at the sight of her, and until then, he hadn't realized how fearful he'd been after last night's conversation that she would leave anyway. When she saw him, she set aside her coffee mug to start out across the dunes. She was clad in an oversize shirt with the ends of the long sleeves flapping, and underneath was the faint outline of her swimsuit. Her hair was pulled back in a careless knot, and as usual on the island, she wore no makeup.

"I can't believe you went for a swim on the first morning without me," she called as soon as she was in hearing range.

He stopped in front of her, seawater sluicing down his body. "I didn't want to wake you."

"We always go for a swim together on the first morning," she said without attempting to hide her disappointment. "It's tradition."

He didn't want to upset her any more than he already had, and he hoped he could find some common ground this morning. Humor might be his best bet.

"Okay, race you if you dare!" he challenged, pretending to take his mark. It felt natural to banter with her, though he had to force himself.

But she wasn't about to let him off so easily. "The first-morning swim has to be with all of us together, right after the sun has risen, and before breakfast. Those are the rules."

"We'll all go together when Peter and Lindsay get here," he said reassuringly. He scooped up his towel and began to dry himself. "What do you say we have breakfast?"

Her eyes lit up. "You're on. There are no traditions about that."

"Would you like to initiate one? It's not too late."

She only laughed, but it was a welcome sound, and they began walking toward the dune path that led to the house.

While Rick went to shower, Trista rummaged in the pantry for food, and when he returned, she had poured corn flakes into two of his mother's blue willow bowls.

"Cereal was all I could find," she said.

"This is what I eat every morning. When I eat, that is. How about you?"

"Power bars, all different flavors. Rice cakes sometimes." Trista sat down at the table, and Rick joined her.

"I've been thinking about last night," he said after a long silence punctuated only by the clink of their spoons.

Trista spared him a wary look.

"Maybe I've become a bit too introspective. Too self-centered."

She pushed a few corn flakes around the bowl, appearing to consider this. "You're entitled, but you can't shut out the world forever, Rick," she said.

"Sometimes I'd like to," he replied softly. "I guess I hadn't admitted it to myself until now."

"Maybe this is a breakthrough," she said.

"Maybe." Suddenly, he wanted to explain himself, even though it wasn't natural for him to want to confide in others. "It wounded my ego when Shorty put me on leave. I understand now that I hadn't been operating at top speed even before the accident. Things hadn't been good between Martine and me for a long time, and I was trying to make the pain go away by staying busy. In hindsight, I realize that I should have dealt with our problems before they blew up in my face."

"Martine could have dealt with the problems, too," Trista said.

"Ah, but I became a workaholic in order to cover up my misery. Martine had an affair. Who's to say if one coping technique is better than another?"

Trista didn't say anything. They were silent for a long time, each lost in thought, but she finished eating first.

"Whatever happened between you and Martine, I don't

blame either of you. It's not up to me to judge or accuse or—well, you know what I'm saying. I care about both of you and wish you the best." As if unconsciously, she spread a palm out on the table, fitting it over the white-painted outline of her hand that his father had painted there when they were ten years old.

"We've outgrown our handprints," he said, placing his right hand over the corresponding outline on his side of the table. "But not each other."

"Not each other," she repeated, a tentative smile curving her lips.

"Well," he said, now that they'd reached a point of seminormality. "Let's get on with our morning chores." He spoke with an air of brisk efficiency.

Trista slid her chair back from the table. "I'm planning to tackle the spiderwebs in the living room now, and I could use some help." She seemed to deliver the words only with some effort, and he understood how it was. Despite his attitude of moving forward, he was merely going through the motions himself, attempting to salvage all he could with Trista after making such a mess of it with Martine. He intended to be on his best behavior from now on because he'd realized that yes, he did need his friends. Some more than others.

"I'll collect the dirty towels," he told her, putting the milk back in the refrigerator.

Trista regarded him, one eyebrow lifted in skepticism. "Big whoop, Rick. What about that leaning tower of beer cans?"

He pretended to be aggrieved. "That's art," he said, but he ripped a large plastic bag off the roll beneath the sink, went into the living room and began to toss the cans into it.

With Trista dusting, Rick mopping and then taking turns

with the vacuum cleaner, they soon whipped the room into shape. When they finished, good humor restored, Rick expressed a hankering for fried chicken and suggested a trip to the Bi-Lo supermarket on the mainland to buy some. "You can tag along with me if you like," he said, hoping she would.

She shook the duster out the kitchen door. "I'd better get the Tolsons' room ready," she said.

"Suit yourself." Rick wasn't sure if she just didn't want to go with him or if she really felt it was necessary to get the cottage all gussied up for Lindsay and Peter.

He jangled his car keys and left the back door slam behind him. But when he reached the bottom porch step, he turned and stuck his head back inside. "By the way, Trista, I really am glad you're here."

A flush rose to her cheeks. "Don't overdo it, Rick. I'm planning to clean the bathrooms anyway."

"I just wanted you to know."

He was rewarded by a tentative but incandescent smile.

After he left the cottage, he drove slowly toward the bridge, the car radio set to the beach music station. Right now, Otis Redding was singing "Sitting on the Dock of the Bay," which had always been his favorite Tappany Island tune, reminding him of all the days he had sat with Trista and Martine on the edge of the old dock on the marsh, swinging their legs over the side and planning—some might say plotting—their futures.

It was to the dock on the marsh that he had gone after Roger Barrineau's funeral when his parents had offered Sweetwater Cottage to Virginia as a place to recover from the brutal murder of her husband. The funeral had been a long-drawn-out affair, featuring eulogies by two of Roger's law partners, both of whom had assured Rick at the gathering at the Barrineaus' house afterward that he still had a place in the firm after graduation from law school. No one realized that he had a fire burning in his gut, one that seared his soul so deeply he'd lost all interest in defending accused criminals.

After everyone had left the house, he and Martine had driven Virginia down to Tappany Island, with Trista planning to arrive later in her own car. As soon as they set foot inside the cottage, Virginia had bolted down the knockout pills supplied by her family doctor and retired to her room. Martine, red-eyed and teary over the loss of her father, had waved Rick away when he tried to comfort her, saying she was too exhausted to relive any part of the past horrible days, so, at loose ends, he'd headed across the street to the dock, alone.

Trista's car, in those days a small blue sedan, appeared on the road as Rick was walking glumly toward the marsh, his hands stuffed deep in the pockets of a windbreaker that did little to soften the blustery wind sweeping out of the west.

She hailed him through her open window. "Hey! What are you doing?"

"Going to spend a few minutes on the dock. Need fresh air."

She parked alongside the road, scrambling out and pulling her jacket with her. She didn't speak as they walked down the dock, and he appreciated her silence. He'd been mulling over things in his mind, winnowing out choices and assessing possibilities.

Clouds rippled in layers on the western horizon—luminous pearl gray, softest peach and a brilliant red fired by the setting sun. Trista's eyes were swollen from all the crying of the past couple of days, and she seemed exhausted. He was grateful for her willingness to keep him company. Roger had been like a second father to him. With Roger's death, Rick saw his life tumbling around him, Humpty Dumpty and the wall all over again. That had been one of his favorite nursery rhymes—once.

"How's Mom doing?" she asked after they'd sat dangling their feet off the dock for a while.

"She went to sleep right away. Poor thing, she's still in shock."

"As are we all," Trista said with feeling. "And Martine?"

"Okay," he said.

"How about you?"

"I'll manage," he said. "I'm more worried about you. It must have been awful, finding out the way you did."

"It was better for me to tell Mom than have the police show up on her doorstep," Trista said. She'd been working at the TV station when an item came across her desk concerning "a prominent local criminal lawyer who was attacked outside the Richland County Courthouse by a former client," and when she burst into the room where the video footage was being edited for that night's broadcast, she saw her own father being gunned down. She immediately tried to locate Virginia, who was out shopping, and after she told her mother the terrible news, it had fallen to Trista to call him and Martine.

When Rick and Martine arrived at the house in Windsor Manor after driving several hours from North Carolina, Trista was the one in charge, talking on the phone with the funeral director, arranging for someone to clean the house and prepare it for a reception following the ceremony, even choosing her father's burial clothes.

Despite the strain of all that, on the dock the day of the funeral Trista had skillfully led him through his own thought processes so that before they stood and brushed the bits of leaves and grass off the seats of their jeans, he had known that he would not join Roger's law firm. He would devote his life to getting criminals off the streets and keeping them in jail; the man who had killed Roger was a two-time convicted felon who had been released on parole for reasons that made no sense to any sane person.

Thinking back to that day, Rick was so caught up in his musings that he was actually surprised when the Bi-Lo supermarket appeared on the left-hand side of the road. He turned in to the parking lot and hurried inside. As he waited at the deli counter, he wondered if Trista still liked drumsticks the best. If so, he'd buy several.

He dialed the cottage's phone from his cell, but Trista didn't answer either that or her cell phone. He belatedly recalled that she usually turned it off when on vacation. So he bought six drumsticks, figuring that if she didn't eat them, either he or the crabs off the end of the dock would.

Chapter 11: Trista

2004

Click: Picture of a stray dog. She is the color of caramels, and her fur is matted with burrs. She's sitting beside the garbage can at Sweetwater Cottage. Her tongue is lolling and she seems to be saying, "Give me a chance. Give me a bath. Feed me!" I snapped the picture. Rick wasn't anywhere around.

After Rick left for the Bi-Lo, I vacuumed the Tolsons' room, put fresh sheets on the bed and made a big pitcher of sweetened iced tea for later. Then I clicked on the television and popped one of my favorite movies into the DVD player. I soon realized, though, that I'd left my glasses in my car and went outside to get them.

"Yo," said a voice behind me as I made my way along the sandy walkway. I whirled to find a spindly guy ambling up the driveway with a letter carrier's bag slung over his shoulder. His skin was the rich color of weathered mahogany, and he had a twinkle in his eye. He carried a fistful of mail and looked slightly familiar.

"Yes?" I said politely.

"Are you R. E. McCulloch? I've been trying to deliver mail to you for months."

"No, I'm not."

"Haven't we met before? My auntie used to bring me over here in the summers, and I'd help her wash windows and drag things out to the trash pile before heading down to the beach to throw a few nets for bait. My name's Stanley Doyle."

I moved a bit closer and peered up at him, the sun in my eyes. "You're Stanley? Queen's nephew? Why, I'm so glad to see you." I had a flash memory of a skinny guy who loved to laugh.

"Queen's *favorite* nephew," he corrected as he pumped my hand, his eyes lighting up.

I smiled at him. "How is Queen?" I asked.

"My aunt has gone to live with her son Bert in McLellanville. He owns a fleet of fishing boats, and she does all the bookkeeping for his business."

Well, life moves on for everyone. I'd missed Queen around the cottage during recent summer visits, and Lilah Rose had been vague about what had happened to her. "Tell Queen I said hey. I'm Trista, and I remember her waffles."

Stanley laughed. "So do I. They were almost as good as her biscuits. Now, who's this R. E. McCulloch? Is that the same Rick, or have you got someone new?"

"That's Rick, all right. You probably remember him."

"Uh-huh, bright kid, great smile. How am I going to

get him to put up a mailbox? Can't deliver the mail if he doesn't have one."

"I'll give Rick the mail, if you like."

"I can't do that. Regulations."

"Okay, I'll make sure Rick gets a mailbox."

"That's a good idea. Been holding mail at the post office ever since I took over as relief letter carrier while the regular gal is out on maternity leave. The U.S. Postal Service doesn't take kindly to being a warehouse for letters addressed to people who are too lazy to put up a proper receptacle." He winked.

"I understand."

"Okay, I'll be watching for that mailbox." He smiled and tipped me a genial wave, then paused on his way down the path. "Hey, it occurs to me that maybe you'd be interested in that mutt over there." He gestured toward the hedge, and in the shadows underneath, a dog was sitting with her tongue hanging. She was light brown with short hair and a long straggly tail. A small dog, only a puppy. I hadn't noticed her before.

"Is that your dog?" I asked.

"Nope, she's a stray. She pads around after me on my route, been doing that for weeks now. I pour her a drink from my water bottle and sometimes give her part of my sandwich at lunchtime. She probably survives by eating food people leave on the beach."

My heart went out to the poor thing. "Why don't you take her home, Stanley?" I asked. When the dog noticed us studying her, she wagged her tail enthusiastically. There was something lovable about the way she cocked her head and blinked at us.

"No, I've got a couple of attack cats who wouldn't take too kindly to the intrusion."

"That's too bad."

"Yup, she's a sweet little old mutt, from the looks of her."

"I'll give her water," I promised. I couldn't bear to see an animal suffer.

Stanley grinned. "Maybe you'll want to feed her, too," he said. He went on his way, humming a tune.

I'd been warned so many times by my mother not to feed strays, a dictum established because Mom had no use for animals. Her one aberration had been Bungie, and that only because she was under pressure from my father, who said Martine and I needed a pet; otherwise our growing-up years wouldn't be authentic. But right now, Mom wasn't here, and this was an attractive pup. My camera was just inside the house, and I went to get it, hoping to capture her sweet expression.

The dog seemed to know she was the center of attention, and her ears perked right before I snapped the shutter. Entranced, I observed her for a few moments. She lay down in the shade of the hedge, an intelligent glint sparkling in her eyes. And there was something more—a warmth, an eagerness.

I hoped she would soon find a home, but I wasn't prepared to provide it and doubted that Rick would, either. I splashed some water from the hose into an old aluminum pie plate I found under the porch and waited while she drank her fill. She gazed up at me, her eyes full of gratitude.

I stroked the soft fur between her ears but realized this might give her the wrong idea about the local hospitality. "Shoo," I said, waving my hands at her. "Go find some rich retired people to hassle."

Turning my back on her, I hurried back inside. Then I settled down to watch Debbie Reynolds charm Gene Kelly in *Singin' in the Rain*. I spent almost an hour absorbed in the costumes, music and plot before the phone rang. Reluctantly, I paused the video and answered the phone at the bar.

It was Lindsay. "Trista, I'm so glad it's you! Can you talk?"

Clicking the TV off, I hitched myself up on a stool. "Rick's out, so sure."

"How's it going?"

I thought about it for a moment. Too long a moment to suit Lindsay.

"Trista? Are you going to answer, or do I have to drag it out of you?"

"I'm glad to report that Rick seems better today. So am I." I hesitated before taking the plunge. "Listen, Lindsay, I couldn't tell you this last time we talked because Rick might have overheard, but you won't believe what I walked in on yesterday."

"Try me."

"Rick was asleep in my usual room."

"So?"

"So he wasn't wearing any clothes. It was embarrassing for both of us."

Lindsay laughed. "I guess so!"

"Rick expected all of us here today, not yesterday. Luckily, I'd stopped at Jeter's and bought enough food for dinner, because there wasn't much in the house. When I first arrived, Rick acted put-upon and uninterested, and as if he didn't want me here."

"This is typical behavior in a depressed individual."

"Lindsay. Too much *Oprah*. Too much *Dr. Phil*."

"My degree is in psychology, remember? Anyway, how are you and Rick getting along?"

"I'm coping. But Lindsay, you remember how the Mc-

Cullochs always kept the cottage in good repair? Well, Rick's been here over a month and he hasn't done squat."

"What's wrong, exactly?"

She quickly outlined the problems. "Normally, Rick would have jumped right in and fixed things. I can't wait until you and Peter get here. You *are* coming, aren't you?"

"Oh, Trista, we'd like to, but Adam has a fever and hardly slept all night. We sent Peter's mom home because she was exhausted. Now Ainsley has broken out in blisters."

"This doesn't sound promising, does it?" I felt acutely disappointed.

"I'm so sorry, Trista. I really am. But we can't leave the kids."

My spirits spiraled downward. "I understand," I told her.

"I suspect that you can best help Rick by getting him to open up, talk about his feelings, that sort of thing."

I expelled a long sigh. "He's not very good at that. Never has been," I said.

"You're long-time buddies. He'll probably emote with you before anyone else."

"I don't think so," I said, last night fresh in my mind.

"Listen, Trista, I've seen the two of you engrossed in earnest conversation more than once," Lindsay said, making me suspect that she'd been watching from the porch the day Rick had told me how frustrated he was over Martine's refusal to have kids. That had been an intense conversation, all right, but no one else was supposed to know about it.

Lindsay covered the phone with her hand, but still, I overheard her admonishing Adam. "No, honey, get back in bed and I'll put on your Muppets video in a minute. And don't scratch." To me she said, "Adam's having a miserable time."

"I'm really going to miss you, girl, but I'd better let you get back to him."

"Good luck with Rick, Trista."

"Thanks," I said. "I don't suppose you and Peter would like to adopt a stray dog," I added hopefully.

"You've got to be kidding," Lindsay replied. "I have two sick kids, a pet rabbit and a pair of goldfish. I'd say we're full up at present."

"Just thought I'd ask," I said. I'm sure Lindsay was still shaking her head in puzzlement when we hung up.

Having lost interest in *Singin' in the Rain,* I opened a can of Cheerwine and wandered out on the porch overlooking the beach to drink it. The day was sunny and clear, a perfect day to be outdoors, and after I'd finished my drink, I decided I didn't want to stay inside. A check of the bikes under the house proved fruitless; their tires were long flat, and the air pump that used to hang from a hook in the storage area wasn't there anymore. Needing some way to burn off my nervous energy, I decided to go for a beach walk, this time in the opposite direction from the one we had taken last night.

I glanced around, halfway hoping the dog was still lying under the oleanders, but she must have moved, because I saw no sign of her. Out in the ocean, a freighter plied its way out to sea, and several wet-suited boys on surfboards rode the swells, awaiting the perfect wave. I'd tried surfing a few times when I visited California with a boyfriend wannabe and had decided after a too-close call with a shark that it wasn't the sport for me. I'd ditched the wannabe, too, since we hadn't had much in common anyway.

Usually when we were on the island, Martine and I competed to find the best sand dollars, and out of habit I scanned the sand ahead as I walked. Alive, a sand dollar is a flat sea animal with a feltlike coating of brownish spines, in many ways similar to a sea urchin. The dead ones we found on the beach are brittle disks imprinted with a five-petaled pattern of tiny holes, bleached white by the sun and about three inches in diameter. Martine was good at spotting them and had, in fact, found several perfect ones, which had always eluded me. I missed Martine, I realized suddenly. Like any sister, she could be a pain in the rear sometimes, but she was witty and she was fun.

As I approached a scattered campfire, its users long gone, I spotted the only sand dollar on my walk so far. I leaned down to pick it up, hoping that this time, finally, I had found the perfect one, but one side of it was broken cleanly off. Still, it was pretty, a delicate souvenir of my walk, and for safekeeping, I wrapped it in a tissue I found in my pocket.

Back at the cottage, I was arranging my new find with the others in the basket on the mantel when Rick sailed in the front door, trailing the tantalizing aroma of fried chicken.

"You're going to have to put up a mailbox," I told him without looking around.

"I don't want any mail." He continued into the kitchen and I followed.

"Well, you're getting it, because otherwise the mailman can't deliver. Remember Stanley? Queen's nephew?"

"Tall beanpole of a guy? Used to drive a pickup truck?"

"That's the one. He's your mailman."

"Stanley was older than us by about five years, and I was always so impressed that he could coax bait fish into his net," Rick said.

"You'll get to reacquaint yourself with him in person once you get that mailbox up."

"Why didn't he give my mail to you?"

"He's supposed to put it in the box," I told him. "Postal regulations."

"My final divorce papers are probably what he plans to deliver," Rick said.

"Oh. He didn't mention that." I wished Rick hadn't told me.

A long moment passed. "I'm working around to the opinion that I might as well start accepting that the marriage is finished," he said, speaking slowly. "Has been finished, I should say. Well. Let's have lunch." The discussion was clearly over.

Rick began taking things out of grocery bags and stowing some of the things in the refrigerator. "You acquired more than fried chicken," I observed as my gaze swept across the array off food on the counter. He'd bought things he knows I like: Evian water, smoked oysters to eat with saltines, and Bel Paese cheese, which I often melt on steamed asparagus. I was touched that Rick had chosen things to please me, and I thanked him as we put the items away.

"Hey, I've got to keep the help happy," Rick said.

"Is that what I am? The help?"

"You do wield a mean dust mop. Here's a plate, so grab some chicken out of the bucket. And was that a pitcher of iced tea I spotted in the fridge?"

"I made it earlier. Shall I pour you a glass?"

"Sure," Rick said.

After I'd poured two glasses of tea and handed him one, Rick gulped a few swallows and sat down at the table across from me.

Encouraged by the improvement in Rick's state of mind,

I found myself apprising him of recent developments with my job and how it was more stressful than I liked. Even though I didn't care to get into my difficulties with Byron, mentioning my job brought out Rick's feelings about his own work, and he said he didn't miss the department or working in Homicide as much as he'd expected he would. That was heartening, indicating to me that he was adjusting to this enforced leave of absence. In my opinion, it boded well for his future.

Suddenly, elements in our relationship had somehow shifted back toward the old harmony and understanding we'd once shared. The pleasure of it filled my heart with gladness. I wanted to say fiercely, *Let's grab this moment in time and hang on to it, never let it go. We're still the same people we were. It's everything else that keeps changing. But the core is still honest and true. Like us.* If Rick was aware of these thoughts spinning through my mind, if his were similar, he showed no sign.

We never followed niceties of etiquette at Sweetwater Cottage, though Lilah Rose and Queen had done their best to encourage us otherwise, and Rick tossed a chicken bone into the wastebasket, placed at the ready beside the table. The thump caused a stir on the other side of the screen door, where the dog had parked herself. When she spotted me looking in her direction, she whomped her tail up and down a few times.

Rick, just noticing her, asked mildly, "Whose dog is that?"

"Nobody's. She arrived this morning along with your mail." I didn't let on how pleased I was that she was back.

"The USPS delivers dogs now? Since when?"

"Of course they don't," I told him. "Stanley says she's been following him around on the route."

"So why doesn't he shoo her away?"

"She likes it here," I informed him. "She wants a home."

"She'd best ingratiate herself with someone else," Rick said. He stood and started wrapping the remains of our lunch in plastic wrap. "Let's go scare up a new mailbox—and I'm warning you right now that I'm not buying any of those tacky molded-plastic things shaped like pelicans or fish that the newcomers to the island are putting up. A plain one will do fine."

"That's okay with me." A thought occurred, and I decided to give voice to it. "And, Rick, somewhere along the way, how about if we run your car through the nearest car wash." This was more diplomatic than stating flat out that the car was a mess.

"You're loads of fun, Trista," Rick said with deliberate irony. "You really are."

I shrugged as eloquently as I could manage while snapping lids on disposable cartons. "I try."

"I don't mind having you around. You've got a nice set of—"

"That's enough, Rick," I warned.

"Acrylic fingernails."

"Very funny," I said, eyeing him from behind the refrigerator door. "As if you ever noticed them."

Rick stood watching the dog. "The mutt is probably hungry," he observed.

"Stanley said she probably survives by scavenging for food on the beach." I was halfway hoping that Rick would show some interest, but he turned his back on that pleading gaze. It didn't help that the dog chose that moment to scratch vigorously at a flea bite.

Rick disappeared into his room, and I unfolded the bit of chicken that I'd saved in my paper napkin. "Sweet doggie," I murmured to the animal as I quietly eased the door open. "I told you to go away."

Thump, thump, thump went her tail, and she scarfed down the chicken in one bite.

No time to toss her a few more morsels. Rick, stuffing his wallet into the back pocket of his shorts, emerged from the bedroom, and I wiped the guilty expression from my face.

"Are you finished with your tea?" I asked him as a way of distracting him from the dog, who was conspicuously licking her chops on the other side of the door. "If so, I'll put that glass in the dishwasher."

He drained the glass and handed it to me, but it was slippery with condensation, and I didn't react in time to catch it as it slid through my fingers. The glass broke as it hit the floor, spraying glittering shards in all directions.

"Oh!" I exclaimed. I felt so clumsy. At least the noise caused the dog to disappear, though I suspected she'd lapsed into lurk mode under the shrubbery again.

"It's all right," Rick said. "It was only an old jelly glass, though it *was* the one with Tweety and Sylvester. My favorite." Rick reached into the closet for a broom as I bent to pick up the larger pieces.

"I'm sorry, Rick. I—"

He grinned at me. "Don't worry. I still have the one with the Smurf on it. Careful—don't cut yourself."

I detected genuine concern in his voice, and something else, too—an absorbed fascination in my bosom. I realized too late that our relative positions provided him with a wide-angle view down the front of my blouse. There wasn't anything salacious about the way he was looking at me, but my predominant emotion was…confusion. To me, Rick was still Martine's husband and therefore unavailable.

They're divorced, I told myself. *The marriage no longer exists. He's free, as free as he was before he married her.* And I—I had never lost my heart to anyone after Graham, though I certainly hadn't lived like a nun. Why would I? I had my pick of prominent bachelors in Columbia, some of them quite attentive. The trouble was that I'd avoided allowing sexual feelings to surface with Rick for so long that this didn't feel natural or right. Yet now there was no reason for avoidance, no sense in denying what was real and honest and true.

"I'll get the vacuum cleaner," I said, my voice sounding as squeaky as if I'd been gulping helium. The vacuum was in the hall closet, and I took my time getting it out while I struggled to understand why I was turning into a gibbering Daisy Duck around Rick.

I'd planned to come here and help him find his way back to normal. But ever since I'd walked in the front door, I'd been forced to confront the fact that I no longer knew what normal was. And even if I managed, by some quirk of luck, to help Rick, what about me? I wasn't doing so well myself.

I noticed a faded color snapshot lying on the floor, which probably had fallen out of one of the photo albums that Lilah Rose filled so diligently. It was of me and Rick, and we were riding a bicycle built for two that we'd borrowed from one of the families down the street. We were about fifteen, and our expressions were joyous and carefree, frozen for all time.

Back in the kitchen, with Rick elsewhere, I cleaned up the rest of the broken glass, thinking that perhaps our relationship was as shattered as the painted images of Tweety and Sylvester on the glass. But as Rick had said, he still had the glass with the Smurf. The same kind, only different.

Maybe that's the way it was with us, too. The same, only different.

Chapter 12: Rick

2004

One summer at the cottage, probably when he was thirteen, Rick had been at odds with the twins for a few days, and, exasperated when no one would talk to anyone else, Lilah Rose had resorted to whisking Trista and Martine off on a shopping expedition to King Street in town. On his own for a whole day, Rick had been at loose ends, and Queen's nephew Stanley had stopped by the cottage to deliver fresh fish after surf-casting on the beach. He found Rick disconsolately picking sand spurs out of his socks and wishing he'd chosen guys for friends instead of two extremely unreliable teenage girls whose emotions blew back and forth with the unpredictability of the wind.

"Hey, Mr. Lonely Man, why don't you help mend some

nets," Stanley had suggested playfully, and Rick, bowled over by the offer of man-to-man companionship after the difficulties of surviving in a household of women, accepted the offer gratefully. With Queen's permission, Stanley carted Rick away in his chugging, old and shiny blue pickup to the white frame house off Center Street where Stanley and some of his brothers and sisters lived with Queen.

Rick had visited the house briefly once before, the time his mother had dropped off a quart of chicken-and-rice soup when Queen was sick. He'd played hide and seek with a few of her young male kinfolk that day, darting in and out of the bushes planted around the house. On the day that Stanley rescued him, those same bushes in the front yard were draped with circular fishnets, and Rick spent an enjoyable afternoon learning to mend them as he and Stanley mourned the vicissitudes of women and devoured a whole sweet-potato pie. Queen had been real unhappy about that part of it, since she'd planned to serve the pie for dinner that night.

This was what was on Rick's mind right after breakfast on the day in the middle of the week when Stanley delivered a bundle of mail, including a letter from Roger Barrineau's former law firm and an envelope from his own divorce lawyer. He stuffed the mail deep into the back pocket of his jeans and shook Stanley's hand.

"Sure is good to see you, Rick," Stanley said. "Put some life back in this old house again, won't you?"

"I'm not expecting to stay," Rick hedged. "This is a timeout from real life so I can contemplate my options. I've got some serious decisions to make, and this is as good a place as any to think it all over."

Stanley blinked off into the distance. "That's always a

good idea," he said, putting the accent on the *i* of *idea*. "At a time like that, you can't just go wheeling off in some direction you don't know anything about."

"Exactly," Rick agreed. He was unbelievably happy to be reacquainted with Stanley. "Say, Stanley, you want to come by once in a while? Drink a beer?"

"What? You on the outs with everybody again?" Stanley studied his face.

"Not everybody," Rick said, deciding not to go into detail.

"I wouldn't mind stopping by now and then when I'm not on duty," Stanley allowed.

"Great," Rick said, grinning. "What have you been up to all this time?"

"Working for the post office, most of it. I married Luella Baker, one of the girls I used to bring over here sometimes to fish."

"Tall girl," Rick said. "Crazy about you." Luella liked to visit with Queen sometimes when she was working in the kitchen, Stanley being their foremost topic of conversation.

"Luella and me, we've got children. A boy and a girl."

"You could bring Luella and the kids, too," Rick suggested. "They could play on the beach while we kick back on the porch."

Stanley pushed his hat back off his forehead. "Sounds like you Mr. Lonely Man again," he said.

"Well," Rick said, paused in sudden realization of something that had escaped him until that very minute. He wasn't lonely now that Trista was here, but he wasn't going to mention that to Stanley. "Anyway," he continued, "this weekend is Easter, and you've got time off. Why don't you join us on Saturday. How old are the kids?"

"Boy's ten, girl's eleven."

"We've got Frisbees tucked away under the house if they'd like that."

"They might. My wife would enjoy the beach. She works at the social-security office and doesn't get to play much."

"Trista and I will put a picnic together," Rick said on impulse. "We'll do it up right."

Stanley hesitated only a moment. "Okay, you talked me into it. I'll have Lu call you, but I'd better get going now. Got lots of mail to deliver today." He turned away before angling his thumb toward the oleander bushes. "If you're craving company, seems like you'd invite that poor dog in. She's been hanging around your place for days."

The dog was sprawled in the shade. "I don't want a pet," Rick said with what he hoped was sufficient forcefulness.

"Looks like you got one anyway," Stanley observed.

"Yeah, well," Rick replied with no enthusiasm whatsoever.

"Be back on Saturday," Stanley told him as he rounded the curve in the driveway.

After quickly perusing his final decree of marital dissolution and wondering why he didn't feel more upset about it, Rick slit open the envelope from the law firm where Trista and Martine's father had been a partner. He unfolded a short letter and scanned it. It was signed by J. Alston Dubose, the member of the firm who had been closest to Roger Barrineau.

Dear Rick,
I recall that Roger always spoke highly of you and was pleased that you'd be joining our firm. I was sorry to learn after his death that you had chosen another path.
After I spoke with Trista the other day, I realized that you could be considering a change in career. If you're ever inter-

ested in pursuing a legal career, our firm is open to you. We have recently taken steps to enlarge our practice in immigration and naturalization law, and your expertise in Spanish would be most useful.

It would be great to hear from you.
With best wishes,
J. Alston Dubose

Trista had been talking to Alston about him? She'd never mentioned it.

From beneath the oleanders, the dog regarded him warily as he marched up the back steps and into the house.

"Trista?" he called. "I want to talk with you."

Trista, who was standing on a stool and dusting the ceiling fans with a tool resembling a cheerleader's pompom on a long stick, frowned down at him as he burst into the room. "You've decided to keep the dog?" she asked hopefully.

"It's not about that."

"You're going to paint the wicker chairs today."

"Maybe." He brandished the letter. "I received this from Alston Dubose. What have you been telling him about me?"

Trista carefully descended from the stool. He noted that she was wearing a pair of tight cropped pants and a snug T-shirt. "I didn't tell him much, Rick. Let me see that."

He relinquished the piece of paper. "Alston and his wife were at a party I attended a month or so ago," Trista said after reading it. "They asked about you and Martine."

"And you said?"

"Either not enough or too much, depending on one's point of view." She handed the letter back to him.

He followed her as she went to the door and shook the

duster outside. From under the swing, he heard a sneeze. That damn dog again.

"What the hell does that mean?" he asked, refusing to be distracted.

"I told Alston you were on leave from the department. I mentioned to Eloise that you and Martine had separated."

He blinked at her. "Why'd you do that?"

"Alston asked me about you, and since he and Dad had often discussed your joining the firm, I decided to bring him up-to-date. Did I do something wrong?" Her glance challenged him as she walked past.

"Informing Eloise of our marital problems doesn't exactly strike me as right."

"Martine had already filed for divorce, Rick. It was a matter of public record." She registered the forbidding expression on his face and sighed. "Why are we talking about this? I'm sorry if I did something I shouldn't have."

He ran a hand across the back of his neck, thinking that he really should get a haircut. "Let's drop it," he said curtly, immediately regretting his tone of voice.

Trista shook her head as if to clear it. "Rick, you and I aren't on the same wavelength lately. Which is why I might as well go upstairs and get ready to lie out on the beach and start on my tan."

He followed after her when she headed toward the staircase to the Lighthouse. "Tris—" He reached for her arm.

She wheeled around, the sides of her neck flushing. "Just when we're getting along again, you trigger over something."

"Noising my private business all over the place is worth getting steamed about," he said indignantly.

"I thought we were going to drop it." Her eyes flashed blue fire.

This deflated him somewhat. "We should," he said, removing his hand from her arm. This wasn't worth fighting about.

Trista sighed. "Rick, have you considered that you're in denial about some important things?" she asked gently. When he didn't reply, she left him alone and pondering the truth.

Rick hated psychobabble but was well aware that it existed for a reason, which was that it was necessary to understanding modern life. These days, if you weren't in therapy, most likely you were acting as your own psychologist. He recognized that some people were better at this than others, and he'd never been much for analyzing himself. But was his lack of feeling when he read his divorce decree a few minutes ago a sign of denial? Or was the divorce simply not as upsetting to him as it had been before?

He had too many questions and not enough answers, so he went into the storage room and began to shake the can of green spray paint so he could get busy refurbishing the wicker chairs. He'd rather be on the beach with Trista, but he agreed that he had a lot to do to spruce things up around the cottage. And he felt better if he kept busy, anyway.

As Rick sprayed the chairs, he forced himself to consider his future. Alston Dubose's job offer was totally unexpected, and working at Barrineau, Dubose and Linder was a possibility that he'd dismissed years ago after Roger's murder. He'd been so angry, so incensed that one of the very people that Roger had tried to help had killed him, that he'd decided to become a policeman over Martine's objections. After the funeral, he had waited until he and Martine were back at their apartment in Durham before he initiated the conversation about his intended switch of career path, and she had freaked out.

"You can't do this, Rick! What about the firm, what about moving back to Columbia? I've put up with this dinky apartment and never having enough money and you with your nose in a textbook all day long only because we'd have a good life once you got your law degree. And now you want to become a *policeman?*"

"Martine, listen to me," he began, but subsided under the onslaught of tears and pleading and impossible demands. If he didn't want to join her father's law firm, how about one in Charlotte? It was a big city, lots going on there. Martine could join the Junior League and the museum guild. They'd enjoy a social life befitting a young, up-and-coming lawyer and his wife. They'd buy a big house on the desirable south side of the city, and he could start a career in politics just as they'd planned.

"Just as *you'd* planned," Rick said resentfully, only to be met by Martine's stony silence.

For the first time in their marriage, Rick walked out of the house. He'd stayed away only for the rest of the afternoon, but when he came back, Martine was subdued and quiet. She hadn't spoken to him for a week, and by that time he'd already signed on with the Miami Police Department. He'd actually been surprised when Martine agreed to go with him.

He'd heard Martine complaining to Trista shortly before the move that she didn't want to live in Florida and that Rick was imposing this awful hardship on her, but somehow Trista had communicated to Martine that this was an opportunity to experience new things, and an adventure for both of them. Good old Trista, he'd thought at the time, always making the best of things, putting a good face on it, cheering him on.

And she was still doing it.

When he had finished painting the chairs and drinking a tall glass of iced tea, he went to the back door and picked out the dog in the shade of the oleanders. She wagged her tail when she saw him. Her ear had a cut on it and it was oozing blood. Flies buzzed around, he could hear them from where he stood.

"Go away," he said to the dog. "You don't belong here."

She gazed at him, her eyes round and intelligent.

"Scram," Rick said halfheartedly. She merely flipped her tail up and down a few times, rearranging the dust into feathery patterns.

Having given up on the dog, Rick was bending now and assessing the contents of the refrigerator when Trista walked into the room. She had showered and changed clothes, and her hair was still damp.

"I won't be here for lunch," she said too airily for his taste.

He slammed the refrigerator door and stared at her. This just wasn't done; when they were at Sweetwater Cottage, no one picked up and went off on his or her own. Everyone did things together.

"And where might you be going?"

"Just—out," Trista replied. Her attention was distracted by the dog, who was standing outside at the bottom of the stairs. "What's wrong with her ear?" she asked.

"Maybe she got in a fight," Rick said, still bewildered that Trista would go anywhere without him. Could she have a date? Who did she know here, anyway? The questions surfaced, leaving him feeling indignant, though he couldn't have explained why.

"We'd better check it," Trista said. She stepped out and bent beside the dog, who gratefully nuzzled her hand as

Trista petted her. "Would you please hand me a clean rag out of the box in the kitchen? And put some water on it from the sink."

When Rick came back inside, Trista took the damp rag from him and began to swab the sore. The dog was patient, submitting without a whimper. Rick was reminded of the efficient manner in which Trista had ministered to him on the night of the prom so long ago, and the memory unsettled him.

"I hope this won't get infected. Rick, Hal may have left some antibiotic cream in the guest-room bath after his dog tangled with that rottweiler on the beach a couple of years ago. How about taking a look."

Deciding that it would be better not to comment about not having wanted the dog around in the first place, Rick trudged back into the house and soon emerged with the antibiotic. Trista squeezed some onto the wound, but as soon as she moved away, the dog pawed at her ear.

"Uh-oh," Trista said, moving to stop her. "We can't have that. Come on, dog. Let's go up on the porch and I'll get you some of that barbecue we ate yesterday."

He followed Trista inside. "You're going to feed her," he said accusingly.

Trista pivoted to face him. "If I don't, she'll rub the medicine off that cut before it has a chance to do any good." She opened the refrigerator.

"Maybe we should relocate that dog to the pound."

"You're aware of what happens to dogs in shelters if no one adopts them," Trista reminded him darkly.

"Why don't you take her back to Columbia with you? Give her a real home?"

"That wouldn't be fair. She wouldn't get enough exercise living in my condo, and I'm not there much." She spoke regretfully and as if she wished things were otherwise.

As soon as Trista carried the dish of barbecue outside, the dog lost interest in pawing at her ear and immediately began to gulp great mouthfuls of pork. "There," Trista said with satisfaction. "This is our good deed for the day."

"Hmmph," Rick said, but he couldn't help smiling at the dog's wagging tail.

They stood watching, their differences forgotten. "Hey," Rick said on a sudden inspiration. "Why don't we ride the bikes down to the docks by the Purple Pelican. Unless you have a hot lunch date, that is." He couldn't resist adding that last part.

"Of course I don't," she said, seemingly amused. She slanted a look in his direction. "I was just going out because you were being disagreeable."

Well, what did she expect when she was making noises about doing something without him? "Wouldn't a bike ride be more fun? I found the tire pump this morning and fixed the tires so they'll hold air. Maybe."

"Okay, you've talked me into it," Trista said. "We could pick up lunch at Jeter's and eat it at the public docks." The docks included a marina, prized because of its location at the mouth of Tappany Creek. Boats heading north on their way home from wintering farther south often put in for a day or two, and it was fun to read their names and home ports off the sterns.

Under the house, their faces speckled with squares of sunlight admitted by the latticework, they brushed spiderwebs from the bikes' wheels and handlebars and then set off. At Jeter's, they bought shrimp-salad sandwiches, and when

Jolly learned what they were going to do, he offered them his old rowboat.

"It's tied up on the easternmost dock. You might as well use her. No good if she just sits there accumulating barnacles," Jolly said.

It was only ten minutes, easy pedaling to the docks. This was a route they knew well: right on Center Street, over the creek bridge and right again. They leaned the bikes against a tumbledown fence and strolled along the dock, past empty berths where fishing vessels tied up in the evenings. The visiting boats displayed the names of faraway ports: Bar Harbor, Norfolk, Quebec. A couple was disembarking from their Boston Whaler with a tub of freshly caught fish, and Rick and Trista stopped to help; afterward, they chatted with a gnarled old man who was mending crab traps.

The weather was sunny, the breeze minimal, and once in the rowboat, which Rick insisted he could manage by himself, Trista occupied the bow and leaned her head back so the sun's rays would reach her neck.

"A suntan looks good on camera," she explained to Rick, who only grinned and said she looked good on camera with or without.

Rick was an expert oarsman, slicing the oars cleanly into the water. The boat skimmed easily toward a neighboring island, the one where the marsh ponies lived.

"Are you sure you don't want me to help you row?" Trista wanted to know after a while, but Rick shook his head.

"Physical activity helps me think," he told her.

"About what?" she asked with interest. She seemed unaware of the pretty picture she made, and he swallowed, forcing himself to concentrate on rowing.

"Wouldn't you say I have a lot to decide?" he asked. "Not

only on a personal level, but professionally, as well? I have little enthusiasm for returning to Homicide," he admitted, finding it hard to say the words. He'd been so committed to his work for so long that it pained him to have landed at a juncture where he actually was considering a change.

She shaded her eyes with her hand. "So Alston's offer is welcome, then?"

"It's appealing." Encouraged by Trista's willingness to listen, he admitted his many misgivings about going back to work at the department.

"If you accept Alston's job offer, you'd be moving to Columbia. Is that what you want?"

He rested on his oars. "I believe it is," he said softly.

After a long moment, Trista diverted her gaze toward the nearest spit of land, which extended from the ponies' island. As they watched, one of the ponies appeared on the beach. "Look," she breathed, pointing.

The pony was a solid swaybacked specimen, its legs short, its mane tangled. It lifted its head, sniffed the salty air. For a split second, it made eye contact with him and then flicked its mane before wheeling and trotting back into the underbrush.

They kept watching for more ponies to appear as he headed the boat toward the wild and desolate lee side of the island, where Rick tossed out the anchor and shipped the oars. As he settled in the bottom of the boat with his back against the seat, Trista passed him a sandwich. She slid down so that she was sitting in the bottom of the boat, too, and they rocked gently on the waves as they ate. They washed down their food with the cans of cold Cheerwine that they'd bought from the vending machine at the docks and munched on the gingersnaps that Jolly had thrown in for free.

As they relaxed, inhaling the familiar scents of marsh and

creek and ocean, Rick told Trista about inviting Stanley and his family over on Saturday.

"I remember Luella," she said, looking pleased. "She always arranged time to talk with Martine and me when she visited Queen, even if it was only a few minutes. That made us feel so special, since she was older and engaged to be married."

"She's going to call you to ask what she can bring," Rick said. "Find out if she knows how to make Queen's waffles."

Trista only laughed. "Doubtful. It was a secret recipe."

They stayed moored in the lee side of the pony island for a long time, talking if they felt like it but often remaining silent. It was good to be comfortable with each other, requiring no words in order to communicate. When it was time to go, it was as if they both arrived at that conclusion at the same time, and Rick moved to resume the oars while Trista stowed the picnic leavings under the seat in the bow.

"If only we'd brought fishing poles, we'd catch our dinner," Rick said regretfully as he headed the boat toward the docks and began rowing.

"Who would clean it?" Trista, sitting tall in the bow, turned and widened her eyes at him. She was notoriously squeamish about gutting fish.

"I'd clean if you'd cook."

"I'd cook if you'd clean up," she said.

"Sounds like we've come full circle," Rick replied with a grin.

At the dock, shrimp boats nosed into their slips and began to unload their bounty, the fishermen shouting to one another as they secured their craft. After tying Jolly's boat, Rick fielded the idea of ducking into the Purple Pelican to scope out the menu.

"Remember their crab casserole?" Trista said. "And how we never could duplicate it at the cottage with the crabs we caught off the dock?"

"And their fried oysters? They're still the best."

When they checked the daily special on the chalkboard beside the door, they exchanged a glance of pure glee and immediately asked to be seated at one of the tables.

"Two plates of fried oysters, please," Rick told the waitress before she had a chance to take their orders, and she appeared with the plates almost immediately, sliding them expertly across the blue-checked plastic tablecloth. The oysters were hot and succulent, and the accompanying hush puppies light and fried just right.

"These oysters are so good," Trista said, digging in. "Have you ever considered that they taste like fried ocean?"

Rick laughed. "Yes," he said. "I do." *Fried ocean,* he thought. Who else but Trista would come up with something like that?

They chattered about her pending visit to her mother, and about Lindsay and Peter, whose happiness they both envied. But they didn't talk about Martine. Never about Martine. And that was okay.

After dinner, feeling mellow and satiated, they rode the bikes slowly home in the dusky light and stored them beneath the house. As they emerged from the latticed space, the cool breeze teased Trista's hair into tangles, and the clouds parted to reveal the ghost of a moon against the blue-gray sky. The sea was calm, whispering on the shore.

The dog met them on the back porch and wagged her tail in delight. Trista bent to pet her.

"Let's open a bottle of champagne," Rick said.

"Champagne?" Trista brightened.

"Why not? We bought it last year to toast Lindsay on her birthday, but for some reason we didn't drink it."

"We went into Charleston that night instead. Lindsay wanted to eat at Blossom." This was their favorite in-town restaurant.

Rick told Trista where to find the champagne behind the bar, and after she disappeared into the house, he paused to scratch the dog behind her ears, which he wouldn't have done if Trista had been watching. The dog was a pretty shade of tan, with a spot of white on her chest, and she seemed forlorn but grateful for this bit of attention that had felicitously come her way. In that moment, Rick felt a pang for all lost dogs, for all creatures who did not have a home.

"Rick?" Trista called through the screen door. "I can't find the glasses."

He continued on inside, poured the champagne and smiled when Trista declared that it tasted like fizzy sunshine. They adjourned to the porch, neither of them surprised when the dog trotted around the house and up the stairs to join them. She sat down politely beside Rick's chair and rested her head on her paws.

"Remember Bungie?" Rick asked, absently inspecting the cut on the dog's ear. "How we thought it would be funny to use her when we competed in our high-school talent contest? Too bad the principal wouldn't let us."

"Are you kidding? Mr. Helms got so wound up over not allowing any live animals on the school premises that he completely forgot to monitor the song we were going to pantomime." Trista laughed.

The song had been Concrete Blonde's "Joey," which was one of those tunes that gets into your head so that you can't stop hearing it in your mind for days. The lyrics were about a drunk, but the three of them had convinced Mr. Helms that the song was about a dog so they could include Bungie in their act. When they finally informed the principal that they were going to scrap the live dog in favor of Trista's dressing up in a furry suit, the principal was so relieved that he didn't pay any attention to the words of the song.

Rick had played air guitar, and Trista in her dog outfit and Martine, cast by default as the dog's owner, acted out the lyrics. They hadn't won first place—that honor had gone to the class treasurer, who also happened to be a pretty cool marimba player—but they'd had a lot of fun.

"Mom made the dog suit, and it was prickly and miserable," Trista said. "I itched for days afterward."

"You lost the coin toss," Rick reminded her. "Otherwise Martine would have been the itchy one."

"Hey, McCulloch, why couldn't I play air guitar? I have about as much talent at that as I have at wearing a dog suit."

"The suit fit you perfectly."

"Next time *I'm* playing the guitar."

"Next time, okay."

They smiled and slapped each other a high five, something they hadn't done in years.

It took a while to finish off the champagne, and in the interlude between their first glass and the last dregs, Trista extracted a solemn promise that Rick would complete a major project around the cottage every day with her help.

"Tomorrow, we wash the windows. The next day, we repair the broken steps."

"You know what we can do with the old rotting wood scraps from the steps? And any other rubbish that results from our labors? We'll build a big bonfire one of these nights the way we used to do."

"And dance around it, like we did one summer on the

longest day of the year," Trista said, smiling at the memory. They'd invited kids from up and down the beach, held an informal contest for the best sand sculpture and roasted hot dogs and marshmallows long into the night.

They sat in quiet companionship, more comfortable with each other than they could have imagined even twenty-four hours ago, but when the moon disappeared behind a growing bank of clouds, Trista stood and stretched.

"Guess I'll turn in," she said. Her face was concealed by darkness.

Rick wanted to reach toward her, to touch her arm. To continue being with her. "Good night," he said, and was surprised when she leaned toward him for a hug. Acting instinctively, he wrapped his arms around her and pulled her close.

"Sweet dreams, Rick," she said, moving away almost immediately, and then she went through the French doors into the house and was gone.

Rick stared out at the dark ocean. He wondered what things might have been like if he hadn't married Martine, if he had followed his heart before Trista ever became engaged to Graham. There'd been times when he could have changed the course of his life and had chosen or neglected to do it, and then, suddenly, it had been too late. He felt a sense of melancholy, of regret, but it was overlaid with a new understanding of himself. That probably wasn't a bad thing, considering that people tend to learn from their mistakes.

Finally, Rick got up to go into the house. At the door, the blamed dog greeted him like a long-lost buddy.

"Hey," he said, nudging the dog away with his foot. "You're not coming in the house."

The dog gazed up at him beseechingly.

"All right," Rick said heavily. "You win. But only for tonight, you hear?"

Inside, the dog followed after him, her toenails clicking loudly on the living-room floor. She stood by while he found an old quilt in the laundry room and tossed it into a corner of the kitchen. "You can sleep on that," he said. The dog blinked at him uncertainly before circling around a couple of times and settling down with her head between her paws.

Afterward, Rick lay awake in his room, listening for the dog, imagining he could hear her breathing as he fell asleep. When he woke up later, it was still dark. He felt a warm weight pressing against his thigh, a sensation he had not experienced since he and Martine had split. The door to his room stood open, admitting a sliver of light from the hall. The door, no doubt, had been nudged open by the pup, who was now sleeping beside him.

He thought about making her go back to the kitchen, but it seemed like too much trouble to force the issue. Soon he fell asleep again, grateful for the company.

Chapter 13: Trista

2001

Click: Rick is stowing my suitcase in my car in preparation for leaving Sweetwater Cottage. Martine is carrying out the small cooler that she filled with Cheerwine and leftover chicken wings for my drive back to Columbia. I took the picture, but Rick didn't respond when I asked him to say cheese.

In the summer of 2001, Rick, Martine and I met at Sweetwater Cottage for our usual couple of weeks in the summer. Lindsay and Peter joined us. I didn't invite a boyfriend to the cottage as I sometimes did. Instead, I'd brought a couple of books and eagerly anticipated reading away the slow, lazy afternoons.

I'm not sure when I detected the tension between Martine and Rick, or perhaps it was the lack of warmth between them that first impressed me. I did notice that when Lindsay was passing around new studio portraits of one-year-old Adam shortly after we arrived, Martine abruptly left her cozy spot on the couch beside Rick and disappeared into the kitchen for a long time. Meanwhile, the rest of us admired picture after picture, exclaiming over how much Adam had grown and how much he resembled his father. He was an adorable baby, big brown eyes and a head of dark curly hair like his dad's.

When Martine returned, she seemed stiff, and though she said all the right things about the Tolsons' photos, I noticed that she was jittery and kept jumping up to refill our glasses. At last, I said, "Gosh, Martine, we're supposed to be on vacation. Chill out for a change. We can get our own drinks."

After that, Martine silently repaired to the chair in the corner, where she gazed out at the ocean. By then Peter had usurped her place beside Rick on the couch, and the two men debated at great length the Gamecocks' chances to trounce their perennial rival, Clemson, next football season.

Still, everything appeared normal in the days after we all arrived. We danced the shag at the Purple Pelican, cooked shrimp pilau, shrimp gumbo and shrimp scampi. Together we shopped at the Old City Market in Charleston and jogged along the shore at dawn. At night, when we were exhausted from so much relaxation, slow ceiling fans stirred up a breeze to cool our sunburned skin.

Usually, summer weather on the island remains beastly hot. Gnats swarm out of swamp and woods, flitting their way into eyes and mouths and noses so that everyone expends too much energy brushing them away in what is jokingly called the South Carolina salute. Heat undulates in waves from the paved roads, and the air grows so heavy that it hardly seems worth the effort to breathe. But that year an unseasonable cool front chose to slide across the Low Country in June and provided a welcome respite from the heat.

On the day the front swept through, we had all spread blankets on the beach and were swimming, sunning and beachcombing, when suddenly the temperature dropped. Lindsay, Peter and Martine opted to head for the house and trudged off through the sand, laughing and childishly swatting one another with damp towels. They left the big beach blanket for Rick and me.

I'd brought a terry cover-up, and once I'd bundled up in it, I was impervious to the cold. I returned to my book, determined to finish the chapter I'd been reading earlier. For a while, Rick sauntered along the edge of the water, bending to inspect shells from time to time and whistling between his teeth.

In the distance, a family of four packed up sand buckets and shovels; the parents were wrapping the children in towels for the walk to their car. As they hurried off, the father carrying the youngest piggyback, Rick threw himself on the blanket beside me. I kept reading.

"Cute kids," Rick said, observing the family as they walked past. He lay next to me supported on one elbow, the sun from the west casting his features in light. Soon we'd have to go inside; the wind was beginning to bluster, making it difficult for me to keep the pages of my book from flapping.

Rick seemed so wistful that I set my book aside and regarded him. "You like kids, don't you?" I said. He'd always shown a real affinity for babies, talking to them, asking pertinent questions of their mothers. Once I'd watched him comforting a Down's syndrome child who had fallen and skinned his knee at a park. No one could have spoken more tenderly to the boy, distracting him as the mother tended the scrape.

"I hope Martine and I will have a couple of children one of these days."

"I can't wait to be Aunt Trista," I said. Since I didn't even have a boyfriend at the time, I considered aunthood my best hope of having a baby to love, at least in the near future.

Rick picked at a bit of sand on the blanket. "Tris, has—has Martine ever mentioned wanting a child?"

I took a few moments to answer that one. "No," I said. It was then that I realized that my sister had never spoken of starting a family. Not even once since she married Rick, as far as I could recall.

Rick rolled over on his stomach. "After we moved to Miami, I hinted that we shouldn't put it off too long, but Martine kept avoiding a discussion. I don't think she sees kids in our future, Trista." He sounded sad and disappointed.

"I wasn't aware of that," I said, surprised. Rick would be a great father, and it was hard to believe that Martine wouldn't be overjoyed to bear his children. Wasn't that what people were supposed to do? Find the perfect mate, get married, have babies?

"I don't know how to get across to her that it means a lot to me," Rick said in a low tone. He was clearly embarrassed about discussing this topic, but I well recalled how we'd often been reluctant to say things that Martine needed to hear. It occurred to me that we'd shorted ourselves at times, and I was impatient. It was long past time for Martine to grow up.

"Tell her," I said. "Plain tell her flat out."

"I have," Rick replied quietly.

I glanced at him, taken aback by the pain in his expression. I remained silent, concerned for Rick, worried for my sister. If Martine had made up her mind not to have children, she wouldn't have them. There was no budging her when she'd dug in hard on an opposing position.

"Do you want me to talk to her?" My own inner hourglass, unfortunately, was trickling fast, but I wasn't in a position to do anything about it. Martine, on the other hand, had Rick, who was ready, willing and able.

"Please don't say anything, Tris. She might resent my talking to you."

"You're probably right."

"Well," he said, sitting up but keeping his face turned away from me, "I shouldn't have brought this up. Having a child should be a private matter between husband and wife. I'm sorry to burden you, but I don't have anyone I can talk to about it, and it's eating at me."

"Oh, Rick," I said softly, and in a moment of crystal clarity, I knew that if I were his wife, I'd have ten kids. Twelve. Whatever he wanted.

He stood and attempted a smile. "Forget we had this conversation, okay?"

"Sure," I said, knowing that I never would. I was shaken by his revealing such an intimate detail of their marriage to me, one that Martine had never mentioned.

We stood and shook the sand from the blanket. Halfway back to the house, Martine came out on the porch and gave us a big wave. "Hurry, you two," she called. "We've opened a bottle of zinfandel, and Peter's dishing out the smoked-fish dip. We might even light a fire in the fireplace."

We waved back and smiled, increasing our pace. Before we got to the house, Rick said, "Remember, we never discussed it."

I didn't reply, but my heart was heavy as we rejoined the group. That afternoon was the first indication to me that Martine and Rick's marriage was in trouble, and it took me by surprise. Up until then, I'd considered their lives perfect.

In October of that year, several months after Rick and I had that conversation, he and Martine visited me in Columbia when Rick gave a talk at a local law-enforcement seminar. The weather was still warm and beautiful, the leaves of the trees beginning to take on tinges of bright yellow, ochre, russet and orange. Martine and I went for a walk together, catching up on each other's lives, and as we passed the recreation area in the development where I lived, some of my friends urged us to join them in a volleyball game, Martine on one team, me on another.

My team won, but in the process of spiking the ball, I popped a button off the waistband of my jeans.

"Oh, great," I said, fingering the loose bit of thread as we scuffed through the leaves on the way back to my building. "Another thing to mend."

Martine laughed. "It's just a button, Tris, for heaven's sake."

"I'm no good at sewing," I said. I'm left-handed and never got the hang of it.

Martine hooked her arm through mine. "Don't worry, sis," she said. "I'll do it for you." She liked to sew.

"That's too good an offer to pass up," I told her, and as soon as we got back to my apartment, I provided her with a needle and thread. I turned up Mozart on the stereo, and we settled down companionably on the living-room couch with a couple of pears and a slab of Havarti.

I peeled a pear, admiring the way Martine's needle

flashed in and out of the denim. "You sure are good at that," I told her.

She smiled. "I had to learn when Rick was in law school. Otherwise I wouldn't have had much of a wardrobe for work."

"Mom and Dad gave each of us a sewing machine for our birthdays the year you married Rick," I recalled. "I doubt that I've had mine out of the case more than once or twice, though I'd never admit it to Mom." Our mother had learned to sew when her family went through its financial crisis, and she deemed it a necessary skill, as important as being a good cook or knowing how to write a decent thank-you note.

"I've more or less given up being my own dressmaker," Martine said. "I like shopping the sales at Dadeland Mall on weekends much better than hunching over a sewing machine for hours on end."

"Mom made us the coolest clothes," I said, warming to the memory of all the matching outfits that magically seemed to appear in our closet. "What was your favorite of all the things she sewed for us?"

Martine thought about this for a moment. "Those red wool plaid skirts and matching ponchos in tenth grade. We felt like models when we wore them."

She was right. I'd almost forgotten about those.

"I'm glad we dressed alike as long as we did," I told her. "We got a lot of attention that way." This realization had come along with maturity, never mind my eagerness to make my own fashion statement when I went away to college.

"Maybe it's not good for kids to get that much attention," Martine said soberly. She reached for the scissors and snipped the thread, handing the jeans to me. "There you go. All set," she said.

I chewed and swallowed. "Did you really mean that, Martine? About the attention?"

She shrugged. "Sort of. When we went to different colleges, it took some adjusting to get used to being only Martine instead of Trista and Martine."

"We did okay."

"Twins are supposed to run in families. Poor Mom, what we put her through," Martine said with a roll of her eyes. "I'd much rather be a twin than have them. That's one reason I'm never having kids."

I froze. For reasons of discretion, this wasn't a topic that I wished to pursue; I didn't want to let on that Rick and I had talked about my sister's reluctance to start a family.

Martine propped her legs on the coffee table and leaned back against the downy couch cushions. "Don't look so shocked. My life is complicated enough the way it is."

I didn't, couldn't, understand what she meant, and I hastened to reassure her. "Of course you're going to have children," I said. "You and Rick would be wonderful parents."

She brushed this argument aside. "I like my job and can't imagine staying home with a couple of rug rats day in and day out." Her vehemence caught me off guard.

"How about a part-time job?" I suggested. "After the kids are in school, you could resume a full schedule."

"That wouldn't work for me. I'm pushed for time now, and with kids…" She let the sentence drift off before resuming. "It's just that my life is full. Rick and I take great vacations. I was able to pick up and come with him on this trip, for instance, without having to worry about babysitters. Rick and I never have to deal with problems like homework and earaches and the class bully. I don't want children, Tris. And most certainly not two at one time." She laughed uneasily.

I loved being a twin and was dismayed that Martine viewed twinhood as a less than desirable situation. "Oh, Martine, I'm sorry to hear that," I said, my heart heavy.

She seemed to pull herself together. "Well. Now you know, and—and—"

To my complete surprise, Martine's face crumpled and she buried it in her hands.

"Martine?" I said tentatively, touching her shoulder. I knew instinctively that whatever was going on here was way beyond our topic of discussion.

When she dropped her hands, her expression was one of raw pain. "I had an abortion, Trista. Rick doesn't have any idea."

I'm sure my mouth fell open at this revelation, and I couldn't bring myself to speak. I suppose I'd better explain something important: our parents had reared us to believe that all human life is precious from the start. I hasten to assure you that we respect other people's beliefs, and none of us has ever told others what to do, but for ourselves, in our family, abortion was not supposed to be an option, and I was beyond shocked.

"You probably think I'm awful," Martine said in a rush.

"Of course I don't," I said, though I was struggling to understand. How could Martine have done it? She was married. Rick wanted children. They could afford them. My mind couldn't make the leap across the chasm of wrong becoming right.

"Don't, Trista. There's condemnation in your eyes, and well, maybe I deserve it. One thing for sure, I'm so ashamed, I can hardly live with myself. I deserve that, too." I glimpsed a darkness in Martine's soul at that moment, a deadness. It frightened me, but in an instant it was gone and Martine was smoothing her hair behind her ears, adopting a matter-of-fact tone.

"I found out I was going to have a baby a few days before Rick was to leave to give evidence at a trial in Colorado, and we had a big argument about something else before he left. I wouldn't have felt comfortable talking to him about being pregnant while we were still barely speaking, so I decided to wait until he got home to bring up the subject. But while he was gone, I was so angry with him for some of the things he'd said that I asked my friend Jane to take me to the clinic downtown, and by the time Rick came home, it was all over. The baby was—gone."

"You mean you never told him you were pregnant?" I didn't care to hear any more of this terrible secret, but I couldn't very well get up and walk away. Martine needed to talk about it, and for her sake, I listened.

She shook her head, her face contorted with anguish. "Never," she said, her voice no more than a whisper. "He'd hate me if he found out." Martine reached her hand toward me, and it was trembling. "Don't tell him, please," she said, her voice hoarse. "I regret it now, but at the time I wanted to get back at him and that was the easiest way."

Now I was the unwilling repository of secrets from both Rick and Martine, secrets that I'd be better off not knowing. This put me in a difficult position, and at the moment, my main objective was to insert space between all of us.

"I won't mention it," I said crisply as we heard a key in the front door. I had given Rick an extra one in case he came back while we were out.

Martine stood and, after one agonized glance back at me, headed down the hall to my small study–cum–guest room that she shared with Rick. As I gathered up what was left of the fruit and cheese, Rick strolled in, ebullient about encountering Shaz, one of our high-school friends, in the corridor of the hotel where the seminar was being held.

"He's hospitality manager at the hotel, and I invited him to have dinner with us. Tris, I hope you don't mind."

"Of course not," I said smoothly, and during the discussion of deciding whether to cook in or go out for dinner, Martine returned, face washed and hair tidy. Rick was so hyped about seeing Shaz again that he didn't notice her puffy eyes or my grim seriousness.

That evening, Shaz brought his wife, whom we'd never met, and after dinner at a neighborhood restaurant, we all adjourned to a nearby lounge for drinks. A guy named Tim, who said he watched my newscast every night, sauntered over from the bar and invited me to dance. Though he didn't appeal to me, I provided my phone number when he asked for it, and we started dating soon afterward. Tim, and the resulting romance, kept me from thinking too much about the irony and sadness of Martine and Rick's situation.

Tim and I broke up about six months later. Until now, I haven't revealed Martine's confidence to anyone. But sometimes when I encounter a beautiful child, clearly loved and adored by its parents, I think wistfully of the baby who might have been.

The baby I would have welcomed if I'd been married to my sister's husband.

If you live far away from the people you love, the bad things that could happen to them always hover in the back of your mind. When Rick called and told me Martine had been in an accident, all sorts of possible mishaps crossed my mind: falling from a ladder while screwing in a lightbulb, diving too deeply into a swimming pool, singeing eyebrows when lighting a gas oven. I was not prepared for what really happened. Martine kidnapped? By a paroled convict? It was beyond imagining, especially after what happened to Dad. Two such incidents in one family seemed so unfair.

"I'll be there as soon as I can," I told Rick. After we hung up I talked to Mom, who wanted to book a reservation to Miami immediately, but I told her it wasn't necessary. After a few minutes, Aunt Cynthia took over the phone and confirmed that Mom was hardly in condition to travel. Her disintegrating spinal disks cause her great pain, and she seldom goes out.

Although I'd steeled myself, I was shocked at Martine's appearance when I arrived at the hospital. Her face was so swollen from bruises and scrapes that I couldn't tell she was my twin. And Rick—as expected, he was stalwart and strong, but he desperately needed rest. After I sent him home, I stood watch over Martine, conferring in hushed tones with the nurses who changed her IV, updating my mother on my sister's condition the next day.

Things were easy between Rick and me while I stayed at their house. He seemed distracted, certainly, but what husband wouldn't be upset, considering what had happened? He gave me the impression that he would have liked me to stay a bit longer, but my cues came from Martine. She didn't urge me to stay on while she recuperated, even though I let her know that I had vacation days due me. She seemed fully intent on regaining her physical health and eager to start rehab, so I made my reservation for a return flight to Columbia and notified my boss at WCIC that I'd be back soon.

On Saturday morning, I woke up and was anticipating a jog with Rick, when my cell phone rang.

"I have to talk to you," Martine said quickly before I even had a chance to ask how she was feeling.

"Is something wrong?"

"No, not from the accident, but can you get over here right away?"

"Well, of course," I said, wondering what was up.

"Hurry," she said. "And don't bring Rick with you."

This was certainly an odd request, but it crossed my mind that Martine might want to spare his feelings. She had not yet related the details of her abduction to me, and I certainly hadn't asked.

I showered and dressed as rapidly as I could. The door to the master bedroom was still closed when I left the house, and I assumed Rick was asleep.

When I arrived at the hospital, my sister was propped up in bed, sipping juice through a straw. In the harsh glare of the overhead fluorescents, and with all the bruises and scrapes on her face, she could have been a refugee from some brutal war, and goodness knows I've seen enough of them in news clips. But she smiled and gestured for me to sit down beside her, which I did, squeezing her hand in silent reassurance.

And then, in a cadence as measured as the beep of the heart monitor beside her bed, my sister informed me with grim determination that she was going to file for divorce from Rick.

Chapter 14: Rick

2004

"That dog needs a name," Trista said as Rick opened the door to let her out a few mornings after she appeared on the back porch.

"A home first, a name second," he retorted, watching the animal as she guzzled water from the pie plate. He had to admit that she wasn't so bad now that Trista had cleaned her up and brushed her. Her coat gleamed, and the white spot on her chest resembled a starched bib. He suspected that she might be part terrier, part boxer, part something else.

Trista angled a sly look in his direction. "She's certainly comfortable sleeping on your bed. You like her, Rick. Admit it."

Rick snorted. "I'll do no such thing."

"Why don't you want to name her?" she asked.

Trista was a persevering woman, and he had to give her credit for that, but he felt compelled to set her straight. "I don't want to be responsible for anything anymore. There's no permanence in life, so why commit to anything, even a dog? Why even name the animal?" He delivered this statement with considerable grumpiness, but Trista shrugged it off, changing the subject without warning.

"When are you going running with me, McCulloch?" she said. "We should get you moving a bit more before I go home."

"You've already made me put up a mailbox and trim the shrubbery. And I shaved yesterday." He passed a hand across his smooth chin, still unaccustomed to being beardless.

She studied him critically. "You look better clean-shaven," she said. "And I'm pleased that you got a haircut. But putting up a mailbox doesn't exactly qualify as exercise."

"I don't have any running shoes."

"We'll get some. I'll remind you."

"You're bossy," he said playfully.

"It's called leadership, McCulloch."

While he was still mulling this over, Trista jingled her car keys. "Luella said she's bringing a cake and chicken for our picnic tomorrow, but we're obliged to buy some fresh shrimp and ingredients for slaw. What do you say we go to Jeter's this morning?"

"Do I have a choice?"

She pretended to think this over. "We could go to Bi-Lo, instead," she said.

"Takes more gas."

"Takes more time," she replied.

"That's why I'm for Jeter's. Besides, I've a hankering for Gummi Bears."

They lowered the top of Trista's Miata, so that her hair whipped around her head in a golden halo as she drove. Rick liked the sensation of the wind in his face, the sun beating on his shoulders as Trista turned the car toward Center Street.

"Anyway," Trista said, continuing their previous conversation without missing a beat, "I'm glad we're not going to Bi-Lo. I'm still mad at them for getting rid of the cows."

Rick laughed, remembering. The supermarket used to feature huge statues of cows perched at the edge of the roof overlooking the parking lot. "Every time the three of us would pass by on the way to or from the island, one of us would let out a loud Moo-o-o-o," he recalled.

"And your mom threatened that if we didn't stop all that horrible racket *'right this minute, you hear,'* she'd send all of us to the slaughterhouse along with those darn cows."

"Which caused Martine to tell Mom that her idea was udderly disgusting," Rick said. He paused thoughtfully. "I wonder why Bi-Lo dispensed with those cows, anyway. One summer they just disappeared, and at first I thought they'd gone to the Mo-o-o-n." He kept a straight face, but Trista laughed.

"Why did we all spend Thanksgiving at the cottage that year?" she asked.

"I don't know—it was something our parents decided to do. Remember how we were so thrilled when the Bi-Lo cows showed up in the Christmas parade?"

Trista swerved to avoid a turtle plodding across the middle of the road, and it pulled its head and feet inside its shell as they passed. "Those cow statues didn't do justice to the Future Farmers of America float or even to the one sponsored by Wholsum Dairy," she said.

Rick chuckled. "They sure didn't. That's because the Bi-Lo cows were really steers, which I had enough discrimination to figure out by the time they turned up in the parade."

"You had to explain the difference to me, and why steers couldn't produce milk."

"I thought you already knew."

"I noticed that they didn't have the proper equipment, but I hadn't added the two things together," she said.

"Dumb."

"Yeah, and that's no bull."

Rick groaned at her pun and they both laughed, feeling silly. It felt good not to be so serious. To like what they were doing at that very moment, which was sharing fond memories of their past.

On the way back from the market, as they passed the sack of Gummi Bears back and forth, Trista suggested crabbing that afternoon, to which Rick readily agreed. But when they arrived at the cottage, clouds were gathering in the western sky. By the time they'd stashed the groceries, wind gusts had begun to howl fiercely around the corners of the house. The clouds seemed infused with a peculiar mossy shade of green, muting the sun and flattening a dulled landscape, and soon the rain came sweeping across the marsh.

As he and Trista hurried around closing windows, the dog whined at the door to be let in.

"She can stay out there," Rick said when Trista suggested otherwise.

"Rick—"

"A little rain won't hurt her," he said curtly, refusing to change his mind even when Trista clamped her lips and went outside to murmur to their unwelcome guest.

The hail began a few minutes after they ate lunch,

marble-size stones making a huge racket as they ricocheted off the roof and bounced on the deck. Thinking to distract Trista from the dog, Rick pointedly embarked on a fruitless search for the weather-warning radio that his father had bought one year. When at last he quit trying to find it, he noticed Trista digging around in the old trunk where they'd always kept a supply of jigsaw puzzles and games. Reaching far down underneath the other things, she pulled out an old red photo album.

"Look, Rick, it's one of your mother's books of snapshots. Oh, this will be fun." She had to raise her voice to be heard over the noise of the hail.

Rick moved in closer. He recognized the album. "Remember that summer when Mom's pet project was organizing all the photos that she'd been relegating to shoe boxes for years?" he asked.

"There are more albums," Trista said. "Way at the bottom of the trunk. And a shoe box full of pictures, too."

Rick pulled them all out while Trista settled down on one of the chintz-covered couches and began to leaf casually through the pages. "Here we are at Jeter's Market, wearing our ILT T-shirts, sitting on the steps and eating ice-cream cones," she said.

He leaned over her shoulder. "Mr. Jeter stopped carrying mint chocolate chip either the next year or the one after that. No amount of begging could convince him to stock it again."

"Yeah, he said Rocky Road sold better. But not to us." She grinned at him.

He grinned back, glad that she seemed to be forgetting about the dog. "Hey, how about a fire in the fireplace?" he suggested. "That might chase some of the chill out of the air." They kept a stash of dry firewood on the back porch.

"Good idea," Trista replied, still flipping through the pages.

As Rick stepped outside to get the wood, the rain became torrential, beating against the windows in concert with the pummeling wind. Lightning, great jagged streaks of it, lit the dark sky; thunder rumbled and roared both near and far.

The dog had retreated to the far corner of the porch, where an overgrown morning-glory vine provided maximum shelter. She gazed up at Rick, good-naturedly flapping her tail and scattering hailstones into the shrubbery in the process.

His arms full of firewood, Rick ignored the dog, but he couldn't do the same with Trista, who stood watching him from the kitchen. "Poor baby," she said to the dog. "I'd let you in if I could."

Rick ducked inside as a flash of lightning illuminated Trista's disapproving face. An instantaneous roar of thunder followed, shaking the very floor and walls. "That dog could hide under the porch stairs until it's over," he said.

"There are snakes there," Trista pointed out. Years ago they'd witnessed a rat snake undulating out from under the stairs.

Rick was halfway across the kitchen before he figured out that the dog had slipped inside. Whether her admittance was intentional on Trista's part, he couldn't fathom, and he certainly didn't approve when the dog shook her wet coat, landing droplets all over the floor, chairs and table.

"I'd better get a towel," Trista said, though Rick wasn't sure if she meant the towel for him or the dog. He wasn't all that dry himself.

As it happened, it was for the dog. Trista crouched on the floor, toweling the mangy animal vigorously and telling it reassuring things that Rick didn't want to hear. Worse, the dog now sported a smug self-satisfied expression. Annoyed with both of them, Rick stomped into the living room and built the fire.

While he was encouraging it to burn, Trista marched in carrying the dog and made a fuss about setting it down beside the couch. Then she began to delve through the photos in the shoe box, and after a few minutes, the dog curled up meekly at Trista's feet. Rick, who was by now hunkered down on the hearth, figured he might as well go on ignoring this blatant disregard for his wishes since Trista was clearly determined not to let the dog go back outside. He tried to be angry with her, but the two of them together made such a cute picture that he really couldn't. And the dog didn't look so mangy now that she was dry.

Trista was oblivious to his annoyance, or perhaps she was only pretending to be. "We can glue some of these loose pictures in the albums," she suggested brightly, studying one of him and her on a borrowed tandem bike. "It would give us something to do until the rain lets up. Come on, we'll spread everything out on the kitchen table." She got up and headed toward the kitchen, the dog trailing after her and Rick bringing up the rear.

When the album and pictures were arrayed on the tabletop, Trista stood back, hands on her hips, and regarded the dog with more than a little fondness. "If we can't give you a real name, I'm going to call you Dog." As if in answer to Trista's comment, the dog flopped onto her stomach and pressed her snout against Trista's foot, glaring up at Rick reproachfully.

"How about if you sort these out?" Trista said when Rick sat down beside her.

He began picking through the photos. Some of them he'd never seen; others were familiar. "Mom always told us that someday we'd be glad to have this record of our family life," he said. "She wanted us to show our kids and grandkids how we grew up here at Sweetwater Cottage because someday they'll be spending summers and vacations here just like we do."

Trista flipped over a page. "Oh my, here's one of the day when we caught the baby alligator." She held up a photo of the three of them displaying their prize catch on the back steps. The gator must have been all of ten inches long; they'd encountered it on a sandy bank in the marsh where it was basking in the sun. Martine had dropped a butterfly net over it and hauled it in, much to the dismay of Lilah Rose and Queen.

"We insisted that your mother take our picture with our trophy," Trista recalled.

"We also released it soon afterward."

"I didn't like the gator anymore after it snapped at me and hissed at Martine," Trista said, but she was smiling as she added the picture to the stack to include in the album.

"Here, this one goes in there," he said, tossing it over to Trista. "Martine and your mom, lolling in the sun on the beach."

"That's Mom and me," corrected Trista. "I had the blue bathing suit, Martine the red."

Rick picked it up again. "I was sure that was Martine," he said musingly.

Trista bent closer. "Notice how my smile quirks a bit to the left in this picture? Martine's quirks to the right."

These were traits that had been more noticeable when the twins were children. "Okay, if you say so," he said. He stared across the table at Trista. If he squinted a bit, if he blurred the lines of her face, he would almost think she was Martine.

"Rick?" she said, puzzled. "Is something wrong?"

"Sometimes I look at you and see Martine." Trista's expression changed when he said it, but even so, he didn't want to be less than honest with her about anything, ever.

"I can't change my features," she said, sounding hurt. "Short of cosmetic surgery, that is."

"Don't even think about it." He regarded her evenly, thinking how beautiful she was, how different in mind and spirit from her twin. Now she didn't resemble Martine at all. How could he have ever thought so? Anyone who was lucky enough to gaze deep into her eyes would see Trista's soul shining from deep within along with her own unique brand of intelligence and wit.

"This is hard for me, Rick," she said slowly. She appeared unsure of herself, a rare occurrence.

"In what way?" he asked, careful to keep his tone even.

"A long time ago you assigned Martine and me to rightful places in your heart—Martine as wife, me as sister. Now it's as if the earth has shifted, as if the tide rushed in and washed away everything that was familiar. I don't have a clue about how I'm supposed to *be*." Her tone was laced with frustration.

"Maybe we have to realign and regroup," he said.

"Easy for you to say," she answered, turning her eyes away. "This situation wasn't of my making."

"Oh?" he replied softly. "Wasn't it?"

Her head jerked around. "What do you mean?"

Now that the opportunity had presented itself, he wasn't about to let it go. "Some things have been weighing on my mind lately."

She remained motionless, caught by surprise. His heart warmed to her; he couldn't help it. Nor was there any reason not to speak of things that needed to be discussed if they were to move on from this point in their lives.

"It threw me for a loop when you became engaged to Graham," he said quietly, watching for her reaction.

"I never knew that," she said.

"At that time, our senior year of college, I didn't expect an engagement," he told her. "I don't think anyone did. We'd met Graham when you brought him home at Thanksgiving, sure, but—" He shrugged expressively. "Well, we just didn't have any inkling that it was serious, I guess."

On the day he'd found out that Trista was planning to marry, he'd stopped by to visit her parents, not realizing that Trista had arrived home earlier from Furman. Graham had stayed behind in Greenville, and she was showing off her engagement ring to the neighbors, who had noticed her car in the driveway and dropped in to say hello. Through his shock, Rick had mumbled a few congratulatory words before excusing himself as quickly as possible.

"I thought I loved Graham," Trista said.

Rick believed her, but he'd never considered the two of them well suited. "Your engagement changed everything. Martine believed that it was part of your campaign to become your own person after you went away to college," he said.

Trista looked stricken and as if she wanted to say something, but he didn't let her. "No wonder Martine felt adrift. No wonder she came on to me when we both thought you'd chosen Graham and a life separate from ours."

She seemed shocked. "Martine came on to you? I thought it was the other way around." He winced at the catch in her voice.

He would never tell Trista how one night Martine had shown up unexpectedly at the apartment that he was renting with two of his frat brothers near the university. She'd brought a fifth of vodka, and they'd gotten very drunk, something they had never done together before. Their inhibitions dissolved by alcohol, their clothes magically discarded somewhere along the way, they had engaged in wildly passionate sex. Thinking back, it was probably not coincidence that they had both recently learned of Trista's engagement.

"She took the lead," was all he said. "I was surprised." After that night, Martine's pursuit had been so relentless that he'd hardly known what hit him. In retrospect, he may have been bewitched by Martine's resemblance to the woman who was forever lost to him. By the time Martine talked him into shopping for a diamond, a romance between the two of them had somehow begun to seem appropriate and marriage the logical result.

"You loved her," Trista said. "You said so."

"Like you with Graham, I thought I did at the time," he said, at a loss to explain the breathless excitement, the mindlessness of those initial reckless couplings between him and Martine. The sex had blotted out the dissimilarities between them, but only at first.

"It's easy to be misled," Trista said. "Easy to believe in something because you so desperately want something to believe in."

"You waited until my wedding day to break up with Graham," he said, trying to keep the overtone of accusation out of his voice and failing utterly. "Why was that?"

"Because I'd only recently figured out that he and I weren't good partners. Because I realized that I didn't love him. Because—"

"But on my *wedding* day?" he said, interrupting.

She stood, a frown bisecting her forehead. "Why *not* on your wedding day, Rick? What difference did it make when you and Martine were already promised? Had set the date? Were sleeping together, for Pete's sake?"

He fought back a hot choking anger at—what? At her? At himself? At Martine for teasing him into a marriage that should never have happened? "If you'd broken up with Graham at any time before the ceremony and I'd found out about it, I'd have called off my wedding immediately. Instead I learned you and he had split just before I took my place at the altar. Hal heard it from Curry Anne, who heard it from Martine on the way to the church." He paused, giving her a chance to absorb all this. When he continued, it was in a softer voice, though the attendant emotion came through loud and clear.

"I deluded myself for a long time, Trista, all through high school when I first began to think about you in a new way." He waited for her to reply to this, but she only stared at him, her eyes enormous, the pupils dark. "I wouldn't have married Martine if Graham was permanently out of the picture. I swear it." His gaze burned holes through her, and she dropped her face to her hands. She didn't raise her head for a long time. When she did, the blood had drained from her face.

"Are you all right?" he asked curtly. He wanted to go to her, to touch her, but he couldn't summon the nerve. It was enough to have said all those things, to get them off his chest.

"I felt light-headed for a moment. Sorry."

"Don't apologize." He wouldn't. Since she'd arrived, every time the brink of deeper involvement seemed within reach, he'd stepped back abruptly as if afraid of something, and distance would be placed between them again. He had no intention of living like that anymore, at least where Trista was concerned.

As she started past him, he could no longer keep his distance. He pulled her roughly toward him and would have crushed her lips with his, but she said sharply, "Don't, Rick. Not now."

He released her, became aware that he'd been holding his breath and let it out. The enormity of the incredible things they'd said to each other swept over him, and he was afraid he'd driven her away for good. Something flickered behind Trista's eyes. Anger? Recrimination? No, it was a more positive emotion, though he was at a loss to identify it.

"Trista," he said as she hurried past, but she didn't acknowledge him. She continued past the dining room and across the living room. Her footsteps rang out sharply as she ran up the metal stairs to the Lighthouse.

Outside, the rain had almost stopped, slowing to a trickle. Rick sank onto a kitchen chair and exhaled a long breath of exasperation. Sometimes he was sure that he had sparse communication skills where women were concerned.

If he'd skipped the heavy stuff and kissed her early in the discussion, he would most likely not have to sleep alone tonight, which might have done more for their relationship than all the talk in the world. He pulled himself back from that idea, considering that premature sex with Martine had blinded him to reality for a long time, and he didn't intend to repeat that mistake. It suddenly crossed his mind that maybe Trista wasn't ready for where he hoped to take this, and maybe she never would be. His throat ached when he considered another lifetime spent without her, and he was suffused with longing.

The dog—well, he supposed he could call her Dog now

that Trista was already doing it—walked over to sniff his hand, probably angling for a snack. Rick thought about sending her outside but quickly changed his mind. He felt sorry for Dog in a way; he understood what it was like not to know where you belonged anymore.

Besides, even if Trista had no intention of sleeping with him, Dog certainly would.

The next morning, Trista had already left for her run when Rick woke up. His first inclination was to find her, since he knew she usually headed for the beachfront park, but after last night's intensity, it might be better to keep things casual. Dog was gone, too, no doubt let out by Trista earlier.

Somehow he felt the need to keep moving, so he wandered back to the bachelor quarters, where plain iron bunk beds covered with brightly colored chenille spreads lined the beadboard walls. A set of weights sat on the rag rug in the middle of the floor, and he hefted one of the smaller ones. He had once been in great shape but had allowed his fitness routine to lapse in the past couple of months. Soon he was working out and thinking that he'd have something to tell Trista when she got back.

Afterward, while he waited for her to return, he tossed slices of bacon into the big old iron skillet, humming tunelessly through his teeth and casting expectant glances down the road every now and then. Trista jogged down the driveway as he was arranging the bacon on paper towels to drain. Dog galumphed alongside her, stopping patiently at the door when Trista came inside.

He didn't give Trista a chance to talk about last night. "Hey, you'll never guess what I did this morning," he said.

As he might have predicted, she was slightly standoffish,

unsure what to expect from him. Her hair was damp from running in the morning mist, and she wore no makeup. She looked healthy and impossibly young, almost as she had when they were teenagers.

She went to the refrigerator and poured herself a glass of orange juice, keeping her back to him. "I can't imagine what else you've been up to, but that bacon smells mighty good," she said.

"Guess," he said.

"Guess what?" She kept her expression blank.

"What I did."

"Well, okay. You brushed your teeth, you shaved, and combed your hair."

"Good start. Go on."

"Got dressed. Decided you were hungry."

"And exercised," he said triumphantly. "I found the old weights in the bachelor quarters and did an abbreviated military-fitness workout. I think I'll be sore tomorrow."

"Well. I'm proud of you. I'm sure it's only weeks till you have a perfect six-pack ab configuration."

"Maybe a couple of months. Let's be fair." He began to whisk eggs in a bowl.

"Do I have time for a quick shower?"

"Sure, all of seven minutes."

"Time me," she said, rushing off and up the stairs.

He considered that things could have been worse. It gave Rick hope when she started singing in the shower upstairs, and he smiled at the sound of her voice. She belted out the song woefully off-key, humming certain parts. He wondered if she always sang in the shower; there was so much he didn't know about her.

By the time Trista returned, her hair hanging damp on

her neck, Dog had retreated from her sentry post at the back door to her favorite spot under the swing. Rick placed a plate of scrambled eggs in front of Trista, and after he spotted her sending a covert look at Dog on the porch, he said, "Yes, there's enough for her, too," as he spooned some onto a plate and set it outside the door. Dog immediately snapped out of her drowsy state and attacked the eggs with gusto, wagging her tail all the while.

"You make the greatest scrambled eggs," Trista said, apparently in a good mood. "So light and fluffy."

Rick shook Tabasco sauce on his eggs. "Queen said every bachelor should know how."

"I wish she'd been as forthcoming with that waffle recipe," Trista said with longing.

"That makes two of us," he replied.

Since he was eager to establish the old rapport between them, he steered the conversation toward mundane and uncontroversial topics. He told her how his mother had recently e-mailed interesting sidelights about her Chinese students, how his brother was having difficulty dealing with the presence of an Alzheimer's-afflicted father-in-law in his house. In turn, Trista mentioned that she had recently enrolled in a Pilates class and spoke of her continuing concern about her coanchor's attempts to steal her turf at WCIC.

Though she'd mentioned problems at work earlier, she hadn't been specific, and Rick, getting up to pour them both another cup of coffee, asked her to elaborate on what was going on.

"Unfortunately," she said as she spread a bit of toast with butter, "while Martine was in the hospital, Byron made a play to become the sole anchor of the evening news. He wasn't successful, but he's persistent." For a moment, she seemed pensive and troubled.

"I'm sorry to hear that," he told her. "What will you do about it?"

"Now that Byron's forced the issue, I have decisions to make," she admitted. "I love living in Columbia, so I'm not eager to move to Atlanta or Richmond, even though anchoring a news slot in either of those places would be a step up. I've had a few hard-to-refuse offers, but I've been putting them off. Now, because of Byron, I need to address the problem."

"I can't picture you anywhere but Columbia," Rick said. "And what's with this Stott guy pulling that kind of crap when you've been so helpful to him?" He recalled she'd been instrumental in hiring Byron in the first place, and he felt indignant on her behalf.

She shrugged in resignation but brightened immediately. "Old friends are the best friends. I should keep that in mind." As he was still computing what this meant in relation to the two of them, she stood. "Say, since we've got company coming today, I'd better get rolling. I'm still a mess."

Before he could comment, Trista was rinsing her plate off in the sink. "I'll be down to start the shrimp boiling after I get dressed. You could start cutting up cabbage for the slaw if you don't have anything else to do." Then she hurried upstairs to get ready for their guests.

Rick was thankful that he'd invited the Doyles. They would provide a much-needed respite from the one-on-one tension between him and Trista. Maybe hanging out with other people for a while was just what they needed.

Shortly before noon, Stanley and Luella, along with their two kids, Daria and Isaac, arrived at the cottage in Stanley's SUV. Trista, dressed casually in khaki shorts and a red-and-white-striped polo shirt, greeted them at the door with Rick. She was all smiles and delight at seeing Luella again and meeting the two children.

Luella had contributed a basket of crispy fried chicken and a huge chocolate sheet cake. She was exactly as Rick remembered her—tall and reedy, with snapping dark eyes sparkling with good humor. Daria was the image of her mother, and Isaac was a perpetual-motion machine. The boy and Dog took to each other right away, and as soon as Rick produced a Frisbee, the two of them took off for the beach.

The adults, accompanied by Daria, who had brought a book to read, settled on the porch overlooking the dunes. The adults occupied wicker rockers, and Daria appropriated the hammock. Trista chatted with Daria about the book, which was *Anne of Green Gables,* one of her own childhood favorites, and later she carried in a pitcher of fresh-made cherry Kool-Aid for Daria and herself; Rick, Stanley and Luella drank beer, while Isaac was interested in neither food nor drink for the time being.

At first they talked about old times and the changes that had been wrought by the recent development of Tappany Island. Soon, however, Isaac churned up the porch steps to beg his sister to come play with Dog, and Daria wasn't hard to convince. The two of them ran down toward the water, where Dog was loping back and forth, waiting for the Frisbee to miraculously reappear.

"Kids," said Stanley after a long drag on his beer. "They run us ragged most of the time."

"Oh, now, Stanley," Luella responded with an affectionate glance. "What would our lives be without them?"

"Peaceful? Quiet?" he asked hopefully.

"You wouldn't like that and you know it," Luella retorted

in her easy Low Country drawl. And to Trista, "He complains a lot, but he's just an old softie."

"So, Luella," Trista said with interest, "tell me how you and Stanley met."

"It was in church," Luella said, looking pleased. "In April. The azaleas and dogwoods were blooming like in a scene from a springtime wonderland. After the service, I walked out behind the church to admire the blossoms, and I started to sneeze from all the pollen."

Stanley grinned at her, sharing the memory. "I walked up and offered her my handkerchief. And that was it." He laughed.

"I didn't even know him," Luella continued. "I thought he was mighty handsome, and I was grateful for the handkerchief. I told him I'd wash it and give it back to him the next Sunday."

"She was new at church. I'd never seen her before and was trying to figure out how I could find out her name, when I noticed her sneezing up a storm in the garden," Stanley said.

Luella leaned forward, obviously enjoying the telling of this tale. "I'd just started to attend services there with my grandmother, who needed me to drive her. I spotted Stanley in the front pew that morning and couldn't take my eyes off him for even a minute. I kept forgetting his handkerchief for several Sundays. Only, I didn't forget it at all. All my excuses for why I hadn't brought it gave us a chance to talk."

"I was pretty sure she'd lost that danged hankie, and good riddance. It served its purpose," Stanley said.

Luella laughed. "Pretty soon I was begging Granny to let me drive her to Wednesday-night services and prayer meetings and covered-dish suppers in the hope of seeing Stanley every chance I got, and her increased social life was taking a toll on her. Thank goodness Stanley proposed in short order."

"I had to, or Lu would have drug that poor old lady to and from church so much it wore her out." Stanley slapped his bony knee and laughed again.

Luella turned toward Trista. "You've never been married, Trista, or have you?"

Trista shook her head, avoiding Rick's eyes. "Engaged once. In a serious relationship a couple of times, but nothing ever jelled. If you know what I mean."

"Sometimes it's not easy to find the right person," Luella agreed. "No point in settling."

"Hey, let's go play with the kids," Rick said, hoping to deflect all serious discussion.

"No reason we get to sit on the porch in the shade," Stanley said with mock resignation. "We might as well all be equally overheated and miserable."

Trista divested herself of her sandals at the high-tide line and looped her hair back in a ponytail. Rick watched her, bemused by the delicate arch of her instep, the curve of her calves. If he had married her in the first place, would he still be looking at her with desire? With longing? Or would those feelings have eroded over the course of their marriage? She saw him studying her and smiled slightly. *I would never have fallen out of love with you,* he said to her in his mind. He wished he could say the words for real, and maybe someday he would.

The children were clamoring for Rick to throw the Frisbee, and when Isaac tossed it, he caught it neatly. "Okay, kids," Rick shouted. "Show me your stuff."

The children raced up and down the beach, avoiding the surf like little sandpipers. Isaac delighted in tossing the

Frisbee to Dog, who ran with everyone shouting behind. The only person to whom Dog would relinquish the Frisbee was Rick, and Trista charged that this was because Rick let Dog sleep on his bed. Finally, after Stanley managed to get his shoes sloshed by a wave, Daria declared that she was ready for food, and Luella said she was hungry, too.

Trista, fit from running, didn't want to quit, but after Isaac joined Daria in pleading for their mother's fried chicken, Rick declared the game over. "We don't want to tire these kids out. We want them to have enough strength left to help clean up."

The children immediately objected, enlisting a willing ally in their mother. "Hey, that's for you and Stanley to do," Luella informed Rick, which only made Stanley laugh and pull her close so he could smooch her on the cheek.

"We got better things to do, honey," he said. "Like maybe after we tire these kids out and they go to sleep at home."

Luella wasn't embarrassed at her husband's obvious desire for her. "Big talker," she said, but she hugged him before they all started back toward the cottage together.

As they walked, Rick slung a friendly arm across Trista's shoulders. "Having fun?" he asked. He was surprised when she leaned into him; it felt natural and right.

"Of course," she replied, smiling up at him. Then Daria yelled, "Race everybody to the porch steps!" and Trista sprinted away, the rest of them in close pursuit.

Trista won, Isaac howled when he stepped on a sliver of metal and they all trooped inside to inspect his cut, which was fortunately not serious.

As Luella and Stanley supervised their children, as he and Trista set out the chicken and cold boiled shrimp and fresh-made slaw buffet-style on the kitchen table, Rick noticed Trista observing him. He smiled at her, halfway expecting her to react like Martine, who would have tossed him an offhand grin if he was lucky. But Trista smiled back so that her eyes lit up, and he detected romantic overtones in her expression.

Perhaps he was mistaken, though, because she immediately began to arrange watermelon pickles in a milk-glass dish, not paying attention to him at all.

Chapter 15: Trista

2004

Click: We are sitting on the porch after dinner with the Doyles, and Isaac snapped this picture with his mother's digital camera. Rick's arm is around the back of my chair, but it's an awkward posture, as if he wants to lower it to curve around my shoulders but doesn't. I appear genuinely happy and relaxed, leaning toward Rick. My hand is almost, but not quite, touching his knee.

As Rick and I played on the beach that Saturday with Stanley, Luella and their children, it was as if I unwound inside. I was beginning to understand that I had been taking Rick's pain into myself, letting it knot somewhere deep inside me until I was near to choking with it. Adding my own uncertainty about what was presently going on between Rick and me, I was awash in misgivings. Not good.

I'd spent a restless night after Rick had said all those things to me in the kitchen the day before. I was incredulous, furious, stunned while he was saying them. At first I'd reacted as though he were blaming me for everything that had gone wrong, but then I understood that he was blaming himself as well. Afterward, I lay alone in my bed, worried that I wouldn't be able to act natural after what we'd said to each other, and we were expecting the Doyles for a picnic the next day besides. In the end, I decided that having company over was a good thing.

Do you know how, when you have guests, you put them first? Well, my reservations and doubts about Rick dissolved that day in the pleasant ambience so often engendered by compatible people. The six of us ate at the round table on the porch, laughed at the funny little things the kids said and talked about old times. Later, Luella and Stanley sat in the living room with us while Isaac and Daria munched on Gummi Bears and worked together on a jigsaw puzzle on the floor nearby, just as Rick, Martine and I had done many years ago.

After promising that we'd all do it again someday before too long, the Doyles drove off. Rick and I went around the cottage picking up glasses, which was when I discovered Daria's book, forgotten in the hammock when they left. Of course I immediately called Luella on her cell phone to let her know I'd found it, and she said they'd try to stop by the next day after church. If not then, Stanley would pick up the book when he delivered the mail on Tuesday.

After Luella and I concluded our conversation, Rick came into the kitchen and said, "How about another piece of that wonderful chocolate cake that Luella left?" His tone was so normal, his expression so bland, that I took heart from it. I figured we were back on an even keel, that things were easy between us again.

"Sure," I said. "Make mine a small one."

We carried our cake out on the porch, sat on the wicker chairs and studied the lights of a distant freighter, trying to imagine where it was going.

"Istanbul," I said, naming the place that had sounded the most far away and exotic of all the cities in the world when I was a kid.

"Timbuktu," Rick suggested.

I didn't state what both of us were thinking, which was that if Martine were present, she'd have said Bangkok, the place she always mentioned when we played the "Where is that freighter going?" game.

"You know what I thought about on the beach today? When I saw you kick off your shoes?" Rick said.

I shook my head.

"Our sixth-grade class picnic," he said. "When your sandal broke."

I remembered, the memory flooding back. "You took it to be repaired," I replied. *At as much risk as a sixth-grader's mind could conceive,* I thought but didn't say.

"I watched you crying to yourself, sitting apart from everyone, and I couldn't bear your sadness. I would have done anything I could to make things better."

I wasn't sure how to reply. "Thank you," I said finally. "How did you pay for it?" I asked, since I'd always wondered.

"I had some birthday money in my pocket. It didn't cost much."

We usually hadn't carried much more than lunch money to school. I was silent, remembering how Rick must have run through the crowded city streets, entered the shoe shop and pushed my shoe across the counter. Then, probably worried that the teacher would call a buddy check and find him missing, he'd waited for it to be fixed, counting out wrinkled one-dollar bills when it was ready.

"That was the day I recognized that there was something new between us," I ventured. "Over and above loyalty to the ILTs, I mean."

"Yes," he said, picking up my hand and inspecting it. "I felt it, too."

"What did you think it was?"

"Something extraordinary," he said in a low voice. "But I was an eleven-year-old boy and didn't have words to put to it."

I ate no more cake. In my mind I was shut out of my classmates' games, worried that I'd ruined my favorite pair of shoes. And I was picturing Rick as the prince who had come to my rescue.

We sat silently, holding hands, and left the porch only when a damp fog rolled off the ocean. Once inside I pulled the doors closed behind us, and when I looked out at the beach, I saw that stars were beginning to show themselves in the sky.

I totted up the fragile happiness we had accrued on that day, hoping to prolong it by including Rick in my personal and private reverie, but then I caught my breath. Rick had moved in behind me and was standing so near that I felt the warmth of his body. His arms slid around me, and I closed my eyes. When I opened them, our wavy reflections stared back at me from the darkening glass, Rick serious and me—well, I thought I was kind of dopey looking, like someone who had just awakened. Which in a way perhaps I had.

"You and I have unfinished business," Rick said into my ear.

I rested my head against his chin. "I'm at a loss how I'm supposed to feel about this," I said.

"Tris," he said carefully, "remember that night after the prom? After Martine had gone up to bed?"

I turned within the circle of his arms. "How could I forget it?" I asked quietly. "Ever?"

He reached up and tipped a light finger along my jawline. "I wish I'd had the skill to explain my misgivings after we made love. I thought I'd ruined everything. Overwhelming emotions surfaced that night, and I was totally unable to handle them. They all but immobilized me, Tris. Maybe it's no excuse, but that's the way it was for me."

I didn't doubt Rick's sincerity and I certainly didn't disbelieve what he was saying. We'd only been eighteen years old, after all. "You could have talked to me," I said helplessly.

"We didn't discuss such things then."

"We talked about everything," I said. "About getting a period and what a jockstrap was for and how some people we knew were having sex."

"We never personalized it," he said.

I realized he was right, but that didn't make any of it easier to bear.

"Anyway," Rick went on, "I endured a lot of sleepless nights that summer." His face was pale underneath his tan; this lent him a vulnerability, a sadness.

Suddenly, this was too much to bear. "Don't tell me these things. Don't."

"We can talk about it now," he said. "We proved that last night. There's nothing—and no one—to stop us."

I considered this. "I was devastated when you ignored me for the rest of that summer," I said. He seemed thunderstruck at this admission, though I wasn't sure why. Surely, since we'd always been so tied into each other's thoughts, on some level he must have known what I was going through.

He swallowed, inhaled a deep breath. "Tris, all that summer I felt so guilty that I'd betrayed your parents' trust. I was terrified that if we kept on sleeping together, you might get pregnant."

"We could have taken precautions."

"Sometimes they don't work."

"I understood what to do," I said. "I'd heard other girls talk about getting birth control pills, being fitted for a diaphragm."

"I didn't want to put our futures in jeopardy."

Of course. I should have known that Rick would have always looked after me. He was my protector, the knight who had ridden to my rescue, but I still was determined for him to know how I was—and who I was—in that long-ago summer.

"I didn't care about any of that. I—I longed for you. I ached for you. I couldn't bear not being wanted after—after—"

The expression in Rick's eyes made me feel as if I were melting from the inside out and reminded me of my sexual awakening on that night so long ago, when I learned what it meant to feel pure wanton lust. My heart quickened, my pulse rushed in my ears and I lifted my face to his.

Rick slowly lowered his lips to mine, seeking, infusing me with a sense of inevitability. As we kissed, my spine relaxed and allowed me to settle against him so that my breasts rounded against his chest. I returned his kiss with passion, and I longed for nothing so much as for him to rain sweet kisses all over my face, down the side of my throat, pushing aside the open neck of my blouse.

It would have been fine with me if he'd never let me go, but he relaxed his hold on me. "I'm not going to make any more mistakes," he said. "Somehow in the next few days we have to decide if we'll continue as friends or become more than that. I've already made my choice, and you know what it is. I want you, Trista. But you're the one who has the final say-so."

"I—" I started to say, but Rick placed a cautionary finger across my lips.

"Careful, let's not go there yet," he said.

Somehow, though, I don't know why this didn't feel like another rejection. Instead, I felt cared for and protected, as if my wants and needs were as important as his. He kissed me lightly on the cheek. "Good night, sweet Tilt," he said softly.

His use of my childhood nickname at that moment touched me immeasurably. I smiled at him. "Good night, Rilt."

He backed away, then turned and walked swiftly to his room. I made my way up the stairs to the Lighthouse, stumbling as I went. Once there I threw myself across the bed and stared up at the ceiling fan revolving slowly above me. My feelings for Rick were powerful. And he returned them. This was hard to absorb after such a long time of regarding him as my sister's husband, unavailable to me forever.

It was a while before I changed into my nightgown, and later I fell into a light sleep, waking frequently to mull things over, but when I awoke early the next morning, Easter, I wasn't the worse for all the waking. I felt energized by a new perspective. One part of me didn't believe anything that was happening. What if I had dreamed it? But no, the memory of Rick's kiss was too, too real. It *had* happened, and everything was different now.

That Easter morning, I swung my feet out of bed and threw aside the filmy curtains. The rising sun was a majestic sight, one that never failed to fill me with wonder. I showered, wrapped myself in my robe and ran downstairs. I didn't hear Rick stirring behind his bedroom door, but I knocked anyway.

"Happy Easter," I called before he answered. "Get up and get ready. You and I are going to church." We hadn't discussed going, but attending Easter worship is part of our tradition. I've always loved the Tappany Creek Chapel and enjoyed the service, especially on this holiday with flowers blooming all around and the little girls dressed up in pastel dresses.

"Mmmfgh," Rick said, or something to that effect.

"Rick?"

"Don't want church."

I might have expected this. Rick tended to avoid joining the rest of us at church on any Sunday morning, though Lilah Rose had always insisted, and I wasn't about to cut him any slack.

"It's Easter, Rick. I'd rather not go alone."

I heard Rick moving around his room before he cracked open the door, his smile making me forget the beard stubble and sleep-encrusted eyes. He glanced toward the closet. "I'm warning you, I may not be properly wardrobed for church."

"I'm not, either. I only brought one dress, forgot to pack pantyhose, and your mother would pitch a hissy fit if I showed up for the service bare-legged."

"My mother," Rick said with a lift of his eyebrows, "is in faraway China."

"Somehow I think she'd know," I warned him. "She could smell out an impropriety like a bloodhound on a case."

"I won't snitch on you," Rick promised with a wink.

"There's a man's suit hanging in the closet of the other bedroom," I said. "It might be one of Hal's."

"I'll check," Rick said.

I hurried back to the Lighthouse, showered and slipped into my silk print dress. I wished I'd packed dressy sandals, which would allow me to go stockingless, but I only had pumps.

The sleeves of Hal's suit were slightly too long for Rick, though the pants fit him fine. When he showed up in the kitchen for inspection, he looked wonderful to my eyes. "Wow," I said, ogling him over the rim of my coffee mug. "You clean up good, McCulloch."

"So do you. You're beautiful."

It was what I wanted to hear, but I didn't feel completely dressed. We set off in Rick's car, and as we rounded the corner near Jeter's, I noticed that the store was open. "Stop!" I said suddenly. "I want to buy some pantyhose."

Rick slowed the car, sparing an admiring glance for my bare legs. "Your legs are tanned and gorgeous."

"I don't feel right," I said.

"For Pete's sake, Trista, are you serious?"

I was. "Stop making this difficult, Rick McCulloch. It'll only take a minute for me to run in, and we're early for the service besides."

Rick rolled his eyes, but he pulled up in front of Jeter's. "Thanks," I told him, favoring him with a broad smile over my shoulder as I marched inside the store. I found the pantyhose I wanted, one size fits most, and paid one of the young girls behind the counter.

"You're Trista Barrineau, aren't you?" she asked as she sorted bills into the cash drawer. "I've seen you on TV. You're taller than you seem on television."

Usually when I'm on the island, I'm not recognized, which is wonderful since I can't go anywhere in Columbia without people knowing who I am. Worse yet, some of them make rude remarks. My personal favorite? "You don't look as good as you do on TV." Well, *duh*. I wear tons of makeup on-screen.

With this girl at Jeter's, I was understandably reluctant to involve myself in a long conversation, but she had an open, likable face. She might have been Goz's daughter. Rose? Ivy? I seemed to remember that his girls were named after plants.

"I want to be a reporter just like you," she confided. "I'm going to take a journalism class in school next year."

"That's a good start," I said warmly, and as I left the store, I realized that providing a positive role model for young people was a worthwhile thing to do and something that I didn't often consider when embroiled in turf wars and intrigues at work.

"You look like the cat who got the cream," Rick said as he backed out and onto the road.

I tore open the pantyhose package and told him what the girl had said and how it had made me feel good.

"That's important," he said. "And if you—"

He stopped talking as I shimmied my dress up my thighs. "What in the world?"

"I bought these pantyhose, and now I have to put them on," I explained patiently. I slipped one of the legs over my foot and smoothed it upward, remaining modest but mindful that Rick quickly averted his eyes.

"You're titillating as hell," he said. "Are you doing this to turn me on?"

I halted my labors to stare at him openmouthed. "My legs aren't anything new to you," I reminded him. I hitched the pantyhose as high as I could, then started with the other leg.

"Sweet blessed Jesus," Rick muttered. At my disapproving glance, he darted his eyes in my direction. "That was a prayer. It *is* Easter, you know."

"I don't understand what all the fuss is about," I said, wishing the seat of Rick's car was more roomy so I wouldn't have so much trouble sliding the hose up over my hips.

"Context. Opportunity. And sex appeal," he said as he wheeled in to the church parking lot. He swerved in to a parking space under a crepe myrtle tree, immediately switching off the engine and turning with his elbow propped on the steering wheel.

I twitched my skirt down and started to get out of the car, but he pulled me toward him so he could kiss the middle of my forehead. "The next thing I want to see you do is take those damn pantyhose off," he said, his voice low in his throat.

I couldn't help laughing, and we walked into the sanctuary with our fingers lightly laced together.

The sermon, delivered by a new, young pastor we'd never met, touched on renewal and hope, which I found particularly apt. The minister shook our hands as we left the church, saying that he'd like to see us at services again. I think he believed we were married, which amused me, and later, a member of Lilah Rose's summer bridge club greeted us and told Rick that it was good to see him and his wife at the service. I waited for Rick to correct her, but he didn't. When I asked him why he hadn't, he merely shrugged.

"It's too complicated to explain," he said briefly, and I suppose I agreed with him. Besides, it was a beautiful morning, the honey-colored stones of the church gilded with sunshine, and the sea, visible beyond the church yard, a sheet of billowing blue. I didn't want anything to spoil it.

On the way home we stopped at the park where a group of small boys were flying kites in the freshening wind. One of them had trouble launching his homemade creation, and Rick ran with it until the gusts pulled it up into the sun-washed blue sky. I sat watching from a low wall, my legs pulled up, my arms draped loosely around my knees much as I had when I'd watched Rick flying kites there years ago.

"We should go for a walk," Rick said when he rejoined me. "That storm the other day washed up a lot of shells. If we search hard enough, you might find that perfect sand dollar you've never found."

He'd already removed his jacket. I glanced down at my shoes and pantyhose. "Well," I said slowly, "I guess they've served their purpose." With that, I ducked down behind the wall and tugged them off, rolled the nylon into a ball and tucked it into the end of a drainage pipe, not caring if I ever saw them again.

We ran down to the beach, where a few families had already staked large umbrellas in the sand. Rick rolled up the legs of his borrowed pants, and I scampered in and out of the waves, as sure-footed as a marsh pony.

"You know, there doesn't need to be any more than this," Rick said, his arms sweeping out to encompass the sea, sand and sky. The wind had blown his hair back from his forehead, and the faint scar from his long-ago fight with Hugh Barfield showed through his tan.

"That's what we always think when we're on the island, but somehow, other things intrude. Money, time, jobs, responsibilities."

"Marriages," Rick said soberly.

"Life," I added.

We grew tired of walking after a while and headed back. Once, we stopped and talked with a man who was photographing arrangements of driftwood, and he offered to take a photo of us. I sat on one of the large silvery logs, and just before the shutter clicked, Rick pushed a lock of hair back over my shoulder.

"Good one!" exclaimed the man, and he wrote down my e-mail address so he could send me a copy over the Internet. I didn't think the picture in his viewfinder was perfect, since Rick's face was slightly turned away from the camera, but the photographer had caught me in a rare relaxed pose, happy and carefree.

And then I found it—the perfect sand dollar. I happened to glance down as we walked, and there it was, lying right on top of the sand as if waiting for me. I picked it up and brushed it off, a lovely souvenir of this special day.

Neither Rick nor I had given a thought to preparing the usual Easter dinner of ham and all the fixings. Instead, we defrosted steaks in the microwave and Rick grilled them outside. I set the dining-room table with Lilah Rose's elegant hand-painted china, threw potatoes into the toaster oven to bake and made a simple tossed salad.

Afterward, we watched a DVD of old *Seinfeld* episodes, shoveling popcorn into our mouths as we hadn't since we were kids. It didn't take long for us to become engaged in hearty debate about which was the best episode ever made, and Rick said that his favorite wasn't in the collection we were watching.

"In the one I like," Rick said, "Elaine and Jerry are sitting on his couch doing this exact same thing, watching TV. And they get into a debate about whether they should sleep together. And—"

"I've seen it," I said, all but dumping the popcorn bowl in his lap. "Are you trying to tell me something?"

"You could take it that way," he said consideringly as he

switched off the TV and leaned toward me. In the sudden quiet, my heart started to beat faster, a series of pitty-pats that echoed in my ears. Rick traced the inside of my wrist with his thumb, and the stirrings of desire uncoiled somewhere below my stomach.

"On that show," I said, choosing my words carefully, "Jerry and Elaine find a whole lot of reasons why they should remain just friends."

"And reasons that they should make love, too."

"But they'd made love before, when they were boyfriend and girlfriend," I pointed out as Rick's hand slid higher.

"They must have enjoyed it," he said softly, "because they decided to go ahead and do it again."

Rick's eyes searched mine, never wavering. By this time, I knew what was going to happen, and I longed for him to put his arms around me. The electricity flickering between us was extraordinary, and I felt an effervescent sense of unreality.

But I was not so mesmerized by Rick that practicalities fled my mind. "Now that you've made it clear exactly where we're going with this," I said unsteadily, "maybe I should hit the shower. I'm still all sandy from the beach."

"Let's take a shower together," he said, nuzzling my temple.

"In the Lighthouse or downstairs?" I asked.

"The Lighthouse. With the dark ocean visible through the curtains and a moon path ready to take us as far as we want to go."

"As far as we want to go," I murmured, imagining Istanbul and Timbuktu and limitless possibilities stretching as far as we could see.

He kissed me, the kiss growing hungrier as I wrapped my arms around his neck and pulled him close. This time when we made love, Rick and I would do so as adults. Without reservation. Knowing the true meaning of our love for each other. Facing the future, whatever it might bring, together.

The doorbell rang. Rick sat up straight.

"Damn," he said. "Who could that be?"

I disentangled myself. Frantically, I ran my fingers through my hair, bringing it back to some semblance of my usual style. "I bet it's Stanley and family, here to pick up Daria's book."

"I'll go see who it is," Rick said. He stroked my cheek briefly. "But let's mark the place where we left off, okay?"

I returned his smile with a quavery one of my own and hurried to get the book, which I'd left in the kitchen. I arrived at the front door just as Rick threw it open.

"Well," said Martine, tossing back her expensively streaked hair. "Look who's here."

Chapter 16: Trista

2004

Click: I'm clutching a copy of Anne of Green Gables to my chest, and Martine is standing ready to stride into the house. Rick is holding the door open, clearly surprised. No snapshot of this moment exists, but it should.

My sister had all the right ingredients for beauty, but when she appeared at Sweetwater Cottage that Easter night, she no longer had the glow that comes from being cherished and loved. Instead, a tenuous line bisected her forehead, and I didn't recall ever seeing it there before, nor was there one on my face when I glanced into the nearby mirror. Martine was not happy. Why this made me sad, I don't know. Maybe because I care about Martine so much. Maybe because I have always loved her, no matter what.

"Your cars are parked outside, but the house was so quiet that I tried my key," Martine said as she shoved aside the stack of photo albums on the couch and accepted a glass of scotch and soda from Rick. "It didn't work. Guess you had the locks changed, right?"

"Hal had to call a locksmith last year after some kids broke in," Rick said tersely. "He didn't want a repeat performance."

"I'm so glad you're back to your old self," I said to Martine. We'd hugged after she walked in, and I was happy that she was so well recovered from her injuries.

"I'm feeling great. Oh, and you won't believe what happened just south of Orangeburg as I was driving up I-95. I got stopped by this handsome highway patrolman? And he recognized me, or thought he did. He didn't even bother with my license. He said, 'Well, if it isn't Trista Barrineau! I watch you on the news every night, and you did a real good job reporting that story about someone trying to bribe one of my superior officers.' And then he handed back my license and said to slow down and have a nice day. I was driving kind of fast, but not too awfully. Anyway, thanks." She beamed at me.

"I wish you'd told us you were coming," I said. "We could have waited dinner. There's leftover steak—would you like a sandwich?"

"I ate earlier. Anyhow, I'm just passing through on my way to Maryland to deliver Steve's SUV to him. He's in Annapolis right now visiting his kids, and after we rendezvous outside Washington, D.C., we're supposed to drive around visiting historic sites for a few days before heading back to Miami." The way she delivered this sentence was the clue that she wasn't exactly in favor of the plan.

Rick drew his brows down, clearly uncomfortable with this topic. I felt a muscle tic in my jaw.

"Anyway," Martine went on, surely aware of the effect her words were having on Rick and me, "I thought this would be a good chance to pick up a few of my clothes that I left. I figured somebody would be here at Easter."

I sneaked a glance at Rick, who was now regarding Martine with a blank expression. *All that police work,* I thought. *He's learned to pull a poker face.*

"You're welcome to take them," he said, and his gruff tone left no doubt that he meant that Martine should do this now and not wait.

"I hope you'll put me up for the night. There isn't a motel for miles."

A blanket of uneasiness settled over me, and Rick seemed to summon every bit of self-control he possessed. "Martine, we're divorced. Don't you think you should have checked with Hal before you decided to stay here? Or asked me?"

She frowned at him. "You've more or less disappeared from view, Rick, and Hal never returns my calls."

"You can stay in the room where Lindsay and Peter usually sleep," Rick said grudgingly.

"Okay, that works for me, and as a bonus I get to visit with my twin sis. Tris, I can never thank you enough for all you did while I was in the hospital. Thanks, hon."

Martine had begun calling people "hon" shortly after she moved to Miami. She used the term of endearment for everyone from the garbagemen to her best friend, Jane. This irritated me, but I'd never told her so.

She treated herself to a gulp of her drink. "Mmm, this tastes good. How about a walk on the beach in the morning, Tris, before I start the long drive?"

"Sure," I said, at a loss. I wondered if she expected Rick to accompany us.

Martine yawned and stretched. "I'm exhausted," she said, uncurling herself like a languid cat. "See you in the morning. Can't wait for that beach walk." With studied indolence, she made her way to the hall and hefted her carryall, continuing to the spare guest room and closing the door behind her.

Rick and I stared at each other. "So much for our plans," he said. "Who would have guessed?"

I searched his expression for any hint of discombobulation at the appearance of his ex-wife. I found none.

"I suppose I might as well turn in," I said too brightly. As I brushed past Rick, who by this time was standing between me and the stairs, he grabbed my arm. "If I had my way," he said, "we'd be in the shower now. Together."

Somehow this was difficult to hear with Martine only a few rooms away. "We'll save it for later," I said, attempting a smile.

"Let's not scrap all our plans," he said softly. "We can manage this, for instance." He slid his hand down my arm to my hand and pulled me onto the couch. Moodily, I settled into his lap and rested my head on his shoulder. Where my hand rested on his chest, I felt his heart beating strong and steady. I tried hard to summon the will to remain distant, to remove myself from his arms and go upstairs where I belonged. I failed utterly. Rick smelled of sun and sand, of the island and the cottage, and his bristly beard stubble rubbed against my forehead. It was bliss.

He kissed me, and I melted. I wanted to keep doing it over and over again, but there was the slight matter of his former wife, who also happened to be my sister, only yards away. No matter how I wished I could recapture our previous mood, it was futile.

His hand stole up to cup my breast, but I wriggled away. I spilled out of his lap, landed on my feet, inserted a room length between us. "We can't do this now," I said.

"Great. I finally make progress toward getting you in the sack, and this happens." He smiled as he said it.

"Let's establish a few ground rules," I said. "First, no sneaking around in the night."

"Agreed," Rick replied, though he appeared less than happy with that restriction.

"And we reconnect after Martine is gone," I said. "Let's make an appointment. One hour after she's out of here?"

"One minute," Rick said, straightening his clothes.

"Make that two, and you're on." I smiled tremulously, and he stood and swept me to him for one more kiss. I still tasted him on my lips as I ran up to the Lighthouse.

"I guess Rick's pretty mad at me," Martine ventured as we sauntered down the beach the next morning. Rick had made himself scarce; his car was gone from its customary place under the oak when I woke up.

I said nothing but picked up my pace. The sun was barely over the horizon, and the air was chilly and damp. The incoming breakers crashed on the shore in great, noisy, foaming white waves.

"Tris?" Martine said. "What about it?"

"Probably," I said. I had no intention of saying anything more, particularly if it would hint at the new direction of Rick's and my relationship.

"Does Rick ever talk about me? I mean, about what happened?"

"About the end of your marriage?"

Martine sighed. "Yeah. About his feelings for me."

I selected my words carefully. "I'm sure he's disappointed that the marriage didn't work out. And hurt. And—well, I'm not comfortable with the topic. Why don't you talk with Rick?"

"I'm so far from where I was when we were married that it would be pointless. I just wondered, that's all."

Fortunately, Dog chose that moment to run up behind us, expecting me to toss the Frisbee, but since it was so windy, I hadn't brought it. She yipped joyfully as a wave ruffled over her paws, then scampered in circles around us.

"How can you stand that stray mutt hanging around?" Martine asked irritably. She picked up a shell and lobbed it in the general direction of Dog, who veered off toward the dunes to chase gulls without appearing to take offense.

"I like her," I said, hugging my sweatshirt tighter around me.

"She smells."

"She does not," I said emphatically, jumping to Dog's defense.

"Maybe you didn't get as close to her as I did this morning when I went out to the car to get my cell phone. She's rolled in some dead fish or something."

Now that Martine had mentioned it, I did detect a rank fishy odor about Dog. "She could use a home," I said.

"Somehow that doesn't surprise me."

"I was hoping maybe you'd want her," I said, optimist that I am.

"I take after Mom. I don't like animals in the house. Anyway, while I'm in post-divorce mode, I don't want to tie myself down."

Rick had said the same thing, more or less. I let out a long sigh.

"I'm breaking up with Steve," Martine said suddenly. "It's over, but he doesn't know it."

"So why are you delivering his SUV to him?" I asked. As far as I knew, that's why we'd arisen at first light, forced down a dry bagel and immediately embarked on our walk. "How about that vacation you and Steve are supposed to take together?"

"After he left on this trip, I realized I'm a lot happier when he's not around. I've got plane tickets out of Dulles for Mexico City three days from now."

"Mexico City!" I exclaimed, gawking at Martine in amazement. "Why?"

"I don't expect you to understand, Tris, but I've longed to bum around the world for ages and ages. Just me and a load of art supplies in my backpack, painting this and that and sleeping wherever and with whomever suits my fancy." Defiance was evident in the way she planted her feet in the sand and in the firm set of her jaw.

"I'm surprised," I murmured. "I thought you and Steve…" I let my words trail off.

"Steve was a way to leave my marriage. No more, no less. I'd wanted out for a long time. But," she continued with a little half laugh, "he left a message on my cell phone last night that he caught the flu when he was visiting his kids. He's decided to hole up in a hotel until he feels better. I don't have to leave here today, really."

"Oh," I said, hoping I wasn't the one who was going to have to ask Rick if Martine could stay longer.

"The worst part about delaying my meeting with Steve is that I rehearsed the breakup speech over and over on the drive up here, and I won't even see him until day after tomorrow at the earliest."

Distracted, I said, "Is that Standard Breakup Speech Number One? 'It's my fault that our relationship hasn't worked, not yours, I'll always care about you and about what happens to you, and I hope we'll always be friends.'"

"I'm planning on some version of that one for sure," Martine assured me, and we grinned at each other. "Hey," she said. "I know my being here is awkward for Rick, so I'll talk to him about staying over an extra night."

"Good idea," I said.

"I may have already worn out my welcome." Her words were rueful, and I kept my gaze focused on the sand in front of us.

I changed the subject. "I was going to invite you to Macon in May so we can celebrate Mom's birthday with Aunt Cynthia," I said. "I guess that's out now that you're going to Mexico, right?"

"Totally. I don't have any idea where my adventures will take me, so you'll have to give them a big hug from me." To her credit, she did sound regretful.

"I wish you luck, Martine," I said with the utmost sincerity. "But please always keep me informed about where you are and where you're going. I'll miss you and will worry about you."

"Of course," she said, flinging an arm around my shoulders. I slipped mine around her waist, reassured that going away didn't mean growing away. She was still my sister, my twin, my other self.

Rick didn't come home all day, and not knowing if he'd be there for dinner or not, Martine and I fixed oysters Rockefeller, the oysters fresh from a late afternoon provisioning at Jeter's. I cooked a batch of red rice. It was one of Rick's favorite menus, but when he came in and found Martine still in residence, he went outside again before she had a chance to ask him if he minded her staying over. Clearly, he did. What Martine would do about the situation, I couldn't imagine. I stuck to my resolution to stay out of it.

During dinner, we spotted Rick on the beach tossing wood scraps and rubbish into a heap. Afterward, when it was apparent that Rick had no intention of joining us, Martine and I cleaned up the kitchen, and later she sat down to flip through Lilah Rose's photo albums. This provided a welcome diversion for both of us, and I brought more from the closet shelf where I'd relocated them. Martine pulled a white one, larger than the others, out of the stack.

"This is our wedding album," she said, sounding less than pleased to be confronted with it. "Imagine Lilah Rose's keeping it at the cottage."

"Rick mentioned that his parents stored a lot of things here when they rented their Columbia house," I said, though the sight of myself in those wedding pictures, my expressions forced and my smiles false, pained me.

As Martine continued to page through the album, the back door swung open and Rick came in. "Just stopping in to grab a jacket," he called.

As Rick stalked across the living room, scooping up a packet of matches from the mantel as he went, I stood and yawned elaborately. "I'm going to turn in soon," I said. "Breakfast in the morning, Martine?"

"Sure, and then I'll be on my way," she said, aiming a worried little glance at Rick.

"Trista, can you give me a hand?" Rick asked.

Martine didn't comment as I followed Rick outside. "What's going on?" I asked as we descended the porch steps to the dune path, glad that we could share a bit of time.

He strode ahead of me for a few moments before turning and taking my hand. "I'm going to build the bonfire, get rid of the scrap lumber lying around. You can help."

I was agreeable, and we quickly gathered enough tinder and kindling so that before long Rick had a sizable blaze going. We stood back and watched it grow. Mindful of the cool wind and the fact that I hadn't worn a wrap, I held my hands over the flames to warm them, Rick standing silently beside me.

I don't know how long we stood there, the flames flickering across our faces, the dunes separating us from the cottage and Martine. The scent of dried seaweed and sun-baked sand and salt swirled around us along with the golden sparks from the fire, and I felt myself calming inside.

Suddenly, the slam of a door shattered the quiet. I turned my head toward the cottage to see Martine marching along the dune path carrying something large and bulky.

Beside me, I felt Rick stiffen. "Here's something for your bonfire," Martine said to Rick, her voice strained.

"Wait a minute," Rick said. "What *is* that?"

"Our wedding pictures for one thing," Martine said, biting the words off sharply. Her hair, so carefully coiffed when she arrived, blew around her head. Cast in the orange light from the flames, it appeared as if it were on fire. Mesmerized by the tableau before me, I froze in place.

"You want to burn them?" Rick said, delivered incredulously.

"Sure, why not? The marriage is over."

"You know how much her photo albums mean to my mother. You don't have the right—" But before he finished the sentence, Martine drew her arm back and hurled the book into the fire.

"Martine! What the hell—?" Rick reached out to grab her, but she eluded his grasp.

In the dark, I hadn't seen the other albums Martine carried. "There's more, too," she said before starting to pitch them in. Horrified, I watched as another one ended up in the flames. Pictures spilled from between the pages, and I spotted the one of Rick and me on the tandem bike. I couldn't bear for that one to burn.

"Stop!" I cried. I whirled around, my eyes trying to adjust to the gloom outside the fire circle.

I noticed a long stick that had recently washed ashore, a rusty nail protruding from one end, and I grabbed it, thinking that I could stab the picture and perhaps the albums and pull them to safety. It worked, but I wasn't able to save the wedding pictures, which were now burning rapidly. The fire was leaping so high that I couldn't remain close to it. Frantically, I retreated and tossed sand on the rescued albums to quench the flames.

Martine turned on me then, tears spilling from her eyes. "All these pictures, all this *tradition* that you love so much." She spat out the word as if it had a bitter taste. "It's pointless. What is it for? Why do we care? It hobbles us to the past, and I hate it."

Stunned, I could only stare. I loved the comfort and familiarity that tradition and remembrance lent to our lives as we each traveled our separate personal journey. On a larger scale, tradition is part of our Southern culture, our legacy and our heritage. Some of it is folklore, some is myth, and of that I was well aware. But also, some of it is truth.

Martine focused her gaze on the spectacle of the white wedding album and its contents still curling and burning in the fire's depths. "This was something I had to do," she said brokenly. With that, she walked swiftly toward the house.

Still shocked, I bent to retrieve the albums I'd pulled out of the fire. The one with the red cover was black and curled, and inside, some of the photos were singed. The other had barely been touched by the flames.

"I'd better go talk to her," I murmured, clutching the albums and the precious memories that they represented to my chest.

Rick paused in his gathering of the other albums, which had been dumped on the ground but appeared unharmed. "Trista, thanks," Rick said. He squeezed my arm. I nodded and kept walking.

As I approached the porch, I spotted Martine pacing in the living room. She was smoking, a habit that shocked me almost as much as her burning of Lilah Rose's photographs. I'd never known her to smoke since our clandestine teenage caper out on the widow's walk of the Lighthouse.

She swiveled as I opened the door, her voice dead calm. "I'm sorry if I scared you, Tris. But I'm not sorry I burned the pictures."

"Oh, Martine," I said sorrowfully. I waited to hear what else she might say, but she remained silent.

"You must harbor some seriously bad feelings about the marriage," I offered haltingly as I set the ruined albums on an end table. Our smiling young faces, only slightly scorched from the ordeal, gazed up at me from the open pages.

My sister's expression softened. "I'm over any resentment I had about Rick, but I'm still angry with myself. We never should have married, Tris. When Rick and I decided to become engaged, I was caught up in all the excitement of graduating from college, and my friends were racking up engagement rings one after the other, and—well, it was immature of me to set my sights on him. Then when Dad died, I settled into a depression that wasn't helped by moving to Miami, and things headed downhill from there."

"I'm so sorry, Martine," I said, genuinely distressed. We all do stupid things when we're young, and sometimes it takes a while to set things to rights. I wasn't proud of the Graham debacle, believe me.

Martine, using a shell for an ashtray, stubbed out her cigarette. She walked over and hugged me. "One thing, Trista. You've always come through for me in times of trouble. Thanks for being such a good sister. Just talking with you today made me feel better."

"I didn't do anything," I objected, holding her close for a long moment.

At that point Rick burst through the French doors, and we both spun around. "Martine," Rick said. "We need to talk."

"No, Rick. We've said all we have to say to each other, and I'll be out of here once and for all tomorrow morning."

He glared at her. "You think it's that simple?"

She rested a placating hand on his arm. "I forgive you for any problems you ever caused me, and I hope you'll do the same."

He walked to the fireplace, braced his hands against the mantel and stood facing it for a long moment. When he turned, the finely etched lines around his eyes seemed to have deepened, and the eyes themselves held the misery of the ages. His voice was deceptively soft. "What about the baby, Martine? The one you didn't have?"

Martine's jaw dropped. "I—I—"

Rick strode across the room until he stood directly in front of us. "I found the pregnancy test you used. It was positive. For a while I was in denial. I wanted to believe that the test was the housekeeper's, though I found it odd that she'd use it at our house while she was cleaning. But Esmelda didn't start showing her next pregnancy until a year later."

Martine's eyes didn't meet Rick's, and I held my breath, wishing that I were anywhere else but in that room with those two people.

"Yes, the test was mine," she whispered, and my heart sank even as a shiver ran up my spine. I'm all for honesty, but in this case, I couldn't help thinking briefly that a lie would be kinder.

"You didn't miscarry, did you?" Rick asked abruptly. "You did—something else."

Now my sister looked him squarely in the eye, and her shoulders slumped with weariness. "That's the main thing I want you to forgive," she said brokenly. "If you can."

All of a sudden, I couldn't breathe, couldn't think, couldn't bear the sorrow burning in the depths of Rick's eyes. He turned away, his shoulders heaving, and I went and slid my arm around them. He pushed me aside, and I knew then that it wasn't in my power to make this right.

"I'm going to my room," I said, my words falling heavily into that leaden silence. And I did, before my trembling legs refused to hold me up. As the two of them stood staring at each other over the ruins of their marriage, exposing their mutual grief and sadness and, yes, revulsion, to each other, I left them to deal with it. Left them to pick up the pieces and heave them at each other if that was their wish. I wanted no part of it. Whatever savage truths were about to be revealed, I didn't want to hear them.

Once I was upstairs, by this time operating on autopilot, I started packing my things. Scooped my toiletries from the bathroom and tossed them on top of my clothes. Grabbed the book I was reading and a couple of items of clothing

I'd strewn here and there, stuffing them into my purse. I didn't bother to strip the bed. I didn't intend to stick around long enough for that. At the last moment, I saw the perfect sand dollar that Rick and I had found on the beach. I paused long enough to wrap it carefully in tissue and bury it deep in my purse.

When I crept down the staircase, Martine was collapsed on the couch, sobbing her heart out. Rick bent over her, and I wasn't sure if he was angry or attempting to soothe her. Other people might have stuck around for the fireworks, but as I've told you before, I sometimes zig when others would zag. I was certain that I was doing the right thing by removing myself from the scene, and neither of them noticed as I walked slowly to the door and let myself out.

As I stumbled blindly down the path toward my car, Dog bounded out of the shrubbery, and with tears streaming down my face, I knelt to pet her for the last time.

"Be good, Dog," I told her. "I hope your ear heals well. And if you hang on until summer, maybe Rick will find you a nice family with some kids to play with." That seemed her best hope for the future, since Tappany Island was still a family place and children could be persuasive in determining whether or not a pet was adopted. I hugged Dog as she bestowed sweet sloppy kisses across my cheeks, and then I spared the cottage one last look.

When I'd arrived at Sweetwater Cottage a little over a week before, the house had been dark and shuttered, the inside dusty and dank. But now the house was lit from the inside. It was a home again. From the path where I stood, I could see into the seldom-used dining room where Lilah Rose's china graced the big mahogany breakfront. The rooms that Rick and Martine had occupied last night were also visible behind the sheer curtains, and the Lighthouse, where in my haste I had forgotten to extinguish the lamp, shone its benevolent golden glow over all. I didn't have my camera, but I didn't need one. This was a view of the cottage the way I wanted to remember it, the way I *would* remember it. Forever.

I had never before left Sweetwater Cottage as I was leaving it on this night, feeling bereft and miserable. Being there had always regenerated me, but now I felt drained and spent. I had no more energy to give to the two most important people in my life, and guilt lanced through me as I considered going back inside and taking up where I'd left off. Just as quickly as the notion entered my mind, it evaporated. For my own sake, I needed to let go.

I had done everything I could for both Rick and Martine. Now they were on their own. And so was I.

Chapter 17: Rick

2004

When Rick woke up the next morning, Martine had gone. So had Trista. He'd been slightly aware of movement in the background while he and Martine had been having it out, but he hadn't focused on what was happening at the time. Trista's absence hit him like a blow to the gut, and all he could think about was apologizing for the ghastly scene of the night before.

First he tried dialing her cell phone. She didn't answer. He called the TV station, but she wasn't there. And then he realized that she probably wouldn't want to see him. He was filled with remorse, but considering their long history, he had to believe that eventually he'd be face-to-face with her again. Until then, it was up to him to hold himself together, to make the best of life as it was. He could have gone around half-crazed because he had let this jewel of a woman slip through his grasp, but nothing would be served by adopting that attitude, and he wasn't about to give up his hard-earned emotional stability.

That day and the ones afterward, he threw himself into repairing the cottage. Never had he worked so hard. He fell into bed exhausted every night, got up and began anew every morning. By the end of the week, the shutters all hung straight, railings had been repaired, porch steps did not wobble. He called his brother and told Hal not to worry about maintenance. Rick would take care of it.

He also informed Shorty that he wouldn't be resuming his previous life in Miami. Rick wasn't yet sure where he would end up when he chose a new direction, and Columbia was still a possibility. But living in Columbia, watching the evening news where he would see Trista every night—well, he wasn't sure he could handle that. And despite all the messages he left on Trista's home answering machine and her cell phone, she never returned his calls. He couldn't imagine what she was thinking, and when he didn't hear from her, all his insecurities began to surface. But he let them go because he had learned that no higher purpose was served by hanging on to the negative aspects of his past and letting them drag him down.

At least Martine was out of his life now, and that was to the good. They'd talked almost all night after she admitted to him what she had done to their baby. He had cried; she had cried; and in the end, he'd forgiven her, which was one of the hardest things he'd ever done. After they'd said all there was to say, exhausting themselves in the process, she had gone to her room. He slept on the couch.

He had no idea if he'd ever see Martine again and didn't

care. Right now he wanted to find his own direction and get his life back on track. When Alston Dubose called him one day at the cottage, he was surprised. Rick didn't know how Alston could have found the unlisted number, but Alston told him that he'd checked an old address book and discovered the number of Sweetwater Cottage scribbled beneath Roger Barrineau's name as one of the places to contact him on summer weekends if he wasn't at home.

"Rick, if you don't want the position in our international-law department," Alston said, "I'll understand. But at least come and talk to us about it. You don't need an appointment."

One of Rick's options was to go on living indefinitely at the cottage, where expenses were minimal. Or he could begin to search for another job. Yet the firm of Barrineau, Dubose and Linder had been part of his plans for such a long time in his youth that he hated to brush them off. He was ready to find out exactly what they had to offer.

So one day three weeks after Easter, he headed for Columbia. At the last minute, he held the car door open for Dog, who pushed all his guilt buttons by wagging her tail and whining pathetically as he prepared to leave. With a yip of excitement, she jumped in, and they set off.

If someone had asked him, Rick wouldn't have been able to say why he took her. Perhaps it was merely the thought of the drive ahead and the loneliness of going it alone. Or maybe it was something more than that.

"I want to see you."

Trista, wonder of wonders, had answered her cell phone, possibly because the unfamiliar number of the pay phone in downtown Columbia hadn't rung a bell when it popped up on her caller ID. He thanked the fates for allowing his cell-phone battery to die en route and for providing a phone kiosk in the parking garage of the building that housed Barrineau, Dubose and Linder.

"Rick?" Trista sounded surprised, but he could read nothing else into her tone.

"I want to see you," he said again, more forcefully.

This statement was met with silence.

"Don't put me off like this," he said, willing to beg but hoping it wouldn't be necessary.

"I haven't heard from Martine since she went to Mexico," she said.

"Martine and I have nothing more to say to each other. I've talked with Alston Dubose about that job at the firm. It's a good one, but I don't want to say yay or nay to his offer without speaking with you, Tris."

A long silence. "I'm at the station. I'll be home after the evening news." She sounded tense and strained.

"I still have the key you gave us when we stayed at your place."

"Great. Go on over and make yourself comfortable. You're at a hotel?"

"Shaz and his wife offered me a bed, but I told them not to expect me until they see me."

"Okay, Rick." A muffled noise, and then she said, "I really have to hang up."

She clicked off, and he stared at the phone in his hand for a moment before hurrying to the car. "She wants to see us," he told Dog, who had waited patiently while Rick was talking to Alston. And then he started the car and headed for Trista's condo, but first he stopped off and bought groceries. As he put them away, he smiled to himself over the big pitcher of red Kool-Aid in the refrigerator.

He walked around the apartment scanning the titles of the books in Trista's bookcase and admiring a favorite painting that Martine had given her. Propped on the desk in Trista's study was the framed picture that the man on the beach had taken of them together on Easter, both of them wreathed in smiles. Next to it she had set the perfect sand dollar that they had found on the same day. The pretty display encouraged him; Trista must still have special feelings about their time on the island together.

She was later than he expected, and when the door opened, Dog erupted into a frenzy of glee. Trista was so surprised to see her that she took a couple of steps backward, and then she dropped to her knees while Dog cavorted about and finally quieted herself so that she could be hugged.

"I can't believe this!" Trista exclaimed. "Dog! I never thought you'd bring her."

"She's missed you," Rick said, thinking how nice it was to see them reunited. "She hasn't been the same since you left."

As Trista rose, he slowly went to meet her. She was wearing a business suit, and her hair was swept back behind her ears. It was a new hairdo for her and one that he found very becoming, but there was a tension about her mouth and an indefinable sadness in her eyes. It cut straight to his heart because he knew that he was probably the reason for it.

She gave him a peck on the cheek. "What are you cooking? I smell food," she said as she went to her study and tossed her briefcase on the daybed. When she came out she was untucking her blouse and kicking off her shoes.

"My famous spaghetti sauce," he told her, retreating to the kitchen. "Care for a glass of Chianti?"

She accepted the glass and lifted the lid on the pan where the sauce was bubbling merrily. "Smells wonderful," she said.

"Mom's recipe."

"How are your mother and father?"

"They'll be back at the end of the summer."

Trista leaned against the counter, and Dog sat down beside her feet, tail thumping joyfully on the hardwood floor. "I'm sorry I was late getting here," she said. "We had a big brouhaha at the station today, but the upshot is that Byron is leaving and I'm going to be the sole anchor of the evening news." Her expression was animated, and her eyes sparkled.

She was more beautiful than he remembered, and though he preferred her in the bright light of the sunshine on Tappany Island, walking barefoot beside him in the sand, he wanted nothing so much as to keep on looking at her. "Congratulations," he said warmly.

"Thanks. Apparently Byron figured out that he wasn't going to be able to nudge me out of position, so he went job hunting far afield and will be taking over the anchor spot at the biggest station in Denver."

"That means you can stop considering a move to Atlanta or Richmond," he said.

"Yes, and that's a relief." She paused before asking carefully, "When will you let Alston know about the job?"

"Tomorrow, I hope." He poured a glass of wine for himself.

"Let's go in the living room. I'd like to wind down from a very eventful day."

"I can imagine." He followed her to the couch and sat beside her. She got up again to open a package of salted pecans, which she poured into a red glass dish that he remembered from the Windsor Manor house. It was all he needed to remind himself that he and Trista had a long history, and it wasn't by any means over between them yet.

He was so happy to see her that he couldn't stop looking

at her. Watching expressions flit across her features, listening to the rise and fall of her melodious voice, took him back to a simpler, happier time. It was as if they had never been apart, as if that awful night at the cottage had never happened. As if all the years had fallen away, and they were starting anew.

She asked if she could help when he got up to boil the water for the pasta, but he told her that he wanted to do everything. She'd had a hard day, and he wanted to treat her the way he would have liked if he'd had a similar day. While he worked in the kitchen, she played with Dog, producing an old tennis ball that she threw the length of the apartment. And while Rick was draining the pasta and grating the Parmesan cheese, Trista disappeared into her room and later emerged relaxed and refreshed, wearing a flowing blue silk caftan.

Rick hoped his eyes expressed his appreciation for her beauty. *Her* beauty, which was inner as well as outer. Trista noticed him staring at her, and a faint blush rose along her neck to her cheeks. The sight of it sent a small tremor rippling through him because it meant that she was still aware of him in that way that he had hoped she would be— as a man, not only as a friend.

"Dinner's ready," he said, though the last thing he wanted to do was eat it. But they sat at the table, and he doled out the spaghetti onto each of their plates, and she exclaimed that the salad was delicious.

"This is one of the nicest things anyone has ever done for me. I'm not accustomed to such a warm welcome," she said, her gesture encompassing the table and the food. She took another sip of wine and leaned back, smiling at him across the table. He'd found a small candle in one of the kitchen drawers, and the glow lit up her face.

"It's a simple dinner," he said. "Nothing special." He thought about the long years of his marriage, of the tension in his house and how the strain had grown commonplace in his everyday life. He didn't want to live that way again. After such an experience, some men might swear off marriage or women in favor of an easy freewheeling lifestyle, but he wasn't that type. He needed a partner, a companion, someone who cared about him. Someone to whom he couldn't wait to return at the end of a long day. He had found her, he cherished her, but there were still questions to answer.

"Why did you leave that night?" he asked quietly, steeling himself for her answer.

Trista regarded him for a long moment before answering. "To allow you space and time," she said. "You and Martine."

He reached across the table for her hand, which she gave freely. It was warm within his, and he raised it to his lips and kissed it. "It wasn't because of me? Because you were angry, or because you thought I still loved Martine, or—?"

She shook her head vehemently. "No. I didn't belong there. Not then, not while you were talking about—that."

A wave of relief swept over him. "I was so afraid you left because of me. I know I wasn't the easiest person to be around when the two of us were alone together at the cottage, but you got me back on track. You made me see that I couldn't go on like that. I was falling apart until you arrived. Drinking, and not eating properly, and hating myself and everyone else—my life was slowly trickling down the sewer, and you saved me."

"You saved yourself, Rick, by opening up to me."

"Maybe so," he agreed, but he knew he wouldn't have found it within himself to take the necessary steps toward recovery if it hadn't been for her prodding, her insistence, her caring.

She looked so young and beautiful that he had to remind himself that they weren't eighteen anymore. Holding her hand fast, he said, "It's a lovely night. Let's go out on the balcony."

Together they walked across the living room and opened the glass sliders to the balcony stretching across the whole front of the apartment. Their vantage point on the fifth floor offered a panoramic view of lights winking on and off in the distance. Across the tops of the leafy trees, they could see the South Carolina state Capitol dome. The breeze was balmy, the moon full.

Rick drew Trista closer so that her temple rested against his cheek. "I remember another lovely spring night," he said. "You had treated the cut on my forehead and rinsed out my shirt. The satin of your dress felt smooth beneath my hands when I put my arms around you."

"But I was also wearing a bra with miserable stays that cut into my skin and left scrapes that were sore for days," she said, her breath sweet on his skin. Her lips curved into a smile against his neck.

He moved his hands upward, sliding them across her ribs one by one. "No bra tonight," he said. "I can tell."

"Mmm," she said, leaning into him. "Is that important?"

He gazed up at the stars for a moment. "Maybe," he said. "I've thought about us a lot. Rick, I've avoided talking to you since I left Tappany Island because I needed the time and space to decide what to do. I prayed for a sign, something that would let me know that we're supposed to be together. If I didn't get one, I'd bow out gracefully from my job at WCIC and pursue some of the job offers I've had in the past. Atlanta, maybe, so I could live closer to Mom and

Aunt Cynthia. Or somewhere out West where I could sink down new roots, California, perhaps, or Arizona."

"Would you be happy so far away from the South? It's in your blood, as it is in mine."

She looked thoughtful. "Something would draw me back every year, a homing instinct. I love Tappany Island, Rick, and the cottage. It's a way of life that I couldn't relinquish easily."

"Nor could I," he replied reflectively.

"Anyway, today I got my sign. Two of them, in fact. When Byron announced that he was leaving WCIC and I learned that I was going to be the sole anchor of the evening news, that was the first. The second was when you called and told me you were here. In Columbia. And wanted to see me. That changed everything."

"Did it?" he asked, drawing back so he could study her face. "Did it really?"

"Really," she said, the word only a murmur.

He kissed her then, thinking of how much this woman had meant to him over the years. Thinking of lost opportunities, and wrong decisions, and hurt feelings, and how love was almost impossible to find. Yet like the perfect sand dollar, once found, it was to be appreciated for its beauty.

For a long time, they kissed each other. Over and over and over, until he knew he'd never get enough of her kisses as long as they lived.

"I love you, Trista," he said.

"Like a sister?" she asked teasingly.

"I guess I deserve that," he said with a bit of embarrassment. "I can't be without you, Tris."

"No one else ever measured up to you, Rick, ever."

He leaned back to look at her. "Did you love me back then? The night of the prom?"

Her eyes filled with tears. "I think I always loved you, even before the sixth-grade picnic, even before you attacked Hugh in that hotel room. But we were so young. Too young." A tear trickled down her cheek, silver in the moonlight.

"The day I learned about your engagement to Graham, I got in my car and drove clear across Georgia and partway through Alabama. I found myself in some nameless little town and checked into a run-down motel where I stared at the walls for two days until I forced myself to drive back to Columbia. I couldn't bear the thought of you with anyone but me."

"I didn't have a clue," Trista said. "I had no idea."

"If we'd stayed together then, we'd probably have drifted apart."

"Maybe," she said, though she sounded unconvinced.

"Maybe we're not supposed to know how it would have turned out. We've grown up, Tris. Our experiences have tempered us, challenged us, changed us."

He brushed a tear away with a fingertip and kissed the place where it had been. She smiled tremulously.

"Hey, McCulloch. I think we should consider making up for lost time," she said.

She led him the length of the balcony to the sliding door that opened into her bedroom. He didn't speak as she pulled back the draperies to admit the light of the stars and the huge silver moon above. Then she wrapped her arms around his neck and kissed him with all the passion that he had been anticipating during the past weeks.

He held her tight so that he could feel her heart beat, and he marveled at life. Second chances didn't often present themselves, and yet he intended to take full advantage of this one.

She shifted away, and as he watched, she lifted the caftan over her head in one fluid movement. When she stood before him, her tall, slim body outlined against the open door and the light behind, she was more exquisite than he had even imagined, and now she was his.

Somehow his clothes obligingly ended up on the floor, and he went to her and just held her against him, rocking slightly as he gloried in the smooth texture of her skin, the kisses she trailed along his jaw and throat, her hands upon his firmness. For a long time, they touched each other, their kisses growing deeper and more intense. When he gazed into her eyes, he saw that they glowed with a special warmth, a deep-down happiness and contentment that he had never seen there before.

How could they have not realized it would be like this? How could they have avoided this all their lives? He didn't know. He didn't know anything except that he loved Trista with all his heart.

"Marry me," he said close to her ear.

"Yes," she said shakily. "Of course."

They eased themselves down on the bed, and he noticed how fragile she seemed. She wasn't—her body was an athlete's, toned by running every day. Her pulse raced beneath his fingertips, and she moaned when he held her full breasts in his hands and kissed the rosy tips one by one. Their eyes locked for a long moment in which he knew—*knew*—that for her, this experience was as moving as it was for him.

He slid on top of her and almost immediately she guided him inside. He felt an astonishing sense of oneness with her, something he had never experienced, as though not only their bodies but their souls had merged. His exultation encompassed her, joined with hers as he grasped her hands and pinned them above her head, gazing into her eyes as her hips curved up to meet his and began to move instinctively.

Together they found their rhythm, felt it echo in their

blood, lost their bodies in its throbbing beat. He felt her release building even as his own surged through him, and he cried out her name as he spun out of control. Lost in the reflection of stars and moon and city lights in her eyes, he could only cling to her as he drifted slowly back to reality. To Trista in his arms.

Which was as real as life could be. After a while, he brushed her damp hair from her face.

"When?" he asked her, knowing she would understand.

"In the fall, at Sweetwater Cottage. On the beach. With our families there, and Lindsay and Peter and their children."

"Attendants?"

"I don't care. I just want to be married."

Everything happens for a reason, Rick decided in those moments. Sometimes we take detours from the path of life, and we go where they lead us. But eventually, if we're lucky, we find ourselves where we're supposed to be. Or where we should have been all along.

"Rick? You're going to accept the job Alston offered, aren't you?"

"I'll tell him so tomorrow." He glanced at his watch; it was after midnight. "Make that today," he corrected himself.

They heard the staccato click of toenails on the oak floor, and then Dog appeared beside the bed. She whined and nosed her muzzle into Rick's hand, which was hanging over the edge.

"We can't go on calling her Dog," he said.

"I thought you didn't want to give her a name," Trista replied as she snuggled closer. "You said you weren't responsible for her."

"That was when I didn't believe in permanence. Things have changed. Besides, every family should have a dog."

"I agree," Trista said.

"How about Joey? Like the title of the song we sang in the talent show?"

"Joey," Trista repeated sleepily. "I like it. It's a boy's name, though."

"Doesn't matter. She's a tomboy, the way she jumps for the Frisbee and runs through the waves."

"Okay, Joey it is."

The dog must have heard because she padded around and jumped onto the bed beside them.

"Is she going to sleep with us?" Trista asked, fading fast.

"I think we'd better get used to it," he said, chuckling in spite of himself as Joey settled into the angle behind his knee.

"I love you, Rick," Trista said.

"I've always loved you," he said, going her one better. "If only I'd had the sense to figure it out in the first place."

For an answer, Trista raised her lips for his kiss, and that was the last thing he knew before he fell asleep.

Epilogue: Trista

2007

We are riding in the car toward Tappany Island, and our six-month-old son is asleep in his car seat behind us. Our dog, Joey, snoozes on the floor beside my feet, her whiskers twitching every so often with doggy dreams. Rick and I hold hands; we still feel like newlyweds even after almost three years of marriage. I've arranged two weeks' vacation from WCIC, where I continue to anchor the evening news, and Rick has scheduled the same amount of time away from Barrineau, Dubose, and Linder. It is the first day of June, and the air already hangs hot and humid.

"Do you think Lindsay and Peter will arrive at the cottage before we do?" I ask, wrinkling my nose at the scent of the marsh wafting from the vents of the air conditioner.

"I explained to Peter about the key in the kitchen window box, just in case," Rick says.

"The same place your mother used to leave it when we were kids," I reply, smiling at him.

"When we talked on the phone, Lindsay asked about Martine."

I exchange a look with my husband. "The last postcard she sent was from Morocco. She'd sketched a picture of a camel on it."

We're quiet for a long moment, because we don't mention Martine often. Neither of us has seen her since that night at the cottage. When she learned of our marriage, she sent us an exquisite set of silverware from Thailand. After that, only an occasional postcard. Every now and then, I feel a pang of sadness because I miss her, but my life is so full that it's only a passing wistfulness, a fleeting wish that we could be closer, knowing full well that because of the circumstances, we probably never will.

Rick squeezes my hand. "Peter said that Adam and Ainsley can't wait to meet our baby," he says. "Ainsley keeps calling him 'Rider.'"

We have named our son Roger Boyd McCulloch after both our fathers, and I laugh at Ainsley's mispronunciation. "Before this vacation is over, Ainsley will be able to say his name. She's already begging to be his babysitter."

"How old is she again?" he asks.

"She's five. Adam is a rambunctious seven."

"He's old enough to learn to fly a kite," Rick says with conviction, as if this is a skill that no boy should lack.

"There are kites in the bachelor-quarters closet," I remind him. "I noticed them when I cleaned."

"Peter and I will dig them out. You know, Tris, I've been thinking."

"About?"

"Us."

Every time Rick waxes reflective, I remember that difficult time at the cottage. That difficult, memorable and wondrous time when we found each other again.

Rick continues to speak. "Here we are, headed for Tappany Island with a new little McCulloch, who is about to experience the joys of the Low Country like generations of McCullochs before him. That's what my grandfather had in mind when he built Sweetwater Cottage—a family resort."

The idea of the rumpled, faded old cottage as a resort tickles my fancy, and I laugh. "I'm sure little Roger will appreciate the place every bit as much as we did. Before long he'll be falling off the dock while fishing for crabs."

"And catching alligators in a butterfly net."

"Riding his bike to Jeter's and reading comic books on the back steps while the guinea hens peck around his feet."

"Not to mention charging boiled peanuts and Gummi Bears to the McCulloch account."

"And we'll be taking snapshots of him every step of the way," I say softly.

"So he can show them to his children."

"And his children's children."

Behind us, our son awakens. He gurgles, grins and sneezes. He's a bonny, happy baby, full of fun. Rick and I delight in being parents. We believe it's the best thing that's ever happened to us except for marrying each other.

We cross the old swinging drawbridge, turning left where Center Street intersects with Bridge Road, and soon we spot the tower and gabled roof of Sweetwater Cottage through the veil of trees.

"We're home again," I say to Rick, and he smiles at me.

"Home," he says. "What a beautiful word."

And it is.

Rick parks under the oak tree, I unstrap our son from his car seat, and we walk toward the cottage with Joey following behind until she trots up the back-porch steps and flops down in her customary spot under the swing. I draw a deep breath of the salty air, notice that the oleanders are heavy with pink blossoms and that beyond the dunes, the sea is a wide, inexhaustible blue. My heart, already full, expands to take it all in.

"We need a picture to commemorate our first summer vacation here as a real family," Rick says suddenly, and he runs back to the car to get his camera and the tripod that will allow him to set the timer so that we can all be in the photo.

Click: Rick and Roger and I are smiling into the camera lens. Rick's arm is curved around my waist, which is already swelling with our newly conceived daughter, and I am gazing up at him with love. I cradle our beautiful son in my arms, and he is clutching a lock of my hair in his tiny baby fist. Holding on tightly, all of us holding on to one another because we know how quickly life can change, how sometimes precious people can be taken from us, how the things we hold most dear can disappear in the blink of an eye.

But we also know the power of undying love. And that's what I hope our children, grandchildren and even great-grandchildren will understand when they look at us—forever smiling, forever young—in this snapshot.

★ ★ ★ ★ ★

Next™

Every Life Has More Than One Chapter™

Award-winning author Stevi Mittman delivers another hysterical mystery, featuring Teddi Bayer, an irrepressible heroine, and her to-die-for hero, Detective Drew Scoones. After all, life on Long Island can be murder!

Turn the page for a sneak peek at the warm and funny fourth book,
WHOSE NUMBER IS UP, ANYWAY?,
in the Teddi Bayer series,
by STEVI MITTMAN.
On sale August 7

CHAPTER 1

> "Before redecorating a room, I always advise my clients to empty it of everything but one chair. Then I suggest they move that chair from place to place, sitting in it, until the placement feels right. Trust your instincts when deciding on furniture placement. Your room should "feel right."
>
> —TipsFromTeddi.com

Gut feelings. You know, that gnawing in the pit of your stomach that warns you that you are about to do the absolute stupidest thing you could do? Something that will ruin life as you know it?

I've got one now, standing at the butcher counter in King Kullen, the grocery store in the same strip mall as L.I. Lanes, the bowling alley cum billiard parlor I'm in the process of redecorating for its "Grand Opening."

I realize being in the wrong supermarket probably doesn't sound exactly dire to you, but you aren't the one buying your father a brisket at a store your mother will somehow know isn't Waldbaum's.

And then, June Bayer isn't your mother.

The woman behind the counter has agreed to go into the freezer to find a brisket for me, since there aren't any in the case. There are packages of pork tenderloin, piles of spare ribs and rolls of sausage, but no briskets.

Warning Number Two, right? I should be so out of here.

But no, I'm still in the same spot when she comes back out, brisketless, her face ashen. She opens her mouth as if she is going to scream, but only a gurgle comes out.

And then she pinballs out from behind the counter, knocking bottles of Peter Luger Steak Sauce to the floor on her way, now hitting the tower of cans at the end of the prepared foods aisle and sending them sprawling, now making her way down the aisle, careening from side to side as she goes.

Finally, from a distance, I hear her shout, "He's deeeeeeaaaad! Joey's deeeeeaaaad."

My first thought is *You should always trust your gut*.

My second thought is that now, somehow, my mother will know I was in King Kullen. For weeks I will have to hear "What did you expect?" as though whenever you go to King Kullen someone turns up dead. And if the detective investigating the case turns out to be Detective Drew Scoones... well, I'll never hear the end of that from her, either.

She still suspects I murdered the guy who was found dead on my doorstep last Halloween just to get Drew back into my life.

Several people head for the butcher's freezer and I position myself to block them. If there's one thing I've learned from finding people dead—and the guy on my doorstep wasn't the first one—it's that the police get very testy when you mess with their murder scenes.

"You can't go in there until the police get here," I say, stationing myself at the end of the butcher's counter and in front of the Employees Only door, acting as if I'm some sort of authority. "You'll contaminate the evidence if it turns out to be murder."

Shouts and chaos. You'd think I'd know better than to throw the word *murder* around. Cell phones are flipping open and tongues are wagging.

I amend my statement quickly. "Which, of course, it probably isn't. Murder, I mean. People die all the time, and it's not always in hospitals or their own beds, or..." I babble when I'm nervous, and the idea of someone dead on the other side of the freezer door makes me very nervous.

So does the idea of seeing Drew Scoones again. Drew and I have this on-again, off-again sort of thing...that I kind of turned off.

Who knew he'd take it so personally when he tried to get serious and I responded by saying we could talk about *us* tomorrow—and then caught a plane to my parents' condo in Boca the next day? In July. In the middle of a job.

For some crazy reason, he took that to mean that I was avoiding him and the subject of *us*.

That was three months ago. I haven't seen him since.

The manager, who identifies himself and points to his nameplate in case I don't believe him, says he has to go into *his cooler*. "Maybe Joey's not dead," he says. "Maybe he can be saved, and you're letting him die in there. Did you ever think of that?"

In fact, I hadn't. But I had thought that the murderer might try to go back in to make sure his tracks were covered, so I say that I will go in and check.

Which means that the manager and I couple up and go in together while everyone pushes against the doorway to peer in, erasing any chance of finding clean prints on that Employee Only door.

I expect to find carcasses of dead animals hanging from hooks, and maybe Joey hanging from one, too. I think it's going to be very creepy and I steel myself, only to find a rather benign series of shelves with large slabs of meat laid out carefully on them, along with boxes and boxes marked simply Chicken.

Nothing scary here, unless you count the body of a middle-aged man with graying hair sprawled faceup on the floor. His eyes are wide open and unblinking. His shirt is stiff. His pants are stiff. His body is stiff. And his expression, you should forgive the pun—is frozen. Bill-the-manager crosses himself and stands mute while I pronounce the guy dead in a sort of *happy now?* tone.

"We should not be in here," I say, and he nods his head emphatically and helps me push people out of the doorway just in time to hear the police sirens and see the cop cars pull up outside the big store windows.

Bobbie Lyons, my partner in Teddi Bayer Interior Designs (and also my neighbor, my best friend and my private fashion police), and Mark, our carpenter (and my dogsitter, confidant, and ego booster), rush in from next door. They beat the cops by a half step and shout out my name. People point in my direction.

After all the publicity that followed the unfortunate incident during which I shot my ex-husband, Rio Gallo, and then the subsequent murder of my first client—which I solved, I might add—it seems like the whole world, or at least all of Long Island, knows who I am.

Mark asks if I'm all right. (Did I remember to mention that the man is drop-dead-gorgeous-but-a-decade-too-young-for-me-yet-too-old-for-my-daughter-thank-god?) I don't get a chance to answer him because the police are quickly closing in on the store manager and me.

"The woman—" I begin telling the police. Then I have to pause for the manager to fill in her name, which he does: *Fran*.

I continue. "Right. Fran. Fran went into the freezer to get a brisket. A moment later she came out and screamed that Joey was dead. So I'd say she was the one who discovered the body."

"And you are...?" the cop asks me. It comes out a bit like who do I *think* I am, rather than who am I really?

"An innocent bystander," Bobbie, hair perfect, makeup just right, says, carefully placing her body between the cop and me.

"And she was just leaving," Mark adds. They each take one of my arms.

Fran comes into the inner circle surrounding the cops. In case it isn't obvious from the hairnet and bloodstained white apron with Fran embroidered on it, I explain that she was the butcher who was going for the brisket. Mark and Bobbie take that as a signal that I've done my job and they can now get me out of there. They twist around, with me in the middle, as if we're a Rockettes line, until we are facing away from the butcher counter. They've managed to propel me a few steps toward the exit when disaster—in the form of a Mazda RX7 pulling up at the loading curb—strikes.

Mark's grip on my arm tightens like a vise. "Too late," he says.

Bobbie's expletive is unprintable. "Maybe there's a back door," she suggests, but Mark is right. It's too late.

I've laid my eyes on Detective Scoones. And while my gut is trying to warn me that my heart shouldn't go there, regions farther south are melting at just the sight of him.

"Walk," Bobbie orders me.

And I try to. Really.

Walk, I tell my feet. *Just put one foot in front of the other.*

I can do this because I know, in my heart of hearts, that if Drew Scoones was still interested in me, he'd have gotten in touch with me after I returned from Boca. And he didn't.

Since he's a detective, Drew doesn't have to wear one of those dark blue Nassau County Police uniforms. Instead, he's got on jeans, a tight-fitting T-shirt and a tweedy sports jacket. If you think that sounds good, you should see him. Chiseled features, cleft chin, brown hair that's naturally a little sandy in the front, a smile that...well, that doesn't matter. He isn't smiling now.

He walks up to me, tucks his sunglasses into his breast pocket and looks me over from head to toe.

"Well, if it isn't Miss Cut and Run," he says. "Aren't you supposed to be somewhere in Florida or something?" He looks at Mark accusingly, as if he was covering for me when he told Drew I was gone.

"Detective Scoones?" one of the uniforms says. "The stiff's in the cooler and the woman who found him is over there." He jerks his head in Fran's direction.

Drew continues to stare at me.

You know how when you were young, your mother always told you to wear clean underwear in case you were in an accident? And how, a little farther on, she told you not to go out in hair rollers because you never knew who you might see—or who might see you? And how now your best friend says she wouldn't be caught dead without makeup and suggests you shouldn't either?

Okay, today, *finally,* in my overalls and Converse sneakers, I get it.

I brush my hair out of my eyes. "Well, I'm back," I say. As if he hasn't known my exact whereabouts. The man is a detective, for heaven's sake. "Been back awhile."

Bobbie has watched the exchange and apparently decided she's given Drew all the time he deserves. "And we've got work to do, so…" she says, grabbing my arm and giving Drew a little two-fingered wave goodbye.

As I back up a foot or two, the store manager sees his chance and places himself in front of Drew, trying to get his attention. Maybe what makes Drew such a good detective is his ability to focus.

Only what he's focusing on is me.

"Phone broken? Carrier pigeon died?" he asks me, taking in Fran, the manager, the meat counter and that Employees Only door, all without taking his eyes off me.

Mark tries to break the spell. "We've got work to do there, you've got work to do here, Scoones," Mark says to him, gesturing toward next door. "So it's back to the alley for us."

Drew's lip twitches. "You working the alley now?" he says.

"If you'd like to follow me," Bill-the-manager, clearly exasperated, says to Drew—who doesn't respond. It's as if waiting for my answer is all he has to do.

So, fine. "You knew I was back," I say.

The man has known my whereabouts every hour of the day for as long as I've known him. And my mother's not the only one who won't buy that he "just happened" to answer this particular call. In fact, I'm willing to bet my children's lunch money that he's taken every call within ten miles of my home since the day I got back.

And now he's gotten lucky.

"*You* could have called *me*," I say.

"You're the one who said *tomorrow* for our talk and then flew the coop, chickie," he says. "I figured the ball was in your court."

"Detective?" the uniform says. "There's something you ought to see in here."

Drew gives me a look that amounts to *in or out?*

He could be talking about the investigation, or about our relationship.

Bobbie tries to steer me away. Mark's fists are balled. Drew waits me out, knowing I won't be able to resist what might be a murder investigation.

Finally he turns and heads for the cooler.

And, like a puppy dog, I follow.

Bobbie grabs the back of my shirt and pulls me to a halt.

"I'm just going to show him something," I say, yanking away.

"Yeah," Bobbie says, pointedly looking at the buttons on my blouse. The two at breast level have popped. "That's what I'm afraid of."

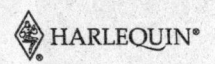

HARLEQUIN

EVERLASTING LOVE™
Every great love has a story to tell™

A love story that distance and time has never dimmed.

While remodeling her home, April finds some old love letters addressed to Norma Marsh. Tracking down the owner, now in her eighties, brings to the surface secrets Norma has kept from her grandson Quinn, about a love close to her heart. A love April begins to understand as she starts to fall for Quinn...

Look for

A Secret To Tell You
by
Roz Denny Fox

On sale August 2007.

www.eHarlequin.com

HARLEQUIN

NASCAR

In August...

Collect all 4 novels in Harlequin's officially licensed NASCAR series.

ALMOST FAMOUS
by Gina Wilkins

THE ROOKIE
by Jennifer LaBrecque

LEGENDS AND LIES
by Katherine Garbera

OLD FLAME, NEW SPARKS
by Day Leclaire

All four on sale August 2007

OLD FLAME, NEW SPARKS

Kellie Hammond's late husband left her ownership of Hammond Racing, but that's not all he left her. Jared "Bad" Boyce is now back in Kellie's life thanks to her husband's last business deal. With both her son and Jared vying to be the star driver, Kellie is torn between the two men in her life—but there's a secret she hasn't revealed to either of them as they square off on the racetrack...they're actually father and son.

Visit www.GetYourHeartRacing.com for all the latest details.

NASCAR0807

HARLEQUIN

Mediterranean NIGHTS™

Glamour, elegance, mystery and revenge aboard the high seas...

Coming in August 2007...

THE TYCOON'S SON

by
award-winning author

Cindy Kirk

Businessman Theo Catomeris's long-estranged father is determined to reconnect with his son, so he hires Trish Melrose to persuade Theo to renew his contract with Liberty Line. Sailing aboard the luxurious *Alexandra's Dream* is a rare opportunity for the single mom to mix business and pleasure. But an undeniable attraction between Trish and Theo is distracting her from the task at hand....

www.eHarlequin.com

HM38962

REQUEST YOUR FREE BOOKS!

2 FREE NOVELS PLUS 2 FREE GIFTS!

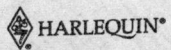

HARLEQUIN®

EVERLASTING LOVE™
Every great love has a story to tell™

YES! Please send me 2 FREE Harlequin® Everlasting Love™ novels and my 2 FREE gifts. After receiving them, if I don't wish to receive any more books, I can return the shipping statement marked "cancel." If I don't cancel, I will receive 4 brand-new novels every other month and be billed just $4.47 per book in the U.S. or $4.99 per book in Canada, plus 25¢ shipping and handling per book and applicable taxes, if any*. That's a savings of about 15% off the cover price! I understand that accepting the 2 free books and gifts places me under no obligation to buy anything. I can always return a shipment and cancel at any time. Even if I never buy another book from Harlequin, the two free books and gifts are mine to keep forever.

153 HDN ELX4 353 HDN ELYG

Name	(PLEASE PRINT)
Address	Apt.
City	State/Prov. Zip/Postal Code

Signature (if under 18, a parent or guardian must sign)

Mail to the Harlequin Reader Service®:
IN U.S.A.: P.O. Box 1867, Buffalo, NY 14240-1867
IN CANADA: P.O. Box 609, Fort Erie, Ontario L2A 5X3

Not valid to current Harlequin Everlasting Love subscribers.

Want to try two free books from another line?
Call 1-800-873-8635 or visit www.morefreebooks.com.

* Terms and prices subject to change without notice. NY residents add applicable sales tax. Canadian residents will be charged applicable provincial taxes and GST. This offer is limited to one order per household. All orders subject to approval. Credit or debit balances in a customer's account(s) may be offset by any other outstanding balance owed by or to the customer. Please allow 4 to 6 weeks for delivery.

Your Privacy: Harlequin is committed to protecting your privacy. Our Privacy Policy is available online at www.eHarlequin.com or upon request from the Reader Service. From time to time we make our lists of customers available to reputable firms who may have a product or service of interest to you. If you would prefer we not share your name and address, please check here. ☐

HEL07

ATHENA FORCE

Heart-pounding romance and thrilling adventure.

A ruthless enemy rises against the women of Athena Academy. In a global chess game of vengeance, kidnapping and murder, every move exposes potential enemies—and lovers. This time the women must stand together... before their world is ripped apart.

THIS NEW 12-BOOK SERIES BEGINS WITH A BANG IN AUGUST 2007 WITH

TRUST
by Rachel Caine

Look for a new Athena Force adventure each month wherever books are sold.

www.eHarlequin.com

AFLAUNCH

HARLEQUIN

Super Romance

Looking for a romantic, emotional and unforgettable escape?

You'll find it this month and every month with a Harlequin Superromance!

Rory Gorenzi has a sense of humor and a sense of honor. She also happens to be good with children.

Seamus Lee, widower and father of four, needs someone with exactly those traits.

They meet at the Colorado mountain school owned by Rory's father, where she teaches skiing and avalanche safety. But Seamus—and his children—learn more from her than that....

Look for

GOOD WITH CHILDREN
by Margot Early,

available August 2007, and these other fantastic titles from Harlequin Superromance.

LOVE, BY GEORGE *Debra Salonen* #1434
THE MAN FROM HER PAST *Anna Adams* #1435
NANNY MAKES THREE *Joan Kilby* #1437
MAYBE, BABY *Terry McLaughlin* #1438
THE FAMILY SOLUTION *Bobby Hutchinson* #1439

www.eHarlequin.com

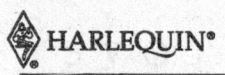

HARLEQUIN®
American ROMANCE®

TEXAS LEGACIES: THE CARRIGANS

Get to the Heart of a Texas Family

WITH

THE RANCHER NEXT DOOR
by
Cathy Gillen Thacker

She'll Run The Ranch—And Her Life—Her Way!

On her alpaca ranch in Texas, Rebecca encounters constant interference from Trevor McCabe, the bossy rancher next door. Rebecca becomes very friendly with Vince Owen, her other neighbor and Trevor's archrival from college. Trevor's problem is convincing Rebecca that he is on her side, and aware of Vince's ulterior motives. But Trevor has fallen for her in the process....

On sale July 2007

www.eHarlequin.com

HAR75173

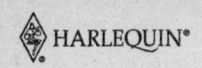

HARLEQUIN®
EVERLASTING LOVE™
Every great love has a story to tell™

COMING NEXT MONTH

#13 A SECRET TO TELL YOU by Roz Denny Fox

When April Trent is renovating an old house in Virginia, she discovers a hidden cache of letters. Written in France during the Second World War, they appear to be love letters to a young American woman named Norma Marsh. When April tracks down the recipient, now in her eighties, she finds herself facing an angry grandson, as well. Quinn Santini wants to protect his grandmother—who has secrets he's never guessed. Secrets that include a love she's kept close to her heart all these years. A love April understands...as she begins to fall for Quinn and his little girl.

#14 THE BRACELET by Karen Rose Smith

A miniature gold daisy, a heart, an envelope, a little girl, a little boy—just some of the charms Brady Malone has given his wife, Laura, for the bracelet he bought her, symbols of their life together. Brady and Laura fell in love in the turbulent late sixties and expected their marriage to last forever. But now, more than thirty years later, after a newspaper article that reveals a long-buried secret of Brady's, they both wonder if a gold *forever* charm will be added to the bracelet....

www.eHarlequin.com